Ra...
THE IMPROPER WIFE

more . . .

Also by Diane Perkins

The Improper Wife

The MARRIAGE BARGAIN

DIANE PERKINS

NEW YORK   BOSTON

Warner Forever is a registered trademark of Warner Books.

Book design by Giorgetta Bell McRee

Warner Books

Time Warner Book Group
1271 Avenue of the Americas
New York, NY 10020
Visit our Web site at www.twbookmark.com

Printed in the United States of America

First Paperback Printing: October 2005

10 9 8 7 6 5 4 3 2 1

To my daughter, Meagan, and my son, Dan.
You've filled my life with joy.

Acknowledgments

This book would not have been possible without the help and encouragement of my writing friends. Thank you, Karen Anders, Lisa Dyson, Darlene Gardner, Julie Halperson, Helen Hester-Ossa, Virginia Vitucci, Mary Blayney, Lavinia Klein, and my Aussie "twin," Marg Riseley. Thanks, too, to Nancy Mayer, Victoria Hinshaw, and Emily Hendrickson from The Beau Monde, who came to the rescue when I had pesky research questions Google and all my shelves of research books couldn't answer. Special thanks to another Aussie pal, Melissa James, whose last-minute feedback made *The Marriage Bargain* a better book.

On another note altogether, thank you, Kathryn Caskie, for sharing your knowledge of promotion to a clueless person like me.

I'm waving, too, to the Wet Noodle Posse (wetnoodleposse.com), my fellow 2003 Golden Heart finalists, a bunch of talented writers who stayed together to lavish support and laughter on each other. Ladies, soon you'll all be writing a page like this!

And last, a heartfelt thank-you to my editor, Melanie Murray, who is always there when I need her, and to the whole Warner Forever team, who make working with them a delight.

The
MARRIAGE
BARGAIN

Chapter ONE

Spring 1816

Mist still clung to the grass in a field on the outskirts of London near the Uxbridge Road. Only the barest peek of dawn glimmered on the horizon. Spencer Keenan paced the length of the field and back, mist swirling around his feet like smoke above a cauldron.

"This is utter nonsense." His friend Blake's voice sounded crisp and clear in the damp air. It was also filled with exasperation.

Spence turned to him. "Nonsense it may be, sir, but the idiot accused me of cheating. What else was I to do but call him out?" He gave a wry grin. "You are my second. You were supposed to prevent settling the matter on the field of honor."

Blake shook his head. "Damnedest thing, Spence. There was no reasoning with these fellows."

As the heavy dew stained his boots, Spence crossed over to where Blake waited. Their other friend, Wolfe, paced nearby. Who else but these two men would

have stood by him through this foolishness? At this un-
godly hour as well.

Spence glanced at them, Blake rocking on his heels,
hands in his coat pockets, Wolfe prowling back and forth at
the edge of the road, checking every two seconds to see if a
coach was coming. Spence saw not the tall, imposing ex-
soldiers they were, but the young, skinny lads he'd be-
friended at Eton. He grinned again, this time at the memory
of standing shoulder-to-shoulder with these two against
larger, older bullies. And of sitting in the dark, risking more
brutality from the upperclassmen for not being abed, nam-
ing themselves *The Ternion,* one plus one plus one,
stronger together than apart. Even Napoleon, the biggest
bully of them all, had been unable to vanquish them.

Wolfe, still searching the fog-filled road, walked over
to where Spence and Blake stood. Spence glanced from
one to the other. Theobold Blakewell, Viscount
Blakewell, with his impeccable breeding and good looks
that never failed to make the ladies swoon. Gideon Wolfe,
as dark as Blake was fair, the son of an East India Company nabob and a half-Indian mother, always ready to
fight anyone who dared take issue with that fact. And finally Spence himself, Earl of Kellworth, resisting the use
and confines of his title ever since the reckless accident
that caused his brother's death eight years before.

Spence laughed out loud. The Ternion stood shoulder-
to-shoulder this day because of one foolish young cub
who dared accuse Spence of cheating at cards. That night,
the whole of White's game room had pleaded with young
Lord Esmund to render an apology to Spence. Blake and
Wolfe had demanded it. But Esmund, looking as frightened as a cornered fox, with hair every bit as red, had

shaken his head like a willful child, refusing to retract his ill-conceived words. And Spence, feeling a leaden dismay, had been left with no other choice but to call Esmund out to this duel at dawn.

Wolfe turned to Spence with a furrowed brow. "The stripling cannot have any skill with the pistol."

Spence, on the other hand, had accrued almost a decade of war in which to hone his skill, but that need not be said.

"As we all well know," agreed Spence.

Blake slapped Spence on the shoulder. "You might actually hit the fellow and kill him, you know. Then what? We all dash off to the Continent before you are hanged for murder?" Blake gave him a teasing expression. "I have had my fill of France, Spence, old fellow. I pray you will make a dumb shot."

"Shoot into the air?" Spence pretended to bristle. "I cannot so dishonor myself."

For all his levity, Spence's gut twisted painfully at the unlikely prospect he might draw the blood of that foolish pup. Spence had spilled the life-blood of many an enemy, but this mere boy was not his foe, and Spence had no desire to end one more young life merely to preserve his good name.

Besides, he no more relished fleeing to the Continent than Blake did. Why, the Ternion had just begun to sample London's delights. There was sport, gaming, and drink aplenty still to enjoy.

Spence set his chin in resolve. He would simply use his skill to make it appear as if he aimed directly at Esmund's vitals. With any luck, the pistol ball would not go wayward and accidentally kill the fellow.

"You *could* kill him, Spence." Wolfe's voice was as serious as Blake's had been jesting.

"I shall try my best to miss him." Spence patted his friend's arm.

Spence paced again. He hated being backed into a corner like this. He detested confinement of any kind, such as a flight to the Continent would impose. Not now when they were free to go and do as they pleased. The Ternion were still young and unfettered. At least Blake and Wolfe were unfettered, and Spence had arranged his responsibilities in a way that very nearly demanded no attention at all.

In time the Ternion must change. Eventually Blake and Wolfe would want to settle themselves, and their adventuring would come to an end.

The familiar restlessness pounded at Spence's chest. How long before Blake and Wolfe desired to marry and set up their nurseries? Not long, he suspected.

For some odd reason he thought about his wife, Emma, residing safely at Kellworth Hall. Blake and Wolfe had never understood the bargain he'd made with her, the wife they had never met. But neither had Blake and Wolfe understood his decisions about his inheritance and property. Spence had managed all these matters very well, had he not? There was no reason to speak to Blake and Wolfe about them now. No reason to mention Emma.

"I have examined the pistols." Blake's voice cut through Spence's thoughts like his boots had split the mist. "An extremely fine set. Made by Manton."

Blake, as any good second ought, had negotiated all aspects of the duel, especially the pistols. He lifted a finger and shook it at Spence. "What foxes me is where a nodcock like Esmund would acquire such a pair."

Spence good-naturedly pushed Blake's arm aside. "Devil if I know."

"I insisted upon firing them both," Blake went on. Blake had been meticulous about the duel, as meticulous as he was about the tailoring of his coat or the cleanliness of his linen. He tugged at the snow white cuffs of his shirt. "Seems to me both pistols pulled to the left."

Perhaps Blake was succumbing to a fit of nerves, Spence thought, because this must have been the fifth time he'd mentioned the pistols pulling to the left. Spence bit down the impulse to tease his friend about turning soft after only a month of civilian life.

As in all else, the Ternion had together sold their commissions, all agreeing they'd had enough of war after Waterloo, when their regiment, the 28th Regiment of Foot, bore the onslaught of wave after wave of French cavalry.

Wolfe gazed toward the road for the hundredth time. "Where do you suppose Esmund found a surgeon willing to risk attendance at a duel?"

Blake shrugged. "His brother located the man." He gave a soft laugh. "Can you imagine what sort of surgeon would take the risk? I pray he is not needed."

So did Spence, who wheeled around and trod into the field again, busying himself in judging distances, searching for a tree branch or rooftop or something in the distance that would make a good place to aim.

The mist thinned as the sky grew lighter, but the morning's unseasonable chill gave Spence a shiver. The plain brown coat Blake and Wolfe insisted he wear had no buttons. "Nothing to give Esmund a place to aim," Blake had told him. "Stand sideways," he'd also instructed. "But turn your head toward him." Spence had listened, nodding agreeably, going along with the instructions as if he did not already know this trick of making himself as small a target as possible.

"I hear a carriage." Wolfe stepped into the road to check.

The dark chaise clattered into view, rumbling to a stop not far from where Wolfe stood. Two men stepped out. Lord Esmund was hatless, and his shock of red hair glowed in the early-morning light. Spence studied him. The fool was in debt to his ears from gambling, and naught but a boy, barely of age, but only five years younger than Spence himself. Esmund was as unfledged as a bird just pecking out of its shell. He played at a man's game, however, and Spence figured he was too green to even know it.

Blake and another young man who, with his red hair, had to be Esmund's brother, Lord John, bent their heads together in conference. A third man stumbled out of the carriage, a bulbous creature with an unkempt coat and a weave to his step.

Wolfe strolled up to Spence. "The surgeon looks as if he's been dipping deep into his medicine."

"His brandy, more like." Spence laughed.

"Precisely." Wolfe looked grim.

Spence and Wolfe tried to overhear the discussion between the two seconds.

"I'll be glad when this is over and we might get some breakfast," Spence whispered.

"It still makes no sense why the boy carried things this far." Wolfe frowned.

"Spence?" Blake called to him as casually as if asking him to gaze upon some interesting shard of antiquity.

He walked over.

Blake's handsome features appeared chiseled in stone, as they always looked before battle. "The pistols are loaded."

Spence nodded as Wolfe joined them, a deep line between his eyebrows. "I dislike this whole matter, Spence. It smells rank."

Wolfe always smelled trouble, but at the moment Spence did not care what drove Esmund to make his false accusation. He merely wanted to get the business over with, so the three of them could set off toward that fine inn they'd passed on the way. He was hungry for eggs and ham and a pint of brew.

Spence glanced at his offender, who shook like a wagon rolling down a stony road. God help the lad. Esmund would be lucky not to shoot himself in the foot.

Spence gave Wolfe a wry smile. "In any event, there's nothing to be done but see it through."

Lord John handed Esmund the pistol. To the young man's credit, he seemed to garner some backbone. His trembling eased a bit.

Returning to his customary cocky smile, Blake handed Spence the other pistol. Its stock was walnut, textured to keep from slipping in a sweating palm. The barrel was heavy and nearly as thick at the muzzle as at the breech. Sighting ought to be more accurate. If this pistol contained some of Manton's secret rifling, it would be more accurate still. All in all, it was a fine weapon.

Blake and Lord John consulted their watches. "Stations, gentlemen," Blake announced.

Spence and Esmund each counted out twelve paces and turned, arms at their sides, pistols pointed to the ground. The scent of new grass and honeysuckle filled

Spence's nostrils. In the distance a cock crowed. The breeze was light but bracing on his cheek. It was like any fine day in the country.

"As agreed, you will fire simultaneously at my signal." Blake used his best captain's voice. Its volume threatened to summon the magistrate from the next county.

Spence drew in a breath, held it, and watched Blake from the corner of his eye.

"Attend!" Blake called, his white handkerchief raised high above his head. "Present!"

Spence's heart accelerated. He raised his arm, glancing from the church spire just visible over Esmund's shoulder back to Blake.

Blake's fingers opened and the handkerchief fluttered from them like a butterfly in flight. Spence fired.

Through the smoke from his pistol, he spied Esmund, frozen in place. Unbloodied, thank God. The barrel of Esmund's pistol swayed up and down, back and forth.

Spence turned his face to him, unflinching. He'd stood fast countless times as French soldiers charged straight for him. Their sabers and pistol balls had not killed him then, and Esmund's swaying hand was more likely to shoot one of the birds soaring overhead.

Suddenly Esmund's face contorted and he emitted a sound more like a sob than a battle cry.

Fire and smoke flashed from the barrel, and the crack of the pistol broke through the air. Spence heard the pistol ball zing toward him. He smiled and thought of how cool the ale would feel on his throat.

The ball hit Spence with a dull thud. Its force knocked him backward as it passed through his coat, through his shirt, and, with a sharp, piercing pain, into his flesh.

He realized with a shock that he had been hit and was falling backward. This was not the way the Ternion should end.

Then, as if time stood still, Spence thought of his wife. He remembered her youth, her vulnerability, her gratitude when he'd married her—in name only. He opened his mouth to beg Blake and Wolfe protect her, because now he could not. The only sound that came from his mouth was a moan.

Emma, he thought as his head seemed to explode against something hard on the ground. *Forgive me.*

Chapter TWO

"My lady, two gentlemen to see you!"

Emma Keenan, Countess of Kellworth, jumped to her feet at the footman's quick approach. The weeds she'd just pulled from the vegetable garden scattered at her feet.

"To see me?" Wiping the dirt from her gloves, she caught Tolley's apparent urgency. Whoever these visitors were, they could not have arrived at a worse time. She looked more like a field hand than the lady of the manor.

"Yes, ma'am." Tolley sounded worried. "Mr. Hale said to fetch you straight away and to make haste."

Such dispatch from the elderly butler did not bode well. Poor Mr. Hale tended to move at the pace of a lame snail. For him to request speed suggested a matter of great importance.

At one time she would have been certain such unusual callers would have come to tell her that her husband had been struck dead on some battlefield, but she knew Spence to be in London at present. His cousin had informed her of that fact.

Shaking out her skirt, Emma nearly ran to keep up with Tolley, who undoubtedly took Mr. Hale's word very seriously. As they crossed through the kitchen gardens to the house, the out-of-breath footman could tell her nothing more about the callers. She and Tolley entered the house from the back, and Emma hung up her wide-brimmed hat and her apron on a hook by the door. She removed her muddy half boots and slipped her feet into the worn pair of shoes she'd left there earlier.

"Tell Mr. Hale I shall be there directly," she told Tolley, before dashing up the servants' stairs to her bedchamber.

Her maid, Susan, nearly as ancient as Mr. Hale, dozed by the window, a piece of mending in her lap. She woke with a snort when Emma closed the door.

"There are callers, Susan. I must change."

"Callers, ma'am?" It took several seconds for the maid to move her stiff limbs out of the chair.

"I must dress quickly."

But Susan could move only so fast, so Emma unfastened the laces of the shabby dress she wore to work in the garden and pulled it over her head. She washed her face and hands and removed one of her better dresses from the clothes press. While the maid's arthritic fingers slowly worked the buttons, Emma stuffed her hair into a fresh cap. It wasn't until she was halfway down the main staircase that she remembered the lace of her sleeves was sadly frayed.

Mr. Hale waited for her in the hall, looking very somber, so unusual for him. He typically was cheerful and the most pleasant butler she'd ever encountered, though she could probably count that number on the fingers of one hand. "Two gentlemen in the drawing room, ma'am."

"Who are they, Mr. Hale?"

His brow furrowed. "Friends of the earl."

Spence's friends. Her heart quickened at the thought of her husband. She mentally kicked herself for it. After these three difficult years, the mention of his name ought not turn her into a besotted schoolgirl.

The gentlemen must be here by mistake, that was it. They must think Spence in residence at Kellworth, not realizing how unlikely a prospect that would be. Spencer Keenan thought nothing of Kellworth. Or of his wife.

Emma hurried into the drawing room, one of the few rooms where the furniture was not covered with sheeting against the dust and dirt.

Two tall gentlemen turned at her entrance, one fair-haired and quite handsome, the other dark and forebiding. Both looked to be in shock, as if powder had suddenly exploded in their faces.

The fair one approached her. "Lady Kellworth?" His voice rose incredulously. "Allow me to make our introduction. I am Viscount Blakewell and this is Mr. Gideon Wolfe. We are friends of . . . of your husband." He had to swallow to get those last words out.

Emma extended her hand. "How do you do."

Blakewell shook it, managing a congenial smile that created two deep dimples creasing his cheeks, but did not reach his eyes. "Forgive us, my lady. We are somewhat surprised at your appearance."

She could not doubt that, trying to surreptitiously fold the tattered lace under her sleeve before turning to shake Mr. Wolfe's hand.

"Where is my husband, gentlemen? Perhaps you may give me his direction so I might contact him."

The two men exchanged dark glances.

Emma could guess what that meant. "He has forbidden you to give me his direction, I suppose?" She gave a derisive laugh. "Well, I beg you would pass on a message from me to him. It is about his estate—"

Mr. Wolfe broke in, his gaze filled with suspicion. "The place looks shabby. Neglected. Why has it not been cared for?"

Emma bristled, tossing the dark man the quelling look he deserved. "I have kept out the elements and made sure its people had food to eat. More than that I've not had the pleasure to accomplish."

Blakewell stepped between her and the indignant Mr. Wolfe. "There is much we do not know." His eyes full of sympathy, he reached toward her as if to pat her on the arm.

Emma stepped out of his reach. She did not know these gentlemen any better than she knew her husband. "What is the purpose of your visit, if you please?"

The two men again exchanged looks that could only be described as stressed.

A muscle near Blakewell's eye twitched. "Do sit down, Lady Kellworth. Perhaps a companion might be summoned to join you?"

Emma felt apprehension, as insidious as a garden weed, grow through her from head to toe. "I will stand, thank you." She managed to keep her voice steady.

Blakewell paused, turning away and pressing his fingers against his eyes before facing her again. "Your husband is dead, ma'am. We come bearing his coffin."

Even though she had guessed what his words would be, Emma felt as if the walls of Kellworth had fallen down upon her. It was difficult to remain on her feet.

She closed her eyes. "How?"

"He was killed—" he began.

Mr. Wolfe interrupted. "Blake, take care!"

Emma could hear Blakewell turn from her to address his friend. "We must tell her. She is Spence's wife, man."

"What do we know of her?" Wolfe countered. "Nothing. We ought to heed what we do."

Emma opened her eyes and raised her voice. "How did my husband die?"

Mr. Wolfe swung away and paced over to the window. Blakewell stared at her a long time, before finally answering her. "He was killed in a duel."

Another blow. His death had not been due to something as honorable as war, or natural as illness. It had been in a duel, a useless way to die, something men chose to do over such trifles as insults or card games or women.

At the thought of Spence fighting over a woman, a surprising shaft of pain nearly doubled her over. She hoped Blakewell had not noticed, and tried to manage a brave stare. "Pray tell me why my husband fought a duel."

Blakewell took a breath. "He was accused of cheating at cards—"

"He cheated at cards," she repeated in disgust.

Nearly as bad as dueling over a woman. Until Spence's abandonment of Kellworth, Emma would not have thought him so lost to honor as to cheat. Had Spence fallen that much in debt?

"He was falsely accused!" Mr. Wolfe cried. "And, if you ask me, he was set up."

"Yes. Yes," agreed Blakewell. He gave Emma an intent look. "He was not cheating, my lady, but need I say this is a delicate matter. Duels are illegal, you must know, and, for everyone's sake, especially for your husband's good name, I beg you will tell no one he died in such a way."

"I wonder you told me at all," she said miserably, hating that these two strangers were informing her of how her husband died. "I wonder why you even brought him here."

"We brought . . . brought Spence here to be buried in the family vault. It was the least we could do."

"The very least," Emma whispered. "When did this happen?"

"Yesterday morning," Wolfe told her.

Yesterday morning. Had it been at the same time she worked on the accounts, trying to contrive some way to pay for the spring planting? Had Spence fallen mortally wounded, drawing his last breath when she'd slammed her fist onto the desk and wished him to the devil?

How could she bear having done such a thing?

Feeling as if she were about to shatter into little pieces, Emma forced herself to lift her chin. "Gentlemen, please be seated. I shall step out to arrange for tea."

She walked out of the room and into the hall, where Mr. Hale waited, the housekeeper, Mrs. Cobbett, at his side. She stood stiffly in front of them.

"Is it the earl?" Mr. Hale asked, his wrinkled face even more creased than usual. "They bore a coffin."

She nodded, tears springing to her eyes. "He is dead, Mr. Hale. The earl is dead."

"I feared as much." The elderly butler's shoulders sagged.

Mrs. Cobbett opened her arms and Emma collapsed into them as waves of grief assaulted her, every bit as unexpected as the news of Spence's death.

She thought she hated him. How many times had she cursed him for leaving her with a crumbling estate, elderly retainers who deserved to be pensioned off, and so little money she could barely keep them all in food? The whole countryside cursed him. The failure of Kellworth to prosper had affected everyone.

But at this moment all she could think of was that tall, handsome soldier, his red coat trimmed with gold, gazing down at her with eyes the color of a summer sky and hair as dark as the fertile earth in which she had just been digging. She could still feel the press of his lips upon her forehead after they had spoken their vows and had been pronounced man and wife.

The very next day he had brought her here to Kellworth, not even staying a night here before leaving for the coast, back to war. How young she had been. How her eyes had been full of stars! Now she could see how blind they'd made her.

At the time she'd thought him the most romantic of men, so sensitive to her youth and inexperience that he'd been willing to forgo marital relations with her, though she had snuggled with him in the same bed that one and only night.

She had always believed he would return. For the last two years, she had dared him to return. Dared him to face her wrath for leaving her with the sorry mess that was Kellworth. But always, always she thought she would see him again.

"There, there now." Mrs. Cobbett patted her back as if she were a small child.

Emma sniffed away her tears and straightened. Mr. Hale, his eyes moist, fished in his pockets and handed her his pristine white handkerchief, folded and warm from being in his breast pocket.

Emma dabbed at her eyes. "Mrs. Cobbett, do we have any tea? I must serve something."

Mrs. Cobbett put her fleshy arm around Emma and Emma leaned on her once more. "Never you worry, m'lady. I've a few leaves saved. And Betty is making biscuits from the flour and sugar left in the pantry."

Emma gave her a wan smile. "What would I do without you?"

Mrs. Cobbett squeezed her once more. "Well, I expect you won't find out anytime soon. I've a good many years left in me, you know."

Emma watched Mrs. Cobbett hurry away, her skirts rustling and her keys jangling. These servants were like family to her. Emma was so grateful to them. After Spence departed from her, it had been left to Mr. Hale and Mrs. Cobbett and the others to teach her how to go on and make her feel at home. The servants and Reuben, of course.

She turned to Mr. Hale. "Can we send Tolley to fetch the vicar? He must hear this news directly and we need his help, I think."

Spence's cousin Reuben had the living of Kellworth Parish. He had also been Emma's steadfast friend.

"I took the liberty of sending for Reverend Keenan already. If he is at home, Tolley should bring him very soon."

Emma found her eyes again filling with tears. "Thank you, Mr. Hale." She wiped them away. "I suppose we must also find a room . . . for . . . for the earl's coffin. And . . . and bedchambers for our guests."

It was difficult to think of all that must be done, but so much easier than thinking of Spence lying in a wooden box.

"I have also taken the liberty of having Master Spence . . . I mean, Lord Kellworth's coffin moved to the gallery. Mrs. Cobbett has sent two of the girls to ready the guest bedchambers in the west wing."

She would endure, Emma decided. These lovely people would hold her together and she would withstand this final blow from Spence.

Emma squeezed the butler's bony hand. "You have anticipated everything. I do thank you."

He squeezed her hand in return and limped off. Emma took a deep breath and walked back to the drawing room.

Still standing, the two gentlemen looked as if they'd been having a very heated discussion. They broke apart, both red-faced.

Emma lowered herself into the most worn of the parlor chairs so she could hide its shabbiness. "Please sit, gentlemen."

Blakewell, the charmer, took a chair near her and leaned forward. "How are you faring, my lady?"

She waved off the question, not needing these men to hear her private turmoil. "Forgive me, but I know nothing of you. Who are . . . Who were you to the earl?"

"We *are* his friends." Mr. Wolfe's voice cracked with emotion. He paused, taking a moment to compose himself. "We knew Spence since school days. We served together in the war. We were closer than brothers."

Such fast friends and she had known nothing of them. If she had, she would have tried to reach Spence through them, to beg him to attend to Kellworth's needs.

"He told us so little of you." Mr. Wolfe's tone made it sound as if that had been her fault.

She straightened her spine. "Perhaps my husband forgot about me, as he forgot about Kellworth."

"He would not have done so!" Mr. Wolfe protested. "Spence would not have allowed his home to fall into disrepair."

Emma might have retorted that Spence had not cared enough even to inquire after his property in all this time, but she was suddenly too weary. Besides, that old, constant ache merely added to her grief.

Another worry arose, adding to the tempest of pain and despair she was trying so hard to control. She would lose Kellworth, as she had lost her childhood home. Zachary Keenan, Spence's uncle, would inherit.

Blakewell shot his friend a quelling look. "Lady Kellworth has had enough of a shock for one day. Let us not tease her with such matters now." He turned to Emma. "Is there anything we might do for you, my lady?"

She did not know which of the two she wished to throttle first. Blakewell, with his feigned solicitude, or Wolfe, with his unfounded accusations.

Mrs. Cobbett herself carried in the tea tray, the look of warmhearted concern on her face enough to spark more tears. Emma blinked them away and busied herself pouring, confining conversation to how the gentlemen preferred their tea.

It occurred to her that she did not know how Spence might have taken his tea. She had never had an opportunity to serve him. She had known him so very briefly, but that March day in 1813 when he walked into his uncle's parlor remained as vivid as if it had been yesterday.

Her mother, hastily remarried after Emma's father's death, had never been much of a presence in Emma's childhood, always gadding about to wherever the *beau monde* frolicked. When the distant cousin who had been her father's heir took over Emma's beloved childhood home, all that changed. Her mother brought her to London and rushed her into a come-out, treating her as if she were some pet project, bent upon her making a spectacular marriage. She had been seventeen at the time, and much too much a country miss to know how to go on in the city. She hated London with its noise and dirt and confusion, and begged her mother to marry her off to some country fellow. Her mother, ever conscious of status and rank and ever as indifferent to her daughter's wishes, found her a successful Member of Parliament instead. Zachary Keenan, Spence's uncle, had been nearly as old as her father, and frightened her with his air of importance and the hungry gleam in his eye when he gazed upon her.

Emma had felt many strong emotions these last three years, anger and anxiety chief among them. But not until this moment had she experienced the same sense of despair she'd felt in that London parlor when faced with the frank admiration of Zachary Keenan, his countenance filled with an expectation that Emma had no idea how to fulfill.

And then Captain Spencer Keenan had walked in, tall, vital, and handsome in his infantry uniform. She had never seen a young man so gloriously handsome. When he was introduced to her as the Earl of Kellworth and Zachary Keenan's nephew, he smiled down with eyes the color of a country sky in spring. She thought her heart would stop beating. When her mother told Spence his uncle was courting her. Emma had turned away, unable to bear the young man's reaction.

At dinner the older Mr. Keenan had been seated next to her. He'd brushed his hand along her leg from under the table, and her cheeks had burned with embarrassment. Later when she fled Mr. Keenan's more ardent advances, it had been Spence who found her and dried her tears.

The next day he called upon her mother. Before Emma knew it, her mother pushed her into the parlor with Spence and closed the door on them. He proposed, not marriage so much as a marriage bargain. He would marry her and settle her on his estate and he would go off to war. She would have the protection of his name and the country life she loved in a home even more grand than the one of her childhood.

Emma had readily agreed. Spence had been to her like a knight of old, charging in on a white steed to rescue her from the evil villain. Never once had she believed it when he said theirs would be a marriage of convenience. She thought the reason he spared her the marriage bed was because he had seen how shaken she'd been by his uncle's fervor. She thought he would initiate a true marriage when his soldiering was done; when she was a little older and more ready to be a wife. And a mother. She believed Spence had spoken so out of love for her, a love as pure and fine as in any tale of courtly love.

How young and stupid she'd been!

She'd not realized how much of that girlish dream had remained, how much she'd secretly hoped Spence would again charge in to remove all the burdens she'd borne in keeping Kellworth together. But now he would never return. She would never see him again.

Emma glanced up at Mr. Wolfe and Blakewell. Her silence had become awkward, but she had no idea what to say to them. Mr. Wolfe stared out the window, and Blakewell's gaze fixed on the contents of his teacup. Neither seemed much aware of her. Were they grieving? She could not tell for certain, though they did seem upset.

A knock sounded at the door, and all three of them looked up. Reuben walked in, and Emma sprang to her feet to greet him. Blakewell and Wolfe also rose.

The Reverend Reuben Keenan took Emma's hand in his. "Mr. Hale informed me of the tragic news. My sincere condolences, my dear Emma."

Emma felt the tears prick her eyes again. "Thank you, Reuben." Reuben's boyishly round face was such a comfort to her, even if his expression was solemn. She presented the vicar to Blakewell and Wolfe.

"Blakewell?" Reuben's brows rose. "Were you not at school with Spencer? I seem to recall it."

Mr. Wolfe gave an audible huff.

Blakewell did not smile. "Both Mr. Wolfe and I were schoolmates of your cousin. You were three years ahead of us."

The reverend nodded affably. "We older boys paid little mind to you younger ones."

He turned to take both Emma's hands and lead her to the settee. He kept her fingers in a steadying grip. "Now do tell what happened to my cousin."

Blakewell and Wolfe exchanged glances, and Wolfe wheeled around and trod back to the window. Emma looked to Blakewell.

He remained standing, as erect as a soldier, hands clasped behind his back. "Spence was killed in a duel."

"A duel!" Reuben's eyes widened. "Surely not!"

"It was about gambling," Emma added.

Wolfe twisted around. "He was falsely accused of cheating."

"What of his opponent?" Rueben asked.

Blakewell responded, "He is bound for the Continent, and not likely to show his face for a year or two." Blakewell finally sat in a nearby chair. He leaned toward Reuben. "The thing is, we wish to keep the circumstance of Spence's death quiet."

"Oh, what does it matter?" Emma said this more to herself, but Reuben answered her.

"It matters because if these gentlemen were present at the duel, they might be charged in Spence's murder."

And perhaps they ought to be, thought Emma, for not stopping such a foolish contest.

Reuben cleared his throat. "We do not wish undue attention from the justice of the peace. Let me deal with Squire Benson. I fancy I may talk him into some tame tale, say a fall from a horse?"

"Spence would never fall from his horse!" protested Wolfe.

The muscle in Blakewell's cheek flexed, but he remained silent.

"We shall say it was a freak accident," the reverend placated.

Blakewell and Wolfe exchanged glances again. Wolfe turned back to the window, and Blakewell said, "Very well."

Men are so foolish, thought Emma. What did it matter how he died? He was gone forever and nothing could change that fact. She must worry more about her own fate now. The anger that had grown over three years crept back. Spence had paid no attention to her care while he lived. Had he provided for her in death?

Before leaving for war that day after their wedding, he told her he'd made provisions for her in the event of his death. Not wanting to hear such words, she'd silenced him before he could go on. Now she wished she had let him speak.

But whatever provisions he'd made had likely come to naught after squandering his fortune.

She supposed she would be forced to go to her mother. Would her mother turn her away? More likely the Baroness Holgrove would get busy finding another match for her daughter, something that would raise her own status in the eyes of the *ton*. Emma had never considered confiding her financial troubles to her mother. Her mother's infrequent letters had contained little curiosity about her daughter, filled instead with lively discourse about the society events of which she'd been part. Once her mother had even asked for money.

"We find ourselves a little short of funds," her mother had penned.

Emma had written back that her husband had total control of her finances and she was unable to do anything on her own. She suggested her mother appeal to Spence directly, but she had no idea if her mother had done so, or if Spence had fulfilled her mother's request.

She forced attention back to Reuben.

". . . I suggest we bury my poor cousin tomorrow. We may send messages to the appropriate people today, and I shall ride to Squire Benson's directly." He turned to her. "Will that suit you, Emma, my dear?"

She shrugged. What did any of it matter? The vestiges of her youthful dreams, dreams she had not even realized she'd harbored, had died with Spence.

The next morning dawned gray, with a light but persistent rain falling like tears from the sky, tears that Emma had forbidden herself. She was determined to get through the day without succumbing to emotion.

She and Susan had unearthed her old black dress, the one she'd worn to her father's funeral. Susan had labored into the night, straining her eyes by the light of a colza oil lamp, to alter it to fit Emma's more womanly figure, but the bodice still strained against Emma's breasts. The black hooded cape she wore disguised the fact, though in church, she feared breathing as it merely pulled the neckline even lower.

No one took notice, however. Few attended the funeral service. Spence had not been popular in the countryside of late. Even sufferings that could not be laid at his feet, such as the high price of corn, were blamed on his neglect of Kellworth. No more than a dozen men attended: Squire Benson, who seemed to have accepted Reuben's tale of Spence's death without question, the estate manager, a few servants, and men from the village. Emma had absolutely forbidden Mr. Hale and Susan to come out in the damp, but Mrs. Cobbett sat at one side of her, Blakewell and Wolfe at the other.

The two men remained so stoic, Emma wanted to shake them. If they were such fast friends of Spence, ought they not show more grief?

Reuben spoke such a loving tribute to his cousin, Emma almost lost her battle with tears, but the two men beside her remained chiseled in granite.

The service ended. Reuben walked over to her and clasped her hands. "My dear, again you have my condolences. I shall see you at the house later."

"I shall attend the interring," Emma said. It was a short walk to the family mausoleum on the church grounds, and she had a sudden wish to see if Blakewell and Wolfe would evidence any emotion at all when their friend was closed up within a stone wall.

Reuben squeezed her hands. "Emma, there are good reasons why women do not attend the . . . the final ritual. A lady's sensibilities are too delicate for such an event, I assure you."

"That may be true for others," she retorted. "But I am not a delicate creature and I will see this to the end, even if it is not customary to do so."

He gave her an intent gaze. "I must protect you from such unpleasantness, Emma. I would wish to spare you any suffering at all."

Emma drew back. This was not the first time Reuben had hinted at his regard for her. She supposed she must face it eventually. It peeved her that Reuben would speak this way at the funeral of her husband, no matter how unlike a husband Spence had been. "I wish to remain."

She did convince Mrs. Cobbett to leave, sparing that woman the distress of witnessing the final entombment. She sent her back to the house with the excuse that she must see to the breakfast they would serve when they returned. Reuben argued no further, but walked silently at Emma's side. The rain filled the silence, broken only by the occasional grunts of Blakewell, Wolfe, Tolley, and Squire Benson carrying the hurriedly and crudely made wooden coffin.

They made slow progress over the muddy earth to the somber stone edifice sitting at the far edge of the graveyard. The family crest, engraved in stone above the thick wooden door, was stained with the white-and-black waste of birds. Emma wished she'd thought to have it cleaned, but she'd never even set foot this close to the building.

The last time the mausoleum had been opened was for the entombment of Spence's brother, Stephen, eight years earlier. Reuben and the servants told Emma that Spence's brother died when the carriage Spence had been driving tipped over on its side. The brothers had been extremely close, everyone said. They would now lie next to each other for eternity.

Reuben turned the key in the old lock and the men strained to open the wooden door, its hinges stiff from nonuse. From the doorway Emma could see the gloomy outlines of several sarcophaguses, side by side. The pallbearers carried the coffin into the mausoleum and slid it into its compartment in the wall. Eventually the compartment would be sealed in a stone, carved with Spence's name, like the one bearing his brother's name. Emma felt tears prick her eyes, but she blinked them away.

Reuben recited the final prayers and walked out to stand next to her while Blake, Wolfe, and the other pallbearers filed out. The mausoleum's interior smelled musty and stale, a contrast to the scent of the clean spring rain.

One of the men began to push the heavy wooden door closed. It was to be over too fast. The whole business had been rushed, ostensibly because of the duel. Emma glanced at Blakewell and Wolfe. They wore expressions as stony and unrevealing as the mausoleum's thick walls.

She bit her lip, her mind racing, until one thought could no longer be ignored. She tapped Reuben's arm. "Reuben. Did you view the body?"

He sputtered in confusion. "View the body? I confess, I did not think of it—"

"Then how do we know it is Spence in there?" she asked in a hoarse whisper.

When Spence went off to war, she'd fancied she would sense if he were killed. She'd sensed nothing. What if Spence still lived? What if someone else lay in that coffin?

"How do we know this is not some trick?" she went on. "We know nothing of these men who brought him here—"

"I recall them from school," he broke in lamely.

"This could be a hoax." With sudden decision, Emma stepped forward. "Stop!" she commanded the man closing the door.

Reuben tried to pull her back, but she jerked away from him. Everyone gaped at her.

She cleared her throat. "I wish to view the body."

"No, Emma!" Reuben cried.

She ignored him. "I wish to give witness that this is indeed my husband. Lord Blakewell and Mr. Wolfe, you will attend me." She was as interested in their reaction as she was in verifying the body's identity.

Both men, betraying some distress at last, followed her into the mausoleum. The light from the open door barely illuminated the interior and it took her eyes a moment to adjust. Emma forced herself to look at the space containing her husband's coffin.

"Open the coffin, if you please," she said.

Blakewell and Wolfe slid the coffin out of its space and set it on the stone floor. Wolfe produced a curved knife from inside his coat and pried loose the nails sealing the plain wooden box. The two men looked away as the lid clattered to the floor, the sound echoing against the walls.

Steeling herself, Emma peered inside the coffin.

It was Spence.

Her husband was not shrouded but lay in a brown coat and once-buff trousers, both stained with blood and soil. His face, shadowed with beard, was still as handsome as when he'd made his vows to her.

She gasped and fell to her knees next to the body. "Oh, Spence."

Unable to stop herself, she touched the lock of dark hair that fell across his brow, remembering how she'd dared touch it once before, the day he'd said good-bye and left for war. She wished she were not wearing her black gloves so she could feel if it was still as soft and silky. With her finger, she traced one arching eyebrow and, still unable to stop, stroked his cheek with the back of her gloved hand.

His eyes flew open and she screamed.

He grabbed her wrist and was pulled upright as she backed away in terror.

"Water!" the corpse rasped. "Give me water!"

Chapter THREE

"M y God!" cried Wolfe. "Spence. My God, what have we done?"

Emma looked around wildly. "Get him out of here. Get him out of that box!"

Blakewell grabbed Spence and, though both men were of a similar size, picked him up, and carried him like a baby to the doorway.

"Fetch some water," Emma ordered to the shocked throng of men looking in. "Quick!"

Blakewell placed him on the ground outside the doorway. Spence, who a moment before had prayers for the dead recited over him, turned his face to the rain and softly laughed. He tried to catch the droplets with his tongue.

"Spence!" Wolfe leaned against the doorway, more white-faced than the would-be corpse had been.

Emma could only think of getting him away from where they had almost buried him alive. "We need transport to carry him to the house. And someone fetch the surgeon. Hurry! He cannot be left out in this chill." Falling to her knees beside him, she pulled off her cape and wrapped it around him. "Hurry!"

Two of the servants ran to do her bidding.

Tolley rushed up with a large cup of water and handed it to Emma. Cradling Spence's head in her lap, she put the cup to his lips. He grabbed the cup and gulped. Blakewell crouched across from Emma and held Spence's hands to keep him from drinking too fast. Emma glanced up and caught Blakewell's eye, nearly as wide with alarm as Wolfe's.

Wolfe groaned. "We almost buried him! By God, how did this happen?" He clasped his arms around himself. "He had no pulse. Tell me I am not mistaken, Blake. There was no pulse."

Blake still held the cup against Spence's lips. "Aye, we felt no pulse. And the surgeon pronounced him dead."

"That drunken sot!" spat Wolfe.

Emma had no patience for their recriminations, deserved as they might have been. "Well, he is alive, gentlemen, and we must get him to the house immediately."

In Spence's delirium, his eyes wandered as if sightless, but for a moment focused on Emma. She pulled off her glove and felt his forehead. He was burning with fever.

"Let us carry him to the church at least," Blakewell said, handing the cup to a man nearby.

Wolfe disappeared into the mausoleum, returning immediately with the coffin's lid. The two men eased Spence onto it, and Emma again tucked her cloak, now damp and muddy, around him. Blakewell and Wolfe lifted the hastily made pallet and started toward the church.

Reuben stood frozen in place, shock still on his face. Emma pulled on his arm. "Come, Reuben."

By the time they reached the church door, the same horse and wagon that brought the coffin from the house

waited for them. Blake and Wolfe set the pallet into the
wagon and Emma climbed in.

The rain that had fallen lightly but persistently all
morning had turned the road to mud, slowing their
progress. On foot, Blake, Wolfe, and Reuben easily kept
pace. Spence mumbled incoherently and struggled to sit.
Emma strained to hold on to him so he would not fall out.
His eyes still darted, but he grabbed her hand and held on
so tight she thought he might crush her bones.

When they reached the house, it took only seconds for
the men to carry him into the hall. Mr. Hale and Mrs.
Cobbett watched with stunned expressions.

"My lady, there is no room ready!" Mrs. Cobbett said
as Blake and Wolfe carried him up the stairway, Emma at
his side.

"Put him in my room," she said.

She led them to her bedchamber. When they entered,
Susan toiled to rise from the chair by the window. "My
gracious."

Blakewell and Wolfe placed him on the bed.

"Help me remove his clothes," Emma said. He smelled
of stale sweat and blood. She could not bear for him to lie
another second in such a condition.

Mrs. Cobbett appeared at the door.

Emma looked over at her. "Have one of the girls fetch
hot water and towels. And we will soon need clean bed
linens."

The housekeeper nodded. "Yes, my lady." She hurried
away.

They pulled off Spence's boots, coat, and waistcoat
without much trouble, but his shirt stuck to his skin from
the dried blood. Wolfe produced his knife again and cut

through the front of the fabric as if it were paper. Susan hobbled over with Emma's water pitcher and towel.

"Excellent, Susan," Emma said. "More towels, please."

Emma soaked the towel with water and pressed it against the bloody cloth, holding it there until it was soaked through. Tossing the towel aside, she carefully picked up the edge of what was left of the shirt and peeled it back inch by inch.

When she reached the wound, he cried out and began to struggle, pushing her away with such force she almost fell to the floor. Blakewell and Wolfe rushed to restrain him, but he fought on, cursing and trying to pull his arms from their grasp. Emma caught her balance again and took another towel from Susan. She dampened the cloth and placed it against Spence's forehead.

"Shhhh," she murmured. "All is well. Rest now."

As she stroked his face, he stilled, staring at her. She continued to gently wipe his fevered brow with the cool cloth until, after a moment, he collapsed back onto the pillows, eyes closed.

"He is not dead, is he?" Wolfe rasped.

"Most certainly not." Emma bit her tongue.

"He passed out," said Blake.

"Let us hurry." Emma returned her attention to the cloth stuck upon his skin.

She pulled it away and saw the wound, an inch-wide hole in his shoulder, inflamed with infection. The ball had missed his heart, but the infection could still kill him.

"Can you lift him so we can remove the rest of his shirt?"

Wolfe cut the shirt again to make the task easier. When the two men gently eased him up so she could remove the remaining tatters, the cloth was just as bloody on his back as it had been on the front. She and Blakewell exchanged puzzled glances, and she again soaked the shirt and peeled away the cloth.

"By God, the ball went through!" cried Blakewell, gaping at the ugly hole it left in Spence's back.

There was a knock at the door. "Hot water, my lady." Tolley carried in a large tin. Behind him stood a maid with a stack of towels.

"More hot water, Tolley," Emma said. "And more towels." She needed to wash off the stench of near death.

After a wide-eyed peek at the half-naked man in the bed, the maid hurried off after Tolley.

"We must finish undressing him." Emma unbuttoned the fall of his trousers as the men laid him back on the pillows.

She could not allow herself to think too much on this task. The only men she'd ever seen without clothes had been sculpted from marble nearly two thousand years ago.

Blakewell and Wolfe removed his trousers.

"When will the surgeon arrive?" Wolfe asked in anxious tones as he dropped the trousers on the floor with the other clothes.

Emma had wondered the same thing. She was not sure how much time had passed since they'd pulled him from his coffin. "It will take half an hour to reach him, if he is at home."

Blakewell removed Spence's underclothes, the last of his garments to go, and Emma caught sight of him.

Even ill and filthy, he took her breath away. His shoulders were broad, his chest and abdomen so firm she could see the muscles under the skin. His waist and hips were narrow, and his male parts . . . Well, her heart quite pounded as she let her gaze linger on them.

She clamped her eyes shut. There was still work to do and she must not be distracted from her task. "We will bathe him."

She called to Susan, "The soap, please."

Mrs. Cobbett entered the room, her arms piled high. "More linens." At her heels was more water and still more towels.

Placing towels around him to catch the water and keep the bedding dry, Emma started at Spence's head, washing and rinsing his hair as best she could. Without being asked, Blakewell began at his feet and legs. He saved her the embarrassment of washing the private parts by reaching them first.

As they finished drying him and replacing the bed linens for clean ones, Spence groaned and his eyelids fluttered.

"Mrs. Cobbett, have Cook make some broth or tea or something." After the housekeeper left, Emma murmured, "I wish we had some nightclothes for him."

Tolley said, "I will find some."

By the time Mr. Price, the surgeon, arrived, a clean Spence dressed in clean nightclothes lay in a clean bed. Reuben came to the door with him. Emma had completely forgotten that he'd come with them to the house.

With a worried frown, he walked over to her while the surgeon performed his examination. "How is he?"

"Quite feverish." Emma kept her eyes on her husband. "He falls in and out of consciousness."

When Mr. Price finished he had four people in the room and several servants hovering outside, all waiting for his word. He gestured for Emma. "I will have to probe the wound to remove any remnants of cloth pushed in by the pistol's ball, but it looks fairly clean. The infection is of prime concern, and, of course, whether he'll regain his wits after that nasty blow to the head."

"Blow to the head?" Wolfe piped up. "We know nothing of a blow to his head."

The surgeon gave him a stern look. "You did not know he was alive, I hear."

Wolfe clenched his fists and wore a thunderous expression. "That drunken sot of a surgeon said nothing about a blow to the head."

Blakewell calmly interjected, "It must have happened when he fell. We tried to find a pulse, sir, and the surgeon in attendance declared him dead. We thought only to bring him home."

Mr. Price pursed his lips and tucked his chin against his neck so he could gaze at Blakewell above his spectacles. "He has a knot near the base of his skull. A blow to the head sufficient to cause such a wound could also cause unconsciousness. Likely it suppressed all signs of life as well. But I would not have been so precipitous to pronounce death in such an instance." He appeared absorbed in thought. "Ah, well, he is not out of danger yet. Much will depend on the next few days."

"What must I do?" asked Emma.

"I have some powders to help with the fever and an ointment for the wound. Change the bandage daily." He shrugged. "Give him broth. Other than that, we simply hope for the best."

He reached for his bag and took out a long, thin set of pincers. "I need you gentlemen to hold him still. This may rouse him."

Only Blakewell and Wolfe responded to the request. Reuben stepped out of the way and averted his gaze. The surgeon inserted the instrument into the wound and Spence cried out. Writhing and struggling, he tried to escape the pain, pain Emma fancied she felt herself.

Finally the surgeon finished and the worried servants returned to their tasks. Spence lay insensible again as the surgeon dressed the wound front and back. He promised to come the next day or sooner should Emma require it. Emma walked him to the bedchamber door, where Mr. Hale waited to escort him down the stairs.

After Mr. Price left, Emma suddenly realized her dress was soaked through and stained with mud and blood. "Gentlemen, if you do not mind, please leave me. I wish to change clothes."

Reuben nodded vigorously and hurried to the door. Blakewell and Wolfe hesitated a moment before joining him, but Blakewell turned and walked back to her.

He bowed and addressed her in a hushed, but emotional tone. "Thank you, my lady."

After washing herself and changing into a clean dress, Emma dismissed Susan and was alone at last with Spence. He was propped up on pillows on her bed, his eyelids fluttering as if he were trying to wake. She felt his forehead, still burning hot. He was conscious enough for her to spoon a little broth into his mouth. When she bathed his face with a cool cloth, for a fleeting moment he smiled.

Later she would have the master bedchamber next to hers aired, cleaned, and readied for him, but for now she was content to have him in her bed. She stepped back and watched him, all the memories of three years ago flooding back, like a happy dream. How she wished he were that man of her girlish fancy! To see him lying, almost peaceful, she could not make herself feel otherwise. She'd battle to save the Spencer Keenan she'd wished him to be, even though she might wind up with quite a different man if he did recover.

He became more restless. His eyes opened and darted across the room.

She came to his side again, sitting in a chair next to the bed, stroking his face. "Quiet now, Spence," she soothed. "Quiet now."

He looked at her, but his eyes were not focused. "Must tell them," he mumbled. "Must tell them."

"You may tell them later," she reassured.

"No time. No time." He tried to sit up, but she put her hands on his chest to stop him. He finally collapsed against the pillows, whispering, "Forgive me, Emma. Forgive me, Emma."

Emma gaped at him, open-mouthed. In a rush, her fatigue, hunger, and all the anxieties of the last three years enveloped her. She rested her head on his pillow and let the tears finally flow.

Stephen?

Stephen was there! Spence could see him in the distance, smiling, teeth as brilliant as the white light that surrounded him. Spence raced toward him, but his brother put up his hand and backed farther and farther away.

"Don't leave," Spence begged. "Let me come with you."

His brother smiled again, a peaceful smile. His voice, no louder than a whisper, easily reached Spence's ears. "Go home, Spence. Go home."

The white light enveloped Stephen and he vanished. Spence plummeted into darkness and pain and nightmares.

The dreams were relentless. He stood on the battle-field, his soldiers formed in a square while the French cavalry rode straight for him. Or he saw glimpses of Blake and Wolfe fighting hand to hand with an enemy whose faces turned into those of their old schoolmates, the older, cruel ones who'd made their lives hell.

Or he rode in the phaeton with Stephen, racing down Kellworth's roads, laughing while the breeze caught his hat and sent it sailing and Stephen shouted at him to slow down. Again they rounded the bend, and again the phaeton toppled over and broke into pieces. Again Stephen went flying. Again Spence leaned over his brother's broken body and heard Stephen whisper his name before choking on blood, unable to draw another breath.

Horrible as the dreams were, Spence preferred them to the darkness, which was as terrifying as when he'd been a small boy and he'd known his mother and father would never return to comfort him.

Not all the dreams were horrible. Sometimes angels appeared, including one whose voice soothed him and whose caresses made him feel safe again. A beautiful angel.

Sometimes the angel would disappear and in her place he'd see Emma in her bridal dress, but she was always too far away for him to see clearly. Whenever he came closer, she disappeared and his uncle's visage, large and threatening, filled the dream. Then the angel took on Emma's face, but altered, ethereal.

Sometimes Spence swore he heard Wolfe and Blake talking. He wanted to answer them, but their faces swam in front of him and disappeared as quickly as Emma's had.

The angel was less fleeting. She appeared when he felt lonely, fed him when he was hungry, gave him drink when he was thirsty. When he shivered with cold, she wrapped him in blankets. When he thought he would burn up, she bathed his face in cool water. But even she could not stop the cycle of nightmares.

Spence opened his eyes, but this time images did not fly into his vision, only to disappear. He was in a room. Its walls remained solid, and sunlight streamed through sparkling windows. Chairs and tables remained on the floor. Familiar chairs and tables, but he could not place where he had seen them before. He heard movement, but his left shoulder ached too much for him to turn toward the sound. He tried turning just his head.

The angel sat in a chair near the window closest to his bed. As ethereal as ever, her head bowed over some sewing, her fingers dainty and graceful as she pulled the needle through the fabric. Her brown hair, loosely piled on top of her head, glistened with gold where the sunlight played upon it, and her profile was worthy of an Italian cameo.

He feasted on this chance to observe her, for now she had become as stable as the walls and chairs. She had the same color hair as Emma, the same full, lush lips, but her figure was more womanly, with high, full breasts and the suggestion of a thin waist and long legs beneath her plain gray dress.

A plain gray dress? He blinked, but she did not disappear. He was awake, he must be. He tried to sit up.

Emma stifled a yawn, trying to concentrate on her sewing and keep from dozing in the chair. She heard the rustle of bedcovers and glanced over to see Spence struggling in the bed. Dropping her sewing on the chair, she hurried to his side, placing her hand on his forehead.

"I believe your fever is gone. Are you in need of something?"

He again strained to move. "Sit up," he said, his voice rasping.

She put one arm around him to help him sit and stuffed the pillows behind his back. "There. Does that feel better?"

He nodded. "Water?"

She poured from a pitcher by the bed and held the glass for him to drink. The effort seemed to exhaust him.

Emma looked upon him with relief. He'd been feverish and delirious for three excruciatingly long days and nights, and she had remained at his side nearly the whole time. The fever had finally broken when the full moon shone high in the sky and Emma had wept again, this time out of sheer exhaustion.

His eyes scanned her, lucid now. "What is this place?"

"This is Kellworth."

"Kellworth?" He looked around the room and leaned his head back against the pillows. "My brother's room."

His brother had been dead almost a decade. "It once was your brother's room."

"Before," he agreed. "How did I get here?"

Emma's heart slowed to a normal rate. He sounded sensible. "Your friends brought you here."

"Blake and Wolfe." He smiled as he spoke their names. He *was* lucid. Emma felt like laughing with relief.

He continued to stare at her. "Who are you?"

She stiffened. "You do not know me?"

"In my dream—" he began. "You look like . . ." He stopped himself. "Angel."

He did not remember her. He remembered his friends well enough, but not his wife. Emma took a step backward. "Shall I summon your friends, my lord?"

He brightened. "They are here?"

"I shall send them directly." She walked stiffly to the door and opened it.

"Wait," he called. "You did not tell—"

Emma did not tarry to hear the end of his sentence, but hurried out of the room. She located Blakewell and Wolfe in the drawing room and announced to them that Spence's fever had broken and he was awake. They ran out to visit him.

Emma stood alone in the room.

He had not recognized her. He had forgotten her that completely. Even when enraged at his neglect, Emma had recalled every plane of his face, every line on his brow, every wayward strand of hair. She felt like weeping again.

She thought she'd learned not to weep. Tears did nothing to feed the estate families or to plant the crops or tend the animals. When Mr. Larkin, the estate manager, brought requests for necessary funds, tears did not help. Money was what was required. Instead of turning into a watering pot, Emma sold something. First she sold the few pieces of jewelry she owned; later she sold items from the house— plate, china, whatever she thought would not be missed. Reuben assisted her, facilitating the sale through a dealer in London.

Tears would do nothing now as well, except embarrass her. She refused to let him know the wound he inflicted— above all the other wounds—by not even remembering her.

She balled her hands into fists and strode out the door. The garden must need tending. She'd not been out of doors for three days. Hurrying to the back of the house where her worn half-boots, gloves, and hat would be waiting, she planned to yank out of the earth as many weeds as dared grow among her vegetables.

The door of the bedchamber creaked, and Spence opened his eyes.

"Spence!" Wolfe rushed over to him and clasped his hand. "Thank God!"

Spence gave Blake a puzzled glance.

"You were very ill, my friend." Blake put a hand on the shoulder that did not pain him.

"We did not know—" began Wolfe.

"—if you would pull through." Blake finished for him. "You gave us some tense moments, I assure you."

Wolfe nodded to Blake and let go of Spence's hand.

"How long?" Spence managed.

Blake sat in the chair next to the bed. "Five days, but for two of those you were insensible."

Spence shook his head. "Don't remember."

Blake tossed a swift glance to Wolfe and back to Spence. "That is no surprise," he said in a consoling tone.

The effort to talk tired Spence more than he could have imagined. How sick had he been? He could remember nothing of it except the dreams and the darkness and pain. "Why here?"

"Why did we bring you here to Kellworth?" Blake asked.

Spence nodded.

His two friends again exchanged glances, but he was too fatigued to ask them what the devil was going on.

Blake gave him his charming smile, the sort that always hid what he was really about. "Seemed the best place for you to recover, and believe me you've been well-tended here."

By the angel, Spence thought. "The angel," he said, laboring to get the words out.

"By God, he's addled!" cried Wolfe.

"He's not addled," shot back Blake, whose eyes flashed at Wolfe, but turned soft when looking at Spence. "You must mean Lady Kellworth," Blake said in a matter-of-fact tone. "Your wife."

It took a moment for Spence to comprehend. "Emma?" he rasped, nearly out of breath. "It was Emma. Emma."

Blake rested his hand on Spence's shoulder again. "Easy now. We'll sort it out later. Do not strain yourself."

She had changed. The Emma he knew had been round-faced and as soft and delicate as a spring rosebud. That beautiful woman could not be Emma.

"Emma," he said again.

Blake smiled at him. "You never told us she was a beauty, Spence."

"A beauty." Spence nodded.

Wolfe spoke. "We thought she had a squint or something. Some reason to hide her away in the country." Wolfe's expression turned intense. "Do you remember the duel, man?"

"Duel?" Spence closed his eyes and could see the field and the young man's trembling arm holding the pistol. "Esmund," he remembered. "Dead?"

"No, he's unharmed," Wolfe said. "But you remember?"

"Red hair," Spence whispered. "Don't remember all . . ."

"I think you need a nice sleep." Blake softly squeezed his shoulder. "Plenty of time to remember later."

"You stay?" Spence whispered.

"We'll stay," Wolfe said.

Spence let his eyes close again, grateful his friends would remain at his side. As he drifted toward sleep, the image of the angel swam before him. "Emma?" he murmured.

He wanted her to return.

Chapter FOUR

Emma did not return to Spence's room that day, or the next. She sent Tolley in with careful instructions to bathe and shave him and change the dressings on the wound. Mrs. Cobbett brought him broth and bread. Emma left the rest of the time to his friends.

At night she opened the door connecting her bedchamber with his so she could hear if he needed help, but that was the extent of what she would do. She resisted the impulse to check on him while he slept. She had done her part, she told herself. She'd nursed him through the fever. He had no need of her now.

Besides, she had plenty to do. Having guests in the house created extra work. For one thing, there was the matter of finding enough food for them all and for their horses. These two young gentlemen ate a great deal, it seemed to her. Even Spence's appetite had progressed, Mrs. Cobbett said.

Half the time Reuben also appeared for dinner or breakfast or both. "Checking on my dear cousin," he would say. He'd always been a frequent and welcome guest at dinner, but this time it vexed Emma to ask Cook to prepare enough food for one more. She did not know why she should be irritated at Reuben. Even when he did not show up, Lord Blakewell or Mr. Wolfe seemed to finish whatever was set upon the table. The wine stores were getting lower and lower as well, and she certainly had no money to purchase more.

Emma reluctantly ordered one of her pigs slaughtered, a fine fat fellow who would have brought a good price at market. She had already given up two others from the litter to divide among the farmworkers, not to mention one more to feed the rest of the estate staff.

The first of the meals the pig would provide sat upon the dinner table in front of Reuben, who had done the carving.

"The roast is excellent, my dear," Reuben said with a familiarity that suddenly irritated Emma. "Cook has outdone herself."

"Thank you, Reuben." She watched with dismay as he took another slice of meat. He, of all people, ought to realize what the meal cost her. He knew more than anyone how tight Kellworth's funds were. Still, she had to admit her pride had made her hide the true extent of her poverty from him. Perhaps if she'd shared exactly how much they lived from hand to mouth, he might leave enough meat for tomorrow's stew.

"And how is our patient this day?" Reuben directed this question to Emma.

She stared down at her plate, pushing her turnips to and fro.

Blakewell spoke. "Spence is quite alert today, I must say."

"That is excellent!" Reuben sliced into his pork, then paused as if he'd had a sudden thought. "I almost neglected to tell you. I have a vial of laudanum from Mr. Price." He handed it to Emma.

She put the little bottle in her lap.

Wolfe gave Emma a pointed stare. "He asks for you, Lady Kellworth."

"Does he?" She sipped the half glass of wine she'd rationed for herself.

"You have not attended to him for two days." Wolfe's voice was accusing.

"Two days?" Reuben's eyebrows rose.

Emma fixed her gaze on Wolfe's. "I have had much to do, sir. The estate requires attention."

His gaze did not waver. "If you ask me, the estate needs a great deal of attention, attention it has not received."

Blakewell favored them all with his dimpled smile. "Let us not quarrel over this delicious meal." He directed a question about the church to Reuben.

Emma eyed Blakewell from under her lashes. The man hid much beneath that charm of his. She actually preferred Wolfe's open animosity. She knew where she stood with Wolfe. What went on inside Blakewell's mind was impossible to discern.

"Lady Kellworth," Blakewell addressed her again in his still-affable tone. "We have sent word to Wolfe's man in London to bring our clothing and Spence's."

Another mouth to feed, thought Emma. "Very good, sir. When may we expect him?"

"Two or three days, I believe," responded Wolfe.

This visit of theirs showed signs of lasting a very long time. Certainly Spence would require a long recovery, and she suspected his friends would stick to him until he was well enough to leave with them. She ought not shoulder this responsibility alone, not when the man responsible for her lack of funds was finally unable to escape her.

Emma decided she would visit her husband, if that is what his friends expected of her. If he was as alert as they indicated, she would demand some money.

After every possible morsel of food on the table had been eaten and Cook's pie totally consumed, Mr. Hale and Tolley removed the dishes and brought out one of their last bottles of brandy for the gentlemen.

Emma put the vial of laudanum in her hand and excused herself. She ascended the stairs to Spence's bedchamber with a determined step.

Spence hung onto the bedpost, too weak to move. His shoulder throbbed with pain and he felt like an idiot for trying to get on his feet.

He panted with the effort of remaining still, resting a minute, hoping to garner enough strength to make another attempt to climb back into bed. He feared he'd wind up in a heap on the floor.

Someone knocked on the door.

"Enter," he responded, forcing some volume into his voice.

He hoped it was that footman Tolley. If it was Blake or Wolfe, they'd give him a scold for getting out of bed.

She walked in.

He almost let go of the bedpost.

He'd begun to think she would never return to his room.

She rushed over to him. "What are you doing out of bed!"

He tried to smile but feared it came out more like a wince. "I meant to test my legs. They do not wish to hold me, it seems."

"Foolhardy." She lent him her shoulder and let him lean his considerable bulk on her as she assisted him back into the bed.

"You are not so recovered as that," she scolded.

He examined her close up as she plumped the pillows and straightened the bedcovers. At seventeen she had been like a rosebud that one could not imagine becoming more beautiful as it flowered. His uncle had not been able to keep his hands off her, and Spence could not bear him to pluck that perfect bud, crushing it with his ardor.

"Emma?" he whispered.

She stepped back. "Yes, I am Emma, my lord."

His gaze flicked over her again, taking in the elegant tilt of her head, the lushness of her figure, the confident stance. This was not the delicate rosebud he'd left here at Kellworth.

She stiffened. "Am I so altered? Or have you merely forgotten your wife's appearance?"

He wrinkled his brow. He'd offended her, of course. "You are altered, Emma."

She wrapped her arms around her chest, and a bit of the vulnerable young girl he married showed in the gesture. "Well, that may be," she murmured.

They stared at each other. He did not know what to say to her. "You tended me. I thank you."

She shrugged. "I saw you through the fever. A wife's duty, that is all."

Her chill rose like a barrier between them. "I am afraid I have caused you much trouble," he said uncertainly. "I do not know why Blake and Wolfe brought me here when London would have been closer."

Her eyes flashed. "They did not explain?"

He strained to sit up straighter, but a sharp pain shot through his shoulder. She stepped forward, reluctantly it seemed, and repositioned the pillows behind him.

"I have a bottle of laudanum from Mr. Price. Shall I pour you a dose?" She took the bottle from a small pocket in her dress.

"No laudanum," he managed.

The wounded who survived best on the Peninsula, Spence had observed, were the ones who forced themselves to keep moving, never giving in to the pain. That was why he'd tried to get on his feet, why he would not cloud his mind with laudanum. He wanted to regain his strength.

She shrugged and placed the bottle on the table next to his bed. "As you wish."

He peered into her eyes. "Do you know why I was brought here?"

She did not answer right away. Finally her chin set in determination. "You were shot in a duel and pronounced dead. Your friends brought you here for burial."

"Dead?" He lurched forward, but the pain accosted him again. "Dead?"

"Yes." Her tone was stiff.

He closed his eyes as the pain hit him again, and brought back the memory of relentless darkness. His breath became more rapid and he broke out into a panicked sweat.

A cool hand touched his brow. Her scent, like a spring garden, filled his nostrils. He opened his eyes, and she leaned over him, looking distressed. "I have made you ill." She bit her full pink lip. "I ought not to have told you."

She lifted her hand and stared at it as if its action had surprised her. In his fevered state her hands had stroked him like that, comforted him, made him feel safe from the darkness.

He tried to give her a smile. "Forgive me. It was a momentary weakness."

She stepped back again. "It was entirely my doing. I will not plague you with more conversation."

She spun around and headed toward the door.

"Wait!"

She halted but turned only her head.

"Stay with me a bit." He tried not to sound too desperate, but the whole afternoon he'd felt panic whenever left alone.

"I have much to do."

"Let others do it," he begged. "Sit with me. Tell me how you go on here, Emma. I wish to hear of you."

She swung around to him, eyes blazing. "You *wish* to hear of me?"

He was shocked at the change in more than her manner. She fairly bristled with anger. "Of course. Have you liked living at Kellworth? Have you been happy here?"

She strode back to his side. "I would believe you wished to hear of me, that you ever considered my happiness, sir, if you had acknowledged even one of my letters."

"Your letters?" His head throbbed and he felt dizzy again. He pressed his fingers against his temple, but the movement sent a shaft of pain through his shoulder. Unable to stop himself, he groaned.

Her voice lost some of its edge. "I shall send your friends to attend you. I suspect you can wait a bit longer to hear of how life has been at Kellworth."

The room started spinning and he shut his eyes to make it stop. When he opened them again, she had gone.

Emma dismissed Susan, declining, as she always did, Susan's offer to help her dress for bed. It was difficult enough to let the elderly maid untie her laces. The woman's arthritic fingers worked so slowly Emma nearly perished from impatience.

After Susan shuffled out of the room, Emma donned her nightdress and sat at her dressing table to take the pins from her hair and brush out the tangles.

She examined herself in the mirror by the golden light of her colza lamp.

Was she so altered? She tried to see what changes three years had brought. She'd grown another inch in that time, and her figure had turned more womanly, but what was it he'd seen that prevented him from remembering her?

Emma jumped up from her seat and hurried to the door connecting her room with her husband's. She'd almost forgotten to open it a crack so she could hear him if he roused during the night.

She returned to her dressing table and ran her fingers down her cheek. Her face was terribly thin, she thought. She was thin all over, though it was less apparent with her large breasts, and disguised by her clothes. She examined her neck, trying to remember if it had always been so long. Her complexion was tinted by the sunlight and her arms firmed by hard work. Perhaps he'd thought her a maid—a garden worker. That was what she was.

She grabbed the brush again and dragged it ruthlessly through her long curls, attacking the knots and trying to think of nothing else.

"Emma?"

The brush fell from her hands and bounced on the carpet. Spence stood at the doorway. Rather, he leaned against the doorjamb, breathing hard.

She jumped to her feet and ran to him. "What are you doing? You must not leave your bed."

He took a careful step inside her room, leaning against a bureau near the door. "Wanted to get up," he panted. "Saw your light."

She came to his side and offered her arm to lean on. "I will take you back to bed."

He pressed against her, and she could feel his firm muscles through the thin layer of her nightdress. "No." He gestured toward a chair.

Feeling no choice, she walked him over to the chair where Susan usually sat, hearing the catch in his breath with each step. He winced as she eased him into the chair. His breath came hard.

She walked over to her water pitcher and poured him a glass of water. He downed it greedily.

"You ought to be in bed." She stood over him.

He looked up at her, his piercing blue eyes even more vibrant than in daylight. "Blake and Wolfe told me what you did."

She squared her shoulders. "What I did?"

He reached out and grasped her hand, the touch surprisingly gentle. "I made them tell me about the duel and about . . . my death." He closed both hands over hers.

"You made them open the casket, Emma. You found me alive. If you had not . . ."

She drew back, but he would not release his grip on her hand. The lamp cast enough light for her to see the deep horror in his blue eyes, the panic he tried to conceal.

She could not help but feel it herself. "You remember it."

The confirmation appeared in his eyes.

He released her hand, and Emma fought an unbidden urge to sweep her fingers through his hair, as she'd done so many times while he'd been feverish.

She knelt down to his level and spoke to him as she would a child determined to stay awake after a nightmare. "It is over now. You must not think of it. You are safe."

Suddenly his arms encircled her. He held on to her so tightly she could barely breathe. She felt him tremble against her, and it seemed that his trembling resonated throughout her whole body.

He released her, leaning back against the chair, running a ragged hand through the very hair she'd wanted to touch. "You must think me daft."

For the moment the thoughts she had of him were as jumbled as her emotions. She did not respond.

He gave her a wan smile. "I seem to have developed a fear of the dark."

She shot to her feet and started for the connecting door. "Is there no fire in your grate? I shall see to it—"

"Come back," he pleaded. "The fire is adequate. It . . . it casts a bit of light. I did not want to be alone."

She stopped and turned back to him, clasping her hands together in front of her. "It will only take a moment to fetch Tolley to stay with you."

"No." His eyes swept the room wildly before his gaze returned to her. "Would you sit with me, Emma? Talk to me?"

Her impulse was to refuse, but how often had she heard in her own voice that same edge of controlled panic, the sense that one was held together by sticking plaster? Even though it would take mere minutes to fetch Tolley, she knew how long minutes could be when one was fearful.

"I know I am delaying your sleep," he went on. "But, a little while, please?"

She walked over to the satinwood armchair adjacent to his chair and sat down. "What do you wish to discuss, my lord?"

His smile turned sheepish. "Oh . . . anything."

There was much too much for Emma to say, and now she was certain he would not be strong enough to hear the half of it.

She put her hands in her lap and waited.

He tried to straighten himself in the chair and grunted with the attempt. The pain still on his face, he said, "You mentioned letters. I never received letters from you, Emma."

But she had sent many. She'd sent them to his man of business. She'd sent them to his regimental offices. She'd even sent them directly to Spain and France, wherever the newspapers said he was stationed. It was impossible to believe he could not have received even one letter. How was she to respond to this? Say, "I don't believe you"?

She responded, "I sent them."

His brow wrinkled and he frowned. She was painfully aware that his breathing still sounded as if he'd run from the village without stopping. He twisted in the chair

again, and something twisted inside her when he grimaced in pain. He closed his eyes, she supposed waiting
for the pain to pass.

He opened them again and rested his gaze upon her for
such a long moment that it was her turn to feel like wincing. "You've changed, Emma."

She bowed her head and examined her hands, noticing
her ragged nails. She curled them into her palms.

"You are not the girl I left here."

No, she'd aged. She knew she had become old and bit-
ter, but it was her bitterness and anger that propelled her
forward, forcing her to find ways to ward off the suffering
that would ensue if the farms failed.

She raised her eyes to him and lifted her chin. "No, I
am not the girl you left here."

His expression turned puzzled, and his breathing
quickened. Impulsively she reached over and touched his
hand. She forced her voice to exude sympathy. It was surprisingly easy. "There will be plenty of time later to talk
of this, Spence. It is best you go back to bed."

The panic again flashed across his face. "A moment
more . . ."

They could not sit here longer. He looked to be at the
end of his endurance.

She stood. "I will help you into your room. I will stay
with you."

He gave her a grateful, hopeful look, but then shook his
head. "You have given up enough sleep on my account."

Her eyes widened in surprise. She was not certain she
liked him knowing she'd remained at his side during the
days and nights of his fever.

She shook her head. "Do not concern yourself with me. The hour is early yet and I am not at all sleepy." She extended her hand. "Come. I will help you to your room."

He waved her hand away. "No, I believe I can do it."

He tried to lever himself up by pressing his hands on the armrests of the chair, but his face contorted in pain. He quickly dropped the hand weakened by his wounded shoulder and tried again using his good hand. His muscles shook with the effort. Emma reached for him, his strain resounding in her as if she, too, endured the struggle.

He managed to stand without her, bracing himself for a moment. Still holding on to the chair, he took a cautious step forward and his legs began to give out.

Emma caught him, nearly tumbling to the floor herself. "Lean on me. I will help you."

They inched their way toward his chamber, but he had weakened enough that Emma needed to bear most of his weight. She stumbled and they both struggled to regain balance.

"I fear I will not make the door, Emma," he gasped.

And there would still be a distance to go, once in his room. Emma glanced toward her bed. "I will put you in my bed."

He did not argue, and they laboriously crept to the side of her bed. He could do little to assist himself getting atop the bed, so Emma used the reserve of her strength to lift his legs and slide them up on the bed. She covered him with the blankets, wondering if she should make a fire in her fireplace, an extravagance she'd learned to forgo except on the coldest of winter nights.

She stepped away from the bed.

He tried to sit up. "Do not leave."

"I am merely tending to the fire." She gestured toward his door.

"Leave it, Emma. Come lie with me."

Lie with him? The idea brought a sudden desire to run from the room. It was bad enough that he lay in her bed.

"Please, Emma. Forget the fire. It is being alone I cannot abide. Not tonight."

In spite of herself, she thought of him awakening in his coffin, struggling to get out, calling for help with no one to hear. Her shoulders sagged and she walked back to the bed.

"Lie with me," he pleaded.

She thought of the expense of leaving the lamp and the fireplace burning in his room. It would only take a moment to tend to them. She thought of dragging a chair over to the bedside. There was no reason she could not sit with him rather than lie next to him in her bed.

He grabbed her hand. "Please," he whispered, his breathing accelerating, a sure sign of panic returning.

With teeth clenched, she crawled into bed, teetering on the edge so as to be as far as possible from him. He immediately scooted closer to her. Lying on his good side, he rested his weakened arm around her so that they were like two spoons in the silver drawer.

He stroked her hair, the hair she just realized she'd not put in a plait. His breath was warm on her neck.

"Thank you, Emma," he murmured, his lips so close she feared she would feel them touch her bare skin.

In no time his breathing lost its labored effort and became even. She felt the rise and fall of his chest against her back and the heat of his skin through the thin layers of nightclothes. His arm rested heavy across her, his fingers entangled in her hair. Emma was afraid to move.

Inside her a tumult of emotion roared.

Three years ago she had felt the same heat, the same breath, the same fingers in her hair. But this time there was no gratitude, no heady infatuation, no hope.

It was a long time before Emma slept.

Chapter FIVE

Spence woke in Emma's room, the morning sunlight greeting him, but she had gone. He was glad of the light, even though it did not entirely banish the dream of being in the coffin, about to be buried alive.

The terrifying darkness had been real, after all, although his fevered brain had not realized it. He now remembered pressing his hands against the rough wood of what must have been the coffin lid, he remembered gasping for air and feeling that there would never be enough. He remembered the pain in his shoulder, radiating down his arm. And he remembered the smell of his own sweat and blood.

His head throbbed and his breathing accelerated. As when he'd been small, he wanted to call for help. Call for Emma.

He opened his mouth, only to shut it again.

Emma had not been happy and flourishing at Kellworth as he'd thought, even though that image had sustained him on many a sleepless night in the Peninsula. He was not precisely certain what caused her unhappiness, but he knew he owed her his life.

Spence forced himself to sit up, hanging on to the carved mahogany bedpost of the bed that long ago had been his mother's. He paused to catch his breath from the effort. This weakness of body and emotion was nonsensical. He was a soldier, for deuce's sake. The things he'd witnessed—the things he'd done—were equally horrific. He had not turned into a quivering dish of jelly then, had he?

But then he'd not been alone. Blake and Wolfe were always nearby and the Ternion had managed to survive.

He had survived this ordeal, too, had he not? He would refuse, simply refuse, to give in to weakness. Spence forced himself to slide off the bed and stand, still grasping the bedpost. He finally let go and took a tentative step. His legs held him. Encouraged by such success, he started across the room, heading for the connecting door. He shuffled carefully, guarding against the dizziness that frequently came over him, focusing his eyes on the floor at his feet, fearing to look around lest he lose his balance and fall flat on his face. Once down, he would not have strength enough to rise.

He had no wish to feel any more helpless than he did at this moment. Especially that feverish loss of control over what was real and what was not.

Emma's scent surrounded him. It comforted him in an odd way, as if she were still lending her slender shoulder as she had done the previous night. A stubbornly male part of him wanted to show her he could make the journey to his brother's old room by himself.

From his first glimpse of her three years ago, Emma had always sparked something primitively masculine inside him. Once when the Kellworth gamekeeper had been teaching his brother and him to hunt, they'd come upon a family of deer grazing at the edge of the park. Scenting them, the tall, proud stag wrapped his neck around the little fawn for a moment before the three ran back into the wood. Spence had been glad Gandy forbade them to shoot. "There not be the numbers of red deer as years past," Gandy had said.

When Spence first spied Emma, he'd felt like the stag, with the instant instinct to protect her and whisk her away. And that was precisely what he'd done.

He gave a dry laugh. Were not the tables turned on him now, though? She was strong and he so weak it felt as if the door were a league away.

Where was Gandy now? Spence wondered as he inched along. The gamekeeper must be well into his seventies. Was he still at Kellworth or retired to a cottage somewhere?

Over the years Spence had largely succeeded in blocking out thoughts of Kellworth. With it, however, he'd also blocked out all those who'd once peopled his world. Like Gandy. Kellworth should have been Stephen's. Spence would have been content to have the rest of the world. Fate had decreed otherwise, however, and had given him Kellworth as well.

Not Fate. Spence's own tearing pace and cow-handed driving had done the trick.

He reached the door and collapsed against the jamb, breathing hard. Stephen's old bedchamber looked too much the way it had when Stephen was alive. His personal effects had been removed, but Spence still could not shake the feeling that any minute Stephen would discover him and chase him out.

The hall door to the bedchamber opened and the stocky, dim-witted footman who'd been attending him walked in, searching the room for him with a wrinkled brow until finding him holding on to the doorjamb for dear life.

"There you are, m'lord," the footman—Tolley, was it?—said, breaking into a cheerful smile. "M'lady said I should look in on you. Said you'd be in m'lady's room."

"Then why did you enter this room?" Spence asked.

This must have been a puzzling question, because Tolley frowned and took a moment to think on it. "Dunno, m'lord." He broke out into an affable smile again. "Is there any service I can perform for you, sir?"

Spence's need for assistance was so obvious, he did not know whether to laugh or to shout at the man. He did neither. "Assist me to the bed, if you please."

"Very good, sir." The young footman lumbered over to him and nearly lifted him off his feet. They made it to the bed in a few long-legged strides, where Tolley easily hoisted him up.

"Thank you, Tolley."

The footman stood at the side of the bed. "Lady Kellworth said I was to ask you if you wanted some breakfast, if you were awake, that is, but seeing as you are awake . . ."

Spence had a giant thirst, but no real appetite for food, but perhaps Emma would bring the food as she'd done when he'd been feverish. He rubbed his chin, scratchy with beard.

"Shave me first, I think." If his wife did indeed enter the room, he wanted to look presentable. Bad enough he felt like a cat's chewed plaything; he did not have to look the part.

When breakfast came, Blake and Wolfe brought it.

"Here you are, my fine fellow," Blake said, carrying the tray to the bed. "The finest in gruel and chamomile tea."

"Chamomile tea?" Spence's thirst pined for something more stout, like a big tankard of ale.

"The formidable Mrs. Cobbett insisted you must have this." Blake set the bed tray over Spence's lap. He grinned. "And how is our favorite corpse today?"

"Kind of you to remind me." Spence grimaced. "My head feels as if it is full of wool, I'm weak as a kitten, and my shoulder hurts like the devil. Other than that I feel splendid."

"Glad to hear it!" Blake laughed.

Spence's hand shook while he poured a little cream from a pitcher into his gruel. He tasted a spoonful and his appetite came back, only he could not make his arm move fast enough for his stomach. When he reached for the teapot, Blake got there first and poured him a cup.

Wolfe pushed two chairs to the side of the bed. "We have sent for Arjun to bring us clothing and other necessities. He should arrive tomorrow."

Arjun was Wolfe's faithful valet, a mysterious Indian man of indeterminate age, who braved every discomfort of the Peninsula with his young master, remaining even through Waterloo. He must have been left behind in London when Blake and Wolfe made their dash to Kellworth.

"Very good. I will be glad to don real clothes and forgo these." Spence pulled at the nightshirt.

Blake grinned. "You look remarkably like my grandfather. All you lack is a nightcap."

Spence shot back a sarcastic look. He probably had appeared ridiculous to Emma as well.

Better not think on that too much. "Tell me, how do things go on for you here? Other than not having even a change of clothing."

Wolfe huffed. Blake nudged him, and gave a very stern look. Spence waved his spoon at them. "What does all this mean?"

His friends traded glances.

Spence looked from one to the other. "I'm losing patience, gentlemen."

Wolfe leaned forward. "Something is wrong here, Spence. There are signs of neglect everywhere. Most of the rooms are closed up, unused."

Wolfe's doom and gloom again, Spence figured. "There is only one family member in residence. I doubt she requires many rooms."

"I've walked around the outside as well. The ragstone needs repair in several places. It must be letting in the damp." Wolfe shook his head. "It looks as if not a penny has been spent on the place in years."

Spence's head began to pound. He took a shaky sip of tea. "That is nonsense. I've arranged a considerable sum for the running of the estate and all the manager has to do is ask if he requires more." Last Spence knew Mr. Larkin was still managing the estate, a trustworthy man, the son of the previous manager and a fixture throughout Spence's childhood.

Blake examined Spence closely. "Let us postpone this discussion for a bit."

Spence waved a dismissive, but tremulous, hand. "What does Lady Kellworth say of this?"

Wolfe's lips thinned before he spoke. "She will say nothing about it."

Ever smiling, Blake broke in. "I am certain there is a very logical explanation. You may tend to the matter when you regain your strength, Spence." He peered at Wolfe. "This is not the time."

Spence frowned. He had arranged matters so carefully. His man of business in London had carte blanche to release funds if either Mr. Larkin or Emma made the request. True, Spence had never closely examined the quarterly reports his man provided, but he'd glanced at them. Nothing ever seemed amiss.

Lifting the spoonful of gruel suddenly required too much effort. He foolishly tried to lift the tray to remove it, but pain shot through his arm. Blake quickly whisked the tray away and put it on a side table.

"Do not trouble yourself over this," Blake insisted.

"It is his estate, man," Wolfe cried. "He needs to know."

"But not now," Blake said in a firm voice, but he still wore his smile. "He does not have the strength."

Blake had the right of it, of course. Spence felt like their voices echoed from far away and it was a struggle to keep his eyes open, but he'd be damned if he let his friends think he needed to be coddled like some bony invalid.

He used his good arm to help straighten up in the bed. "Send for Mr. Larkin—the estate manager—if you would be so good. I will speak to him today."

Wolfe nodded, his expression smug. Blake tossed Spence a wary look. They left the room a moment later, bearing the breakfast tray. The door had no more than closed before Spence fell into an exhausted sleep.

When Spence woke, still propped up on the pillows, it was to the sound of loud voices outside his room.

He heard Wolfe's voice raised. "I tell you, Lady Kellworth, it was he who requested it. You cannot countermand an order by your husband."

"I have already done so." Emma's response was at equal volume. "He is far too ill to discuss estate matters with Mr. Larkin."

"I believe that is for Spence to decide," shot back Wolfe.

Blake, ever the conciliator, interjected, "Leave it, man."

Emma went on hotly, "If you cannot respect my wishes in this matter, I will bar you from his room!"

This was his little fawn, the one who needed the strong arm of his protection? Spence had seen French cuirassiers cower when faced with an enraged Wolfe.

"Now see here—" Wolfe began.

Emma stopped him. "I am quite serious, sir. I am going to visit my husband alone and I will thank you not to hover around the door when I do."

"Come on," Blake insisted.

The door opened and Spence caught a glimpse of Blake dragging Wolfe away; that is, until his vision filled with Emma, striding toward him like one of the Furies of Greek legend.

When she caught him watching her, she checked her advance. "You are awake."

"Indeed."

Her hazel eyes glittered in a face flushed pink, as if she had been out of doors, or perhaps merely flushed with anger. Wolfe regularly brought high color to women's cheeks, most often due to anger. Emma's hair was tamed into a knot on top of her head. Almost tamed, to be more accurate. Sunlight from the window dusted gold on the tendrils that escaped, framing her face and caressing the long nape of her neck. He remembered how he had wrapped her curls in his fingers the night before, as if holding on to a safe tether.

He caught his breath. "Your voices woke me."

She averted her gaze with an angry expression. "I see." She quickly recovered and met his eye with a challenge. Quite un-fawnlike.

"Would you care to explain why you prevented Wolfe from carrying out my request to see Mr. Larkin?" he spoke quietly, still daunted by her unexpected strength.

She stepped closer to the bed, the distracting clean scent of a spring day accompanying her. "You are not sufficiently recovered."

He deflected the issue of his health. "Wolfe says that the estate is in disrepair."

She brought the subject back. "He ought not to have taxed you with such matters while you are ill."

He took a breath, ready to issue a stern order as he had done so many times to the soldiers in his company. He set off a coughing spasm. Each cough felt as if someone poked fingers into his shoulder wound.

Emma poured him a glass of water and thrust it under his nose. He seized the glass with a shaking hand and brought it to his mouth.

Deuce! He was furious with himself. Angry that he could not even muster the strength to issue a curt order. And even angrier that this woman witnessed his weakness.

Hand still trembling, he tried to put the glass back on the table. She took it from him, her fingers brushing his.

She gave him a stern look filled with suppressed emotion. "After three years, you cannot complain about waiting a few more days. You can see Mr. Larkin and anyone else you please after you are a little more recovered."

Something was amiss. Whatever it was pulled on that part of his conscience he'd so carefully buried under a mountain of rationalization. Her delaying the discussion only made it tug harder, but his whole body ached from the coughing fit, and his head felt heavy. Even this brief allusion to estate problems made him yearn to close his eyes and return to oblivion.

"Is it so very bad, Emma?" he asked, his voice a mere whisper.

She straightened her spine. "I suspect you will think it of no consequence at all."

That response puzzled him even more.

Spence tried to think logically, but the lure to sleep clouded his brain. There must be some compromise. He always found a compromise when conflict seemed insurmountable. His arrangements for the estate were a compromise, a way to leave him free to pursue the adventure he craved. His marriage to Emma had been a compromise for them both, he'd thought. Now he was not so certain.

"You never told me, Emma, how you go on here."

Her eyes narrowed. "That, too, will seem of little consequence if you wait two or three days."

He frowned. She merely sparked more questions, but his little fawn held the reins firmly in her graceful fingers. He detested this feeling of powerlessness. On the other hand, it would be a great relief to not be required to think.

Still he could not entirely release the matter. "I would like for Blake and Wolfe to speak with Mr. Larkin." He paused in uncertainty. "It is still Mr. Larkin, is it not?"

"It is."

He went on, ". . . to Mr. Larkin and anyone else they please. Will you see to it, Emma?"

Her green eyes flashed. "It is not necessary. I give you my word I will tell you all when you are stronger."

"Tell me something now," he pleaded. "I may go mad with imagining if you do not."

She blew out a breath followed by a long intake of air. "Very well. The decrease in funds has meant that priorities have had to be made, but we have managed, my lord."

"Decrease in funds?" Spence struggled to remember the accountings he had read so carelessly. He leaned forward, feeling the agitation of long-delayed guilt. "Decrease in funds?"

His breathing accelerated and his head spun as if he'd been whirled around.

She dampened a cloth and patted his face. Her voice became softer. "There is nothing you need worry about today. I promise."

He wanted to believe her. He wanted to sleep, to avoid further speech, and, more so, to avoid whatever was wrong here at Kellworth. He closed his eyes.

"Allow them to ask questions, Emma." His voice sounded as weary as he felt. "They are my friends."

"As you wish, my lord," she said stiffly.

Her hand continued to bathe his face with the cool cloth until his breathing slowed and he felt himself sinking into sleep. As if from a great distance he heard the rustle of her skirt and her light footstep as she crossed the carpet. He heard the bedchamber door open and shut again, and he knew she had gone.

Emma left Spence's bedchamber furious at those gentlemen he called his friends. She went in search of them, eventually finding them in the courtyard at the rear of the house, Mr. Wolfe pacing and pointing to where weeds grew between the flagstone. He would probably not remark upon the flourishing herb garden, would he? Emma could tend to the herb garden herself, but weeds between flagstone were not high in importance to survival.

"Gentlemen." She crossed the yard. They both watched her, Wolfe with hands curled into fists. "The earl wishes for you to speak with Mr. Larkin on his behalf. I will instruct Mr. Larkin and Mr. Hale that everyone on the estate must answer any questions you wish to ask."

Wolfe gave a triumphant smile.

Emma glared at him. "I have only one stipulation."

He immediately looked ready to attack. "Which is?"

She met his eye with a steady gaze. "You do not discuss any estate matters with the earl until *I* say he is strong enough." She leaned forward for emphasis. "Until *I* say so, Mr. Wolfe."

Blakewell stepped forward. "That sounds like a very sensible plan, does it not? We do thank you, Lady Kellworth, for allowing us to tend to Spence's interests."

She wanted to smack Blakewell's conciliatory smile right off his face. "You may thank the earl when he is stronger. You may visit him as you have done, but I will have no repeat of taxing him with matters he is too ill to attend to."

"Quite fair." Blakewell nodded. "Is that not so, Wolfe?"

Wolfe averted his eyes. "It will be as you wish, my lady."

"Good," she said. "If you will pardon me, I shall speak with Mr. Larkin and Mr. Hale."

"One moment, Lady Kellworth," Wolfe said. "There are questions I would like to ask you."

Emma straightened. "Ask anything you wish of the others, Mr. Wolfe, but I will answer only to Lord Kellworth. I consider this a private matter and none of your affair."

She turned on her heel and strode off, not waiting for comment or looking back.

Before dinner Mr. Larkin asked to speak to Emma.

She met him in the library.

"Those young gentlemen grilled me, my lady," he reported. "I told them how the estate funds were cut and how you used your allowance to keep Kellworth going. Mr. Hale told them the same thing."

"You have done what the earl requested." Emma still bristled at the intrusion, but she would not let Mr. Larkin see that.

"Tomorrow they insist upon inspecting the property," he added.

She expelled a resigned breath. "Show them whatever they wish to see, Mr. Larkin."

Later over the dinner table Emma endured Wolfe's glowering glances.

Reuben came to dinner again this night and as usual had no difficulty making unremitting conversation. Emma was grateful. Without him, the dining room would have been as silent as a tomb.

She shuddered and took a quick sip of her wine. Perhaps a tomb was not the best simile, considering Spence's narrow escape.

Blakewell, apparently as facile in conversation as Reuben, engaged the vicar in a lively debate about some obscure point of theology. Emma did not trouble herself to follow the lively discussion. In a way she and Wolfe were kindred spirits. Neither pretended there was no tension in the room.

Blakewell and Reuben both paused at the same time, Blakewell to sip wine, Reuben to stuff another forkful of pigeon pie into his mouth.

Wolfe seemed to seize the opportunity. "Reverend Keenan, what do you know about what has been happening on the estate?"

Emma gasped.

Blakewell nearly choked on his wine. "Wolfe!"

"I want to know." He gave his friend a defiant shrug. He turned to Emma. "Do you have any prohibition against my questioning Mr. Keenan?"

She returned a narrow-eyed glare.

"Emma?" Reuben looked to her for direction.

"You may speak as you will." She certainly did not owe any explanation to friends who attended duels and left the loser for dead, but she would not be accused of imposing silence on anyone else.

Wolfe repeated, "Tell me. What do you know about what has been happening here on the estate?"

"I do beg your pardon." Reuben blinked. "What do you mean 'happening on the estate'?"

Blakewell avoided looking at Emma but seemed as interested in Reuben's answers as Wolfe.

Wolfe went on, "I mean, the place is in disrepair. It is virtually closed up. There are few servants, and Lady Kellworth appears each morning in very shabby dresses."

Reuben blushed, darting a glance to Emma. "I . . . I believe there are economies the good Lady Kellworth engages in. Money has been quite tight for some time."

"But, why, sir?" Wolfe persisted. "Why the need for economies?"

Reuben reached for his glass and downed the remainder of its contents. "Well . . . it . . . um . . . We have been given to believe my cousin gambles."

"Fustian!" shouted Wolfe. "Who says such a thing?"

"Talk from London." Reuben wore a guileless expression. "My father told me of it."

"It is not true!" Wolfe nearly jumped out of his seat.

Blake lost his smile. "Spence gambles no more than other gentlemen. We have never seen him drop large sums."

"I do not have an explanation, then." Reuben fussed with the edge of the tablecloth. "I do know that Lady Kellworth has done well in these difficult circumstances. I have helped her out on occasion, but there is not much I can do."

Emma peered from one man to the other. Spence's friends did not know of his gambling? That surprised her. On the other hand, they seemed to have known little of her as well. Maybe Spence hid his vice from them. Or maybe they merely lied to protect him. He'd fought a duel over a card game, had he not?

She wished she had not set up this prohibition against taxing Spence's strength. He had as many questions to answer as he could possibly think to ask.

Chapter SIX

The next day Blakewell and Wolfe toured the estate with Mr. Larkin, searching, Emma was certain, for some evidence to blame her for Kellworth's deterioration. Let them search, she thought. She could not be faulted for making the crops a priority. They were the estate's main source of income. The only action for which she had the slightest guilt was disposing of bits of Kellworth plate and porcelain, small items she had no right to sell. The proceeds had enabled her to purchase livestock—her precious breeding pigs among them. Did not food have more value than a small Worcester bowl or a pair of Derby figurines or Sheffield candlesticks? She hoped Spence would think as much.

She intended to tell her husband everything she had been forced to do to keep his estate and its people afloat. She could hardly wait to do so. She'd waited three years for the opportunity to let him know in no uncertain terms what suffering he'd caused. With the privilege of his title came responsibility, and he had shirked it.

Wolfe's valet arrived at Kellworth while the two gentlemen were still on their tour. To Emma's surprise, he was an

India man, or at least she thought so. His dark complexion and features resembled engravings she had seen of natives from that part of the world; however, his clothing was as English as the best gentleman's gentleman, a well-tailored, plain black coat and black breeches. She was surprised as well to see him arrive in a splendid carriage. It seemed Mr. Wolfe must be a man of means. Perhaps he would leave generous vails for her servants, if he ever left Kellworth. Perhaps he might even be prevailed upon to pay for the keeping of his team of matched roans.

As Tolley hurried out to attend to the valet's arrival, Emma waited with Mr. Hale by the servants' entrance.

"He appears a grand valet, does he not?" she said to Mr. Hale.

"Grand indeed, my lady," the butler agreed.

"I suppose I ought not greet him here." She gave a wan smile. "He might mistake me for the housekeeper."

Mr. Hale retained his dignified stance, but his eyes twinkled. "I think no one would mistake you for a housekeeper, my lady. Mrs. Cobbett, by the way, is readying a room for this fine man. One look at the carriage, and she said she must change his accommodations."

Emma sighed. "Did you ever before have to worry about Kellworth not being grand enough for a valet?"

He straightened his arthritic spine as best he could. "The grandeur of Kellworth has always rested in its family, ma'am."

Emma touched his arm. "And in the excellent staff who care for them."

Tolley peeked in the door, holding his cheek with one hand. "There are three trunks to come in. The earl's and the other gentlemen's."

Three trunks. She suspected they intended to stay until Spence was well enough to leave.

"Tolley, what is wrong with your face?" Emma asked.

"Toothache, my lady." He ducked back out the door.

Emma turned once more to the butler. "Mr. Hale, when it is convenient, please bring the valet to be presented. I shall wait in the library."

"Very good, my lady." Mr. Hale bowed.

A few minutes later Emma sat at the desk amidst shelves of leather-bound books. The windows of the library leaked and she worried the damp might eventually damage the books.

She shook her head. A master glazier would be needed to reseal the windows, and the services of such a craftsman would be an extravagance. She must think of another way to preserve the books, perhaps move them to a drier room. She made a mental note to speak to Mr. Hale about it.

She opened a drawer and removed the record book in which she tallied her accounts. Flipping through its pages, Emma wondered if perhaps Spence could beg money from the wealthy Mr. Wolfe, enough to repair the leaking window, replenish the wine stores, and replace her precious pig. A man's friends helped him out in such ways, did they not?

She was still frowning over her figures when Mr. Hale entered the library, followed by the valet. "This is Arjun, my lady. Mr. Wolfe's gentleman," he announced.

Emma rose and nodded cordially. "How do you do, Mr. Arjun. You must inform Mr. Hale or Mrs. Cobbett if there is anything you require. We wish you to be comfortable."

The man's near-black eyes met hers for a fleeting second before he lowered them in deference. "Merely Arjun, my lady. Your servants have been most hospitable."

She expected an exotic accent to go with his dark appearance, but there were only the cultured tones of an educated man. "Thank you for bringing the gentlemen's belongings."

"I am at their service." He bowed.

After Arjun left with Mr. Hale, Emma figured the day was too far advanced for her to return to the garden. Tolley had been busy and now would have to deal with Arjun's trunks. He would not have time to tend to Spence. Mr. Hale had enough to do and she certainly could not send in one of the maids. She had no choice but to look in on Spence herself.

Carrying a pitcher of fresh water in one hand, she knocked lightly on the bedchamber door. Hearing no sound within, she crept in quietly.

Placing the pitcher on the table beside the bed, she paused a moment to make certain Spence was resting well. He lay against the pillows, eyes closed. His complexion had neither the sweat-gilded flush of fever nor the sickly pallor of the previous day. If such a thing were possible, Spence looked more handsome than he had the first time she had seen him walk into his uncle's drawing room. Three years had etched tiny lines at the corner of his eyes, and the planes of his face were more sharply masculine. His lips had more definition, the top lip perfectly bow-shaped and just a tad thinner than the bottom one. The corners of his mouth naturally turned up, as if he smiled even in repose.

Emma experienced that flash of awareness she remembered when he was first presented to her, that flare of excitement that had marked every brief hour she'd spent with him back then.

His eyes opened, and she stepped back. It took a moment for him to focus.

"Emma," he murmured, blinking sleep away.

She'd hoped he would have remained asleep. "I am sorry to disturb you. Tolley is busy, so I must check on you and bring you fresh water."

With his one good arm, he pushed himself more upright on the bed. "You do not disturb me, Emma. How do you go on today?"

In spite of herself, she felt like that green girl of long ago, so thrilled that the young soldier showed an interest in her. It angered her to be so affected by him.

"I am as always, sir," she responded in clipped tones.

His eyes crinkled at the corners and his voice deepened. "I wish you would tell me what is wrong, Emma."

She curled her hands into fists, not to curtail her anger, but to suppress the long-dormant yearnings his voice threatened to loose.

She met his eyes. "We will speak of this when you are stronger."

His gaze did not waver.

She turned away to fill his glass with water before he could respond to her.

He took the glass from her hand and sipped. "Thank you." He glanced at her again, but without the same intensity. "Would there be any ale, Emma? I've a great thirst for ale."

Ale? She supposed the servants had some ale to drink with their meals, but it would be as carefully rationed as the wine had been.

"I shall see to it, my lord."

There was a knock on the door, and Tolley entered with a trunk on his shoulder. His usually affable face was all contorted. "Your trunk from London, my lord." He winced as he spoke.

"That is excellent." Spence peered at the footman. "Are you unwell, Tolley?"

The footman set the trunk down in the corner of the room. As soon as he'd done so, he clapped his hand against his cheek. "Toothache, m'lord."

"Is it very bad?" Emma asked, wondering how she could afford to send him to the village to have it pulled.

Tolley winced again. "I'll manage, ma'am."

"Do you need him, Emma? Perhaps he could have a day to rest." Spence reached over to the bedside table. "You are welcome to the laudanum, Tolley. I'll not be using it."

Spence's offer showed the sort of consideration Emma once believed typical of him—before he showed that thoughtfulness was easily forgotten. Out of sight was indeed out of mind for the Earl of Kellworth.

Tolley took the vial from Spence's hand. "Thank you, m'lord."

Emma added, "You are excused from your duties, Tolley. You may tell Mr. Hale the earl has ordered it."

"Yes, m'lady." Tolley bowed and left the room.

"I believe I have just shot myself in the foot," Spence said.

Emma swung round to him, alarmed. "What did you do?"

He chuckled. "Figuratively, I meant. I was looking forward to getting out of these nightclothes. Now I have no one to assist me." He gazed over at the trunk. "Perhaps if Arjun packed a banyan for me, I could manage it myself. Would you mind looking, Emma?"

All she wished to do was flee the room, but she walked over to the trunk and unlatched it. Inside were neat stacks of white shirts and neckcloths, and underneath fine new coats and other clothing. Everything appeared to be new. Of course. After leaving the army, he would have needed new clothes.

She pressed her lips together, trying to guess how much this finery must have cost, how much food she might have purchased with such a sum, how many repairs might have been accomplished. How it might have felt to have even one new dress for herself.

"Do you see a banyan in there?" He leaned forward as if he would be able to see it.

She carefully lifted out the fine white linen shirts and two coats of superfine before she found the blue-patterned chintz robe.

"You cannot do this yourself," she said, carrying the garment over to the bed.

"I shall give it a go." His smile was uncertain.

Emma sighed. She *had* seen him fully naked, and had bathed his feverish body more than once. "I will assist you."

The gaze of his piercing blue eyes did not waver. He covered himself to the waist with the bed linens and pulled at the hem of his nightshirt so that he no longer sat upon it. As efficiently as if she were removing dustcovers from the furniture in the unused rooms, Emma pulled the nightshirt over his head.

Except for his bandage, he was bare to the waist, exposing the muscles of his chest, peppered with dark hair. Her breath caught. He continued to watch her.

"Your wound is healing well," she said, dropping her eyes to his bandage. Tolley had done a clumsy job of it, and it had shifted, exposing the wound. The skin around the wound was no longer an angry red, but a much healthier pink. "It must be rebandaged."

She leaned close to him, feeling his gaze still upon her as she carefully unwound the cloth. She made the mistake of glancing up to meet those intense blue eyes, which were now only inches away. His breathing accelerated. She quickly turned away, reaching for a clean cloth and the bottle of lavender water.

"I shall bathe it before giving you a clean bandage." She pressed the damp cloth against the wound.

He flinched, and again her gaze met his. "Did I hurt you?"

"Never." His voice again resonated inside her like the lowest tones of a pianoforte.

Setting her chin, she focused on the task, moving as quickly as she could. She applied the ointment the surgeon had left, covered the wound and wrapped the bandage around his chest, under his other arm. The feel of his warm flesh beneath her fingers remained even after she finished.

When she picked up the banyan, her hands shook. "Put your injured arm in first," she instructed, gently guiding the sleeve so he would not have to move his arm too much. In spite of herself, her heart raced. She was much too aware of his eyes upon her, the rate of his breathing, the warmth of his skin.

She adjusted the banyan over his shoulders and he wrapped it around himself.

Before she could get away, he took hold of her hand. "Thank you, Emma."

She pulled it from his grasp. "It needed to be done."

She wrapped the old bandage and the nightclothes into a bundle and turned to leave.

"Must you go, Emma?"

She could make up an excuse. Say she had urgent business to attend to, like the feeding of the pigs or the weeding of the garden. She swung back to him.

His eyes pleaded. "Sit with me by the window. I long for fresh air and sunshine."

She frowned. "You ought not to get out of bed."

"I must." Adjusting the banyan around him, he swung his legs over the side of the bed.

Reluctantly, she offered her arm.

He waved it away. "I think I can do it. Stand nearby to catch me if I'm mistaken."

As if she could catch a falling six-foot-tall man. The strain of moving was all over his face, and he grunted as his feet hit the floor.

His legs held. "I need to get my strength back."

The way to regain strength was to rest, but she did not argue further. Rather, she walked by him, close enough for him to lean on her if need be.

They slowly made it to two side chairs in the small alcove by the bay windows overlooking the park at the rear of the house. He levered himself into one of them. "Would you open a window for me, please?"

She hesitated, concerned he would catch a chill.

He gave her a somewhat desperate look. "Emma, I cannot be closed up in here a moment longer. I need the air."

His panic was clear. Had he been thinking of the coffin? Of being trapped in it?

She'd felt trapped in London, when they met. She remembered how she'd thought she might perish if she could not escape the walls surrounding her and find a place with fields and trees and space to run. Even Hyde Park had been no release. Any time she'd spent there had been confined in a curricle, seated next to Spence's uncle.

Yes, she could recall feeling suffocated.

She lifted the sash, opening the window as wide as it could go, though the window was taller than she. Spence struggled to his feet again to lean against the window frame and take deep breaths of the cool spring air. Like gentle fingers, the breeze ruffled his hair.

"I forgot this fragrance," he said, still inhaling deeply. "Kellworth in the spring. No other place smells like it."

She knew what he meant. The fresh grass, the newly tilled earth, the garden's new riot of flowers. It was how hope might smell, had she dared to believe in hope.

He turned to go back to the chair and lost his balance. Emma seized his arm and held on until his feet were again firm beneath him.

He gave a dry laugh. "You have rescued me again, Emma. I nearly tumbled out the window."

She shook inside from more than his close call.

He grimaced as he sat himself in the chair. "I detest feeling this weak."

She released his arm. "You will recover."

He looked up at her. "I am impatient."

Of course. He would be eager to be well, to be away, to be back to life away from her, where he would not have to give Kellworth or his wife a second's thought.

She folded her arms across her chest and spoke stiffly. "If you do not take care, your convalescence will be longer still."

His blue eyes looked puzzled, but she turned and started to straighten up the room. Or rather, to rearrange items that needed no rearranging.

"Sit a moment," he begged.

Girding herself, she marched back to the chair and sat, folding her hands in her lap.

He tilted his head, as if thinking. "I know better than to ask how you go on. You will scold me and say I am not well enough to hear it."

She recognized his attempt at good humor. She simply did not wish to respond to it.

But he would not make it easy to evade him. He smiled at her. "Tell me what you did today."

He could not truly wish to hear the events of her day. Of rising early and dressing herself so that when Susan shuffled up the stairway, she would not have too much to do. Of searching for some mending so her maid might feel useful but not be overtaxed. Of checking with Mrs. Cobbett and Cook in the kitchen to figure how to stretch the food so that the guests would be satisfied and would not question the meagerness of the fare. Of donning her wide-brimmed straw hat, old boots, and gloves so she could tend the vegetable garden and check on her pigs.

It would not serve for him to hear all that.

"I worked in the garden," she said.

He nodded, clearly wanting her to go on.

"And then Mr. Wolfe's valet arrived."

"Arjun." He nodded. "What did you think of him?"

It was easier to talk of something that had nothing to do with either of them. "He looked to be from India, but he spoke like an Englishman."

"He is a bit of a mystery. I do not believe Wolfe knows the man's story, except that in India, his family served Wolfe's mother's family for over a generation. Wolfe's mother is half Indian, an aristocratic family, but he dislikes talking of this."

Wolfe would be unhappy talking of anything with her, Emma was certain. She was unlikely to discuss his parentage, under any circumstances.

Their feeble conversation faltered, and Emma feared he would return to the subject of Kellworth, so she asked a question. "You have known Mr. Wolfe and Lord Blakewell a long time?"

A softness came into his eyes. "A very long time. We were schoolmates. We've been nigh inseparable since."

It was on the tip of Emma's tongue to remark that a wife should know her husband's best friends, but she bit it back, and turned to look out the window.

"Thank you for welcoming them here, Emma." His voice turned low again.

She gave a sarcastic laugh. She had not precisely welcomed them. It would be more accurate to say she tolerated them. "This is your house, Spence. How could I do otherwise?"

One corner of his mouth turned up, an endearing expression, and she was irritated that it affected her much as it had when they first met.

"I think of Kellworth as yours," he said.

She took a sharp breath, barely able to hold back the diatribe she'd practiced in her mind for three years. In their marriage bargain she'd not bargained for hardship and want.

Even so, she loved Kellworth as if it *were* her own. She rose and walked over to the window. She longed to see the estate prosper again, to see the house restored to its original beauty, but could not discuss this with him. Not yet.

"Have . . . have you been sleeping well?" she asked instead, her tone polite. He had not come into her room again, terrified of being alone. He had not again slept holding her in his arms.

"Tolerably well," he replied, his voice uncertain. "The lamp you set in my chamber is a great comfort. As is knowing you would hear me if I called you."

There was a rap at the door and Mr. Hale entered. "I beg pardon, m'lord, but your cousin, Reverend Keenan, has come to call on you."

Spence glanced at Emma, with a look that seemed regretful. He turned back to the butler. "Of course, Mr. Hale. Ask him to come in."

Reuben must have been waiting in the hallway, because he walked in directly. His step faltered when he spied Emma. He strode over to Spence's chair.

"By God, you are out of bed!" Reuben spoke jovially. "I confess to being astonished!" He thrust out his hand, and when Spence raised his to shake it, Reuben covered the hand with both of his. "How are you feeling, Cousin?"

"A bit better," Spence replied.

Reuben turned to Emma. "And you, Emma? It is good to see you."

"I am well," she said. "Will you come for dinner, Reuben?"

He gave a polite nod. "I would be delighted." He spoke as if it had been an age since he'd dined at Kellworth instead of only a day.

She walked over to the bundle of soiled clothes and bandages. "I shall inform Mr. Hale to set you a place."

It was an excuse to leave the room. She glanced back before walking out the door.

Spence was gazing at her. "Good day, Emma."

"Good day," she mumbled, and hurried out of the room.

She carried the bundle to the back stairs, intending to take it to the laundry. From below came the sounds of retching. Emma hurried down.

On the landing Tolley knelt over a chamber pot, vomiting. The exotic valet Arjun was at his side.

Arjun looked up at her approach. If he was surprised to see the lady of the house carting laundry down the servants' staircase, he gave no indication.

"What is wrong?" she cried.

"He has not yet been able to explain," replied Arjun calmly. "In a moment, perhaps."

Emma dropped her bundle and hurried back to her room to fetch some water and a clean cloth. When she returned, Tolley was seated on the landing floor, leaning against the banister.

She dampened the cloth and crouched down to wipe his face. "Are you all right, Tolley?"

"Yes, m'lady," he moaned.

"Give him a sip of the water," Arjun suggested.

She handed Tolley the pitcher, but stopped him from drinking too much.

"Forgive me, ma'am," Tolley gasped. "I tried to make it to outside."

"Do not think of it," she said. "You must have more than a toothache. Shall I summon Mr. Price?"

Tolley strained to reach into a pocket of his coat. He handed her the vial. "I think it was the laudanum, ma'am." He clasped his hand over his cheek. "My tooth pains me still."

Arjun extended his hand. "May I see it?"

She gave him the vial. He opened it and sniffed.

Tolley coughed and winced in pain. Emma gave him another sip of water. "I took the laudanum and was about to lie down to rest, but I felt I would be sick. My pardon, ma'am. I grabbed the pot and ran, but I did not make it in time." He took hold of the banister and pulled himself to his feet. "I shall tend to this." Swaying on his feet, he gestured toward the pot.

"No, you shall not," Emma insisted. "You must return to your bed."

He hesitated, but she gave him a firm glare. "I insist, Tolley."

Nodding, he lumbered up the stairs.

Emma held her breath against the stench and reached for the chamber pot.

Arjun stopped her. "I will tend to it, my lady."

Somehow she felt she would be better suited to the task of carting away vomit than this pristine gentleman's gentleman, but she took a step back. "Thank you, Arjun."

He nodded, but regarded her with a furrowed brow.

"Yes, Arjun?"

He handed her Tolley's empty vial. "The vial did not contain laudanum, my lady."

Her eyes widened.

"The vial held a syrup made from the ipecacuanha root," he said.

This meant nothing to her.

"Ipecacuanha is known to induce vomiting," he went on. "The young man appears quite robust. He will suffer no ill effects, do not fear. With your permission and his, I will provide him something to relieve the toothache."

She blinked. "But it was supposed to be laudanum."

He shrugged, then turned to pick up the chamber pot.

As he started down the stairs, she stopped him. "What if he had not been robust?"

"I beg your pardon?"

"What if the person taking the vial had not been robust? What if he had been quite ill?"

Arjun paused. "Someone very sick might be endangered."

Emma remained still as the valet proceeded down the stairs, but as soon as he was out of sight, she proceeded to the library, asking a passing maid to inform the vicar she wished to speak with him before he left.

A few minutes later Reuben entered the library. "What did you wish of me, Emma? You know I would do anything you asked of me."

The tone of his voice set off warnings. She so wished he would not imply this unwanted devotion toward her.

She held out the medicine vial. "This was not laudanum, Reuben. You gave Spence an emetic."

His jaw dropped and he staggered. "Grant me mercy. Tell me I did not do such a thing!"

She shoved the bottle at him. "Smell it!"

He leaned over so the vial reached his nose. "Dear God." He collapsed in a chair and wiped his brow. "My cousin looked too well to have been harmed by it. Say it is so."

She did not sit. "He did not take any of it. But if he had—in his weakened state—"

He held up his hand. "Do not go on, my dear. Do you not think I know what the result might have been? I would never forgive myself if Spence came to harm at my hand."

"I want to know how this happened, Reuben." Emma glared at him.

"I . . . I . . ." He took a breath. "I do not know!" He covered his mouth with his hand, then blurted out, "I must have mixed up the vials! I asked Mr. Price for something for dysentery. I had a touch of it, you see. He gave me the laudanum for Spence at the same time!"

She put her hands on her hips. "Did you not discover that your medicine tasted like laudanum?"

His round cheeks trembled. "I never took any of it. My . . . problem resolved itself." He rose to his feet. "Here, I will bring the laudanum when I return for dinner."

"Never mind. Spence will not take it." She could not believe Reuben would be so heedless.

"I must take more care," he wailed. " 'He who ignores discipline despises himself, but whoever heeds correction gains understanding.' "

"That is all very well—" began Emma.

"Proverbs, you know." Reuben reached for her hand. "Tell me what you wish me to do about this and I will do whatever you bid, my dear lady. You have had trials enough without my adding to them."

She pulled her hand away. "There is no need to turn maudlin, Reuben. There is nothing for you to do."

"I shall confess the whole to my cousin," he continued. "And beg for his forgiveness."

"You will do no such thing," she scolded. "I will not have you telling Spence things that will only distress him."

His eyes widened in shock. "Do not tell me you have a *tendre* for him, after all that has transpired!"

She certainly did not wish to discuss the cauldron of feelings she had for her husband with Reuben.

She made herself give him a level gaze. "I have compassion for the sick, no matter who it might be." There was only a twinge of guilt at lying to the vicar.

He stared at her for long enough that she wished she could squirm. "If only . . . ," he began, then cleared his throat. "I fear for my cousin and his companions. 'Those who sow the wind shall reap the whirlwind,' you know."

She could agree on that, but would do so secretly. She had made a point never to discuss her husband with his cousin. It seemed . . . disloyal.

"You may go, Reuben. I am needed elsewhere. I just wanted to speak with you first."

He looked wounded. "I wish you would rest yourself. You work too hard, Emma, my dear. Shall I have Mr. Hale order us some tea?"

She gave a little laugh. She did not even know if there was any more tea. "I am not tired, and I really must not tarry."

He gave up, bowed, and turned to walk out of the room.

Before he reached the door, Emma said, "Come for dinner at the usual time, Reuben. It is kind of you to lend your company."

He smiled and departed with a happier step.

Chapter SEVEN

Throughout the next week Spence grudgingly accepted the annoyance of everyone withholding information from him. Not knowing what caused Emma's chill or Wolfe's worry or Blake's determined cheerfulness became another obstacle to surmount, like the weakness in his legs and the pain in his shoulder. He concentrated on getting his strength back.

At Tolley's recommendation and Wolfe's insistence, Arjun took over Spence's treatment. Tolley's toothache had been miraculously cured from some sort of bark Arjun had given him to chew. During Tolley's ministrations Spence heard every detail of the tooth treatment, including how Spence's laudanum had given him nothing but the vomits.

What Emma thought of Arjun's doctoring, she never said, but then, Spence saw very little of her. Sometimes he lay awake at night thinking of calling out to her, but pride prevented him. He had once been Emma's valiant, now he'd turned into her burden, and, for some plaguing unknown reason, she was furious at him. He had failed her, but he did not yet understand what had happened or why.

The only way he could make the discovery was to recover; therefore, he threw himself wholeheartedly into Arjun's odd regimen, refraining from meat, learning to sit still and think of nothing but one word, moving his muscles in gentle prescribed patterns. His balance improved, and using a cane Tolley unearthed from the attic, he soon navigated around the room by himself.

That evening he asked Tolley to dress him and he braved the staircase to appear in the dining room for the first time. Mr. Hale hastily set a place for him at the head of the table. Little of the food served met Arjun's strictures, but Spence was not that hungry. He did chuck Arjun's rules out the window for one forbidden glass of wine. Emma had served a sauternes that must have predated the war. Spence swished the sweet liquid in his mouth, savoring its rich taste as long as possible.

Though Blake and Wolfe had greeted his entrance at dinner with enthusiasm, throughout the meal Emma's expression remained grim. He suspected it was in anticipation of what was soon to come. If he had recovered sufficiently to take the stairs, he had damned well recovered enough to listen to her account of matters here at Kellworth—and of what volatile emotions lay between the two of them. He would not rest until his questions had answers.

His body apparently took it literally that he would not rest. Sleep eluded him that night, even though the exertion of attending dinner ought to have exhausted him. True, he'd not tarried with Blake and Wolfe and their port after the meal. He left the room with Emma and had been rather proud to show her how he could climb the stairs unassisted. When he looked back after reaching the top, she still stood staring at him as if he were the Tower's executioner.

Now he could hear her in her bedchamber and could see the lamplight from the crack in the doorway. More than once the past week he'd thought of begging for Emma's company at night, of lying next to her, holding her and feeling totally safe, but he did not want her to see all his weakness of mind.

He had forced himself to forgo the lamp and make do with a glow from the fireplace and moonlight from the window. He repeated Arjun's word over and over and soon mastered the panic of the darkness. He almost felt himself again.

Spence was still too weak to fear giving in to his masculine urges, the ones that on his wedding night gave him a battle quite different from any in the war. She had been so very young. He knew he'd have no time to show her what lovemaking could be. His uncle had frightened her enough with kissing and pawing at her. She would have needed a slow, gentle introduction. And what if he had got her with child and then returned to the Peninsula? That worry alone convinced him he must leave her the very next day.

Though not as terrifying as the confines of a coffin, Kellworth could be another sort of entrapment, one that bound him with memories and regrets. Even this bedchamber was a torture of memories. Stephen was everywhere in it. Spence could picture his coat and boots thrown casually aside. He could see Stephen turn and smile at him, could remember them both as boys scrapping on the floor. And just when he succeeded in banishing Stephen from his mind, the tall, shadowy figure of his father emerged, gone so long Spence could no longer remember his face without looking at the portrait below stairs.

He'd been only five years old when his parents perished at sea on their return from Naples, an excursion meant to acquire more treasures of antiquity to adorn Kellworth. Spence wondered if Emma had left the Roman or Greek statues in their various corners. The statues always stood like ghosts to remind him of what had been stolen from him.

But better for him to sit cross-legged on his bed and concentrate on the strange word Arjun had given him than let his mind travel in that direction. The direction in which his thoughts meandered was a mere indication he was bored. This mundane country life was like death to him.

Spence glanced back at the light glowing from Emma's room. He imagined her seated at her dressing table, brushing her luxuriant hair. His fingers flexed with the memory of her soft curls. He recalled the scent of her, a scent so much like Kellworth she might have been spawned from its stones.

He sat up. Why wait until the morrow for their confrontation? There would be no interruptions at this time of night, no other tasks to perform, no distractions, except perhaps the recall of her soft curves beneath her thin muslin nightdress.

Spence reached for his cane and eased himself off the bed. Earlier he'd refused the nightshirt Tolley tried to hand him, and he could not visit her dressed only in his drawers. He hobbled over to the bureau and fumbled around before his fingers found his banyan. Grimacing at the shot of pain when he shoved his arm into the sleeve, he wrapped the robe around him and quietly walked to the door, opening it wider.

Emma sat at her dressing table exactly where he'd fancied her to be, brushing out her hair. In the dim light from the lamp, her hair looked as dark as his own, giving her an exotic, sultry air. Emma the rosebud had opened into full glory.

"Emma?"

Her brush stilled and she turned. Even in the darkness he could see her apprehension. She did not speak.

He entered the room, carrying but not using the cane to emphasize how well he had recovered. He stopped near the chairs by the windows and gestured to them. "Shall we talk?"

She turned back to the mirror, and he watched her straighten her spine and rise. She lowered herself into the chair but remained poised, like a Scottish Kellas cat ready to pounce.

He braced himself. "I am ready to hear it, Emma. Do not hold back. I am ready to hear everything."

Her gaze did not waver as he took the chair opposite her. The moonlight from the window bathed her in a soft light, making her look as angelic as his fevered mind had fancied her. Her white nightdress completed the celestial impression, except that it clung to her body, revealing the very real woman underneath.

Desire stirred within him—a desire he knew himself still too weak to indulge—but it pleased him to feel so much a man in her presence.

When she did not speak, he murmured, "Tell me why you are unhappy."

She blinked and her hands curled into fists in her lap. She seemed to steel herself before speaking. "My unhappiness ought to be no surprise to you, sir. Everyone at Kellworth has suffered. Did you not think we would?"

As it had so many times this week, the feeling that he'd missed something important, something he ought to have known, returned. "But why, Emma? Why have you suffered?"

Her eyes shot daggers at him. "We suffer from lack of funds and well you know it."

The puzzle was no closer to being complete. He tried to remain calm. "You mentioned this before. What lack of funds?"

Her contempt could not have been more visible even in a noonday sun. "Do not toy with me, Spence. You cut the funds for Kellworth within my first year here. You ignored me when I begged you to send money, and so I had no choice but to economize where I could. When your *friend* Mr. Wolfe runs to you with his tales of how the house needs repair, ask him if the farm was neglected. Ask him if we saw to the crops and to the people—"

Spence held up his hand for her to stop.

She did not. "We let as many servants go as we could. They had to seek employment elsewhere, and now most of them are far from their homes and families. Loyal retainers like Mr. Hale and Susan stayed on, as well as others like Tolley, who would not find good situations otherwise, but the older ones deserve to be pensioned off. It is hardship for them to work—"

He could barely assimilate all this. He remained caught at trying to discern what she meant by cutting the funds. He had never cut the funds. He would never do such a thing. He wanted everything at Kellworth to remain as it had been when Stephen was alive.

Spence had no desire to live at Kellworth, but he cared about the property and he cared about the people. The people of Kellworth, the house servants, stable workers, even the farm laborers, raised him after his parents died. They were always more present to him than his uncle had been.

"—I begged you to release more money," Emma continued. "I told you what we had to endure. Why did you not answer my letters?"

He tried to take a breath. "Emma, I never received any letters from you."

She huffed.

He tried to calm himself, by forcing his muscles to relax as Arjun taught him, but his voice took on a frantic quality. "I knew of no decrease in funds and I received no letters!"

She glared at him. "Do not speak fustian to me, sir. You forbade me to write to you except through your man of business, but I sent you letters in every way I could think of. To the Regiment, to Spain or France, or to wherever I thought you might be. Had I known of the existence of your friends, I would have sent them letters as well."

He shot back. "I did not forbid you, Emma. Going through Mr. Ruddock was meant to be the most efficient means of contacting me. But I received no letters."

She crossed her arms over her chest. "It is no effort for you to say you received no letters. Would you sit here and admit to me you left us only a pittance? No, I daresay you would deny the whole."

If he'd possessed more strength, he would have jumped to his feet. "No man would dare accuse me of lying. I warn you, do not you do so."

She laughed. "Why? Will you challenge me to a duel? I do not recommend it, considering the result of your last one."

His fingers curled into fists. "I received no letters. But then you never answered my letters. I assumed you had no wish for a correspondence."

She blinked, but the hard look returned to her face. "There were no letters from you. You are attempting to turn this around."

She'd accused him of lying again, but he let it go. He'd sent his letters through Ruddock as well. Ruddock had a lot to answer for. Spence wished he could get his hands around the man's throat right this moment. Had Ruddock been playing it light and fast with the money and with Emma's comfort?

He frowned. "I never decreased your funds."

Her nostrils flared. "We have not had enough funds for almost three years. Kellworth has suffered. The whole village has suffered because of it."

He moved forward to touch her hand. "But I did not decrease the funds. Why would I do such a thing? It is nonsensical. I had no need of money."

She snatched her hand away. "Not even for your gambling debts?"

The wind whooshed from his lungs, leaving him as dizzy as he'd been the week prior. It was as if he'd plummeted from a great height. He pressed his fingers to his temple. "Emma, I have no gambling debts. I never wager more than I can afford to lose."

Her eyes flashed.

"This is the truth." He spoke in a firm voice. "I draw no more than my yearly portion, no more or less than I've drawn for years."

She glared at him.

He leaned forward, looking her directly in the eye. "Who told you this? Who told you this gambling story?"

Her voice was tight as she responded. "Mr. Ruddock sent letters to Mr. Larkin and to me about the decrease in funds. He did not explain the reason. Reuben discovered it from your uncle, who was privy to the information."

Why would his uncle be privy to Spence's financial dealings? Uncle Keenan was no longer his guardian. He'd been out of Kellworth's affairs ever since Stephen had reached his majority.

The only answer was that Spence's money was being embezzled and as a result Kellworth had suffered. He had assumed all was well, but had never checked closely.

Spence's anger and resentment broke into his voice. "Listen, Emma. I will tell you again. I did not lie. I did not know of the decrease in funds. And I did not gamble myself into debt."

"Oh?" She lifted her chin. "Was your duel not about gambling? Did you not nearly die from it? You were accused of cheating, were you not? What gentleman would cheat at cards except one who could not afford to lose?"

The notion that she thought him a cheat as well as a gambler made his eyes burn. "I did not cheat at cards."

She shook her head. "I suppose the opponent in the duel accused you as a lark."

"I do not know why he accused me," Spence said. "He was little more than a foolish boy."

She gave him such a look of loathing that he felt like she'd slapped him in the face. "How very honorable to shoot at a mere boy."

He wanted to protest, to tell her he'd fired above Esmund's head. If he'd aimed for the heart, he'd be in France now instead of Esmund.

Spence looked into her face and saw only contempt. He did not know which was worse. That something had happened to Kellworth's funds, or that Emma thought him a liar, a cheat, and a bully.

His eyes narrowed. "You can ask Wolfe and Blake. They will tell you I speak the truth."

She laughed again. "And I am expected to believe them more than I believe you? These friends of yours were as quick to judge you dead as they were to judge me the cause of Kellworth's decline. I hardly credit what they say."

"It is the truth nonetheless." He sounded damnably defensive.

She stood, her fisted hands held rigidly at her sides. "You did not cheat. You did not decrease the funds. You did not receive my letters. Let us suppose you are telling the truth—a great supposition indeed." Her voice trembled and she faltered for a moment. "Even so, the fact remains that you did not once come to check on matters here at Kellworth. Not once. You did not come during the peace. You did not come after Waterloo. Did you even think of us? Did you think of us while you enjoyed yourself wherever you were? Paris, Belgium, wherever it was? Where have you been since Waterloo? That was nearly a year ago. In that whole year, did you not once think of us?"

Spence felt as if he'd been socked in the gut. She was correct. He, Blake, and Wolfe had frolicked in the newly conquered Paris. They had adventured through a Europe free of Napoleon before returning to England over a month ago. Once in London, he'd thought to inform Ruddock of his temporary residence at Stephen's Hotel, but he asked no questions about Kellworth. He'd gone everywhere but Kellworth. Thought of anything but Kellworth.

He had not thought of Emma, either.

She suddenly gave a cry, something anguished, like a rabbit whose leg was caught in a trap.

She rose to her feet and marched to the door, opening it with a yank. "Let me ask you this, Spence. How am I to afford to replenish the wine stores and continue to feed your friends? How am I going to feed the other people of Kellworth at the same time? What will happen if the roof continues to leak? Or if the barn falls down? I am sick to death of worrying over such things. I will gladly cede these problems to the earl, now that he is here. Let such problems keep you awake at night, Spence." Her voice was almost a sob. "I've had quite enough conversation. I wish you to leave my room."

He felt glued to the chair, not by weakness but by a mixture of anger, fear, and guilt. He'd never wanted the responsibility of Kellworth. He'd wanted freedom and adventure. Now the weight of responsibility ensnared him, trapping him as surely as the coffin had done.

Emma was correct. No matter what the explanation for the missing funds, missing letters, and the gambling debts, responsibility for her suffering and the suffering of Kellworth must be placed squarely at his door. He ought to have checked on them. He ought to have acted the earl at least to that extent. What a foolish, selfish idiot he had been to entrust the well-being of his wife and his people to some man of business in London.

His parents had cared more for their own pleasure than for Kellworth and their sons. Spence was no better.

Emma waited by the connecting door, and he finally managed to make his aching muscles work well enough to get him to his feet. Relying heavily on the cane and feeling like a feeble, foolish, reprehensible old man, he shuffled across the room.

He no more got through the doorway than she slammed the door behind him. He heard the key turn in the lock.

Chapter EIGHT

The next morning Emma took breakfast after her gentlemen guests had gone out to ride or shoot or whatever they did to pass the time now that they had finished poking their condescending noses into her business. Yawning, she poured herself a cup of tea and sipped it eagerly.

She had not slept well at all after her late-night encounter with Spence. She ought not to have been surprised that he denied any responsibility for the privations at Kellworth, but how dare he confront her at such a late-night hour, and in her chamber!

She had carefully planned her confrontation with him. She had compiled several lists to show him. Lists of the servants gone and those remaining. Lists of repairs to be made. Lists of household goods needed. Lists of money owed in wages and to shopkeepers. Lists of food and wine to replace what had been devoured by his friends. She'd envisioned herself throwing the lists in his face and stalking out of the room.

Unfortunately, the lists had been in a drawer in the library. Nothing had gone as she'd wished.

Spreading a piece of bread with some of the plentiful blackberry jam Cook put up, Emma eyed the lone boiled egg left on the sideboard.

She sighed.

Spence would leave when he recovered, she knew, but one thing was certain. She would not allow him to leave before he had secured a future for the people of Kellworth, a future without deprivation.

Ironically, had Spence died, Kellworth would have been saved. His uncle would have inherited, and such a status-seeking man as Zachary Keenan would not squander his property on a roll of dice or a turning of a card.

Had Spence died, she would have suffered, but not Kellworth. Although Spence had assured her that he had provided for her in the event of his death, he had also promised her a comfortable life. She no longer believed anything he said. She believed him three years ago—and look what had happened. She could put no more stock in him than she could put in her own mother. As a child she'd quickly learned that her father never broke a promise, and her mother never kept one.

Emma shook her head. No use to think of the past. What was important now was to determine some means of salvaging Kellworth, if that were at all possible. There must be plenty more valuables not entailed against selling, items that might generate enough money to keep them all from total ruin. She would discover what, then procure Spence's permission to dispose of them as needed.

She glanced again at the egg that Cook would certainly use in some way to stretch out the next meal. It had been a long time since she'd eaten an egg for breakfast.

Spence entered the room.

"Good morning, Emma." His voice was solemn.

He leaned on his cane, his strain palpable, as he crossed the room to reach the head of the table, adjacent to her seat. He leaned against the table for a moment as if to catch his breath.

She stood. "I will fix you a plate."

"Perhaps that would be best." He levered himself into the chair.

She sliced off another two pieces of bread and spread them with butter and jam. With only a momentary hesitation she added the precious egg in its cup.

When she placed the plate in front of him, he gave a wan smile. "I wonder if eggs are a part of Arjun's diet. I don't expect they are, for I have a great hunger for one."

"Shall I remove it?" She reached for the plate, but he put his hand on her wrist, a warm and intimate gesture.

"Leave it." Mischief lit his eyes. "I shall simply not tell Arjun of it."

Emma's brow wrinkled in dismay. That would be like lying, she thought. A very minor case of lying, to be sure, a lie of omission and to a very minor purpose. To a servant. About an egg.

Still, it reminded her of his other lies.

Her thoughts must have shown on her face, because he picked up the eggcup. "Was it for you, Emma? I do not need it."

She shook her head, even more disturbed by his thoughtfulness. "I rarely eat them."

He placed it back down. "Arjun would likely approve of you."

He was trying to joke with her. Why? Surely he knew she was still angry at him.

Emma nibbled on her bread and jam and watched him tap and peel the eggshell from the egg. "I expected you to breakfast in your room."

He looked up, the blue of his eyes as affecting as always. "I am determined to stay out of that room as long as I can."

The undercurrent of emotion in his voice did not escape her. She did not wish to think on it.

She lifted the teapot. "Do you care for tea?"

"Please."

This would be a good moment to mention her lists and to emphasize his responsibility to his people, she thought. She merely needed to think of how to start.

He spoke first. "Emma, I have errands that need doing. I no longer know who in the household to ask."

She tried to keep her expression bland. "It depends upon the nature of the errand."

Without hesitation he said, "I wish for someone to fetch Reuben. I want to speak with him today."

"You want to speak with Reuben? Why?" As soon as the words escaped from her mouth, she realized she had been presumptuous to ask him, the earl, his business.

But he answered her as if it were the most usual of occurrences. "I want to know exactly what my uncle told him."

Her brows knit. "Reuben set off for London yesterday to apprise his father of your presence here."

His spoon halted in midair. "To London? Deuce. I wish I had known."

"He sent around a message. I did not think it important to tell you."

He shook his head. "No reason you should have told me. It is merely that I could have asked him to check on this business of Kellworth's funds."

She stared at him. He sounded so genuine.

"I suppose I could send a draft to the bank at Maidstone," he went on. "Assuming there is money to be had."

"Money?" She could not help repeating.

He gave her a serious look. "I did not gamble the money away, Emma. I have had no difficulty receiving my own money. I can only hope the bulk of the fortune is intact. I will send a draft to the bank for as much as you think necessary, and I suppose shall discover eventually if there were funds enough to redeem it."

"I have prepared a list . . . ," she began, but she let her voice trail off. She was acting as if the funds would truly be there.

"I will make this up to you, I promise." His voice turned low. "You and Kellworth will have all you need. That was our bargain, was it not?"

"Our bargain." She set her jaw. She would believe in this money only when she held it in her hands.

"I wish to speak with Larkin." His manner was all that was agreeable. It made her suspicious. "If he can take time to travel to Maidstone this day, the money shall be in our hands shortly."

He scooped out the last of the egg, then took the remaining eggshell out of the cup. He tapped on it with his spoon, making a cross-shaped hole in its bottom.

She peered at him. "What are you doing?"

He winked. "When the witches go sailing, they sink."

Her eyes widened.

He grinned and leaned forward, a conspiratorial gesture. "Witches live in eggshells and make boats of them. Surely you knew of it."

She could not help but giggle. "That is nonsense. Superstition."

He wagged his brows. "Superstition it may be, but I take no chances."

Her smile faded. But he did take chances. He played at games of chance. She dare not believe his denial of it.

"It is a jest," he said in a quiet voice.

A jest that almost made her forget she could not believe in him.

She started to rise. "I have much to do."

"Stay a moment," he pleaded. "Tell me what supplies you need. Perhaps Tolley can go into the village to purchase them."

She gaped at him. "You have no money. You just said you must send for some."

"Wolfe will have money." His tone was quite matter-of-fact. "I will pay him back."

She gave him a look of dismay.

He peered at her. "You never asked Blake or Wolfe for money, did you?"

"Certainly not." Although with the passage of a few more days, she would have been forced to, or else there would have been nothing for them to drink and precious little to eat.

"They would have given you what you needed, Emma."

She waved her hand dismissively. "I have no reason to trust them with my personal affairs."

"They are my friends," he said. "I would trust them with my life."

Giving him a scornful look, Emma stood. "And we have seen how well they guard your life, have we not?"

She turned on her heel and strode out of the room.

* * *

Spence rested his head in his hands as he sat at the library desk, wading through the lists Emma left him. He had discussed the situation a bit with Mr. Larkin, who answered his questions with the air of a disapproving grandfather. His reputation as wastrel was solid at Kellworth.

According to Larkin's brief discourse, matters at Kellworth were dire. The manager had taken the bank draft and left immediately for Maidstone. Dropping everything in his haste, Spence thought.

He picked up one of Emma's lists, one detailing which servants had been let go. The names were as familiar to him as his own, though he'd not thought of them in years. They were the Marys and Bessies and Toms of his childhood, children of the village and of the tenant farms, who had grown up expecting a home and livelihood at Kellworth. Now they were scattered about the countryside, far from mothers and fathers, sisters and brothers.

More fuel for his guilt.

He picked up another list and another. Countless repairs were enumerated. Could three years of neglect have accumulated so much that needed doing?

He sank his head in his hands again. No one had taken real responsibility for Kellworth since Stephen died. No one but Emma, but Spence had not seen that she had the means.

He looked at another list. Necessities were listed—food, wine, candles, coal—it went on and on. He read through them again.

Emma had listed nothing for herself. No bolts of cloth, no gloves, no lace, no ribbon. Somehow the lack made him feel even more loathsome.

There was a quick rap on the door, and Blake and Wolfe burst in, smelling of the out-of-doors and of horse.

"Look at you, dressed and downstairs!" Blake smiled so widely it looked as if his dimples had sliced his face.

"Are you feeling well, Spence?" Wolfe's countenance, by contrast, included a furrowed brow.

Spence gestured for them to sit. "I confess I'm fatigued already."

Wolfe pointed to the papers on the desk. "Has Lady Kellworth set you to work?"

The smile froze on Spence's face. "She has not set me to anything, Wolfe. It is merely time for me to attend to my duties—"

"I daresay there is plenty to attend to," broke in Blake cheerfully. "What have you there?"

Spence picked up the sheets of paper. "Lists. It appears Kellworth has need of many things."

Wolfe made a derisive sound. "That bears repeating. The place is crumbling around our ears."

"Not only repairs, Wolfe." Spence pointed to one of the lists. "Stores for the kitchen, candles, wine, soap. Many things. I do not know how Emma managed."

"She spoke to you, then?" Blake asked.

"Last night." Spence refrained from telling his friends he had sought the interview in her bedchamber. "She told an extraordinary tale. Kellworth's funds were apparently cut severely almost three years ago. Without my knowledge, I might add."

Blake nodded. "We heard the same from Larkin, your manager here. And from everyone else, for that matter."

"I told them you did not do it," Wolfe said.

"Indeed." He frowned. "I need to discover who was responsible for the cut and why it was done. Lady Kellworth was told I gambled Kellworth's fortune away."

"Ha! We heard that as well," Wolfe cried. "It would be more likely you'd won the fortune."

"More accurate to say I break even." Spence smiled. "Most of the time."

Blake and Wolfe disclosed their own assessment of Kellworth, telling him how all focus had been on the farm, livestock, and needs of the people who worked so Kellworth produced income. They also detailed the neglect and disrepair, not indicating anything Emma had not put in a list. Spence tried to imagine how Emma had shouldered this burden alone. Now he knew why her dresses all seemed old and worn. A sick feeling of shame rested in the pit of his stomach. He wondered if it would ever leave him.

"I would wish to have a few words with your man of business, if I were you," Wolfe remarked. "You have only Lady Kellworth's word that he decreased the funds."

"And Larkin's," Blake reminded him.

Wolfe gave Blake a skeptical look.

Spence spoke in a voice that brooked no argument. "Lady Kellworth suffered on my account, Wolfe. Do not imply any of this to be her doing."

Wolfe opened his mouth, but then shut it again, as if thinking better of saying more.

At that same moment Blake shot to his feet. "Lady Kellworth."

She stood in the doorway, cheeks flaming, her expression brittle. She had overheard Wolfe's ill-chosen words.

Spence and Wolfe stood, Spence with more effort. "Come in, Emma," he said.

Blake rushed to smooth the unpleasant moment. "You must pardon our dirt, Lady Kellworth. Wolfe and I discovered Spence out of his room and we could not resist a look."

Gazing directly at Spence, she took a step inside the room.

"We were discussing the situation at Kellworth," Spence explained.

She looked from Blake to Wolfe. "Indeed?"

Blake and Wolfe both glanced away.

She glared at them. "Did you forget my one request to you, gentlemen?"

"Request?" Spence asked.

"I asked your friends to wait until I judged the time to be right before speaking to you of Kellworth." Her voice was stiff.

"I assure you, my lady, we meant no harm," Blake said.

Wolfe glowered. "He asked."

She returned a withering glance.

Spence leaned against the desk. "I did ask them, Emma. The fault is mine."

"I asked as well, Spence," she said in low tones.

Blake walked over to her. "You did indeed, my lady. You have our sincere apologies for going against your wishes." He bowed. "Allow us to make it up to you. Perhaps there is some service we might perform for you? Wolfe and I would be delighted to do whatever you wish."

She stared him in the face. "It is odd—is it not, Lord Blakewell—that you and Mr. Wolfe have not seen fit before this moment to ask if I needed anything. You were content to eat my food and drink my wine and criticize my care of the house without one thought that I might need some assistance from you."

Blake and Wolfe had the grace to look ashamed. Spence's cheeks burned as well. Even his friends had failed her.

The charm left Blake's voice, revealing a truer emotion beneath. "Forgive me, my lady."

Wolfe managed a bow.

She looked from one man to the other, her chin high. Without speaking she spun around and left the room.

Blake collapsed in a chair and rubbed his brow. Spence lowered himself into his seat.

Wolfe paced in front of them. "She ought to have asked us. How else were we supposed to know? We would have done what she asked."

"Stubble it, Wolfe," cried Blake. "She only made the one request and we even failed to keep that one."

"Deuce," muttered Spence. A crushing fatigue came over him, enough to make his limbs tremble.

Since they'd been boys, he'd hated to be separated for too long from the Ternion, but now, for the first time, he realized he wanted them to be away.

He riffled through the lists and found the one detailing supplies Emma required. He handed it to Wolfe. "Go into the village with Tolley and purchase as much of what is on this list as can fill the wagon. If I am not mistaken, you are not short of funds, Wolfe. Buy what Emma needs."

Wolfe took the list and skimmed it. He did not argue.

Spence went on. "Tomorrow I need for you both to perform a task for me."

They nodded.

"Return to London. See what you can discover about this business with Kellworth's funds. I cannot do it myself at present and I believe I have ignored this matter long enough. I'll write some letters to give whatever permission necessary." He stood, hoping for enough strength to make it upstairs. "And, for God's sake, discover if there is enough money left to see to what must be done here."

Leaning heavily on his cane, Spence started across the room. Before reaching the door, he turned to Blake and Wolfe. "One more thing. When you go to the village, buy Emma something nice. A hat or lace or something. And find out if the dressmaker is still in the village. Tell her to call on Lady Kellworth. Tomorrow, if she is able. Have her bring her nicest cloth."

"We will attend to it," said Blake.

Spence attempted a grateful smile, but the effort was beyond him. "I'll write those letters a bit later."

With his last reserve of energy Spence hobbled out of the room and up the stairway to his bedchamber.

Emma stormed off to the garden. She was so furious with all three men she thought she would explode. She did not care if the sun was bright this day, she attacked her weeds as if each one had the name Spence or Blakewell or Wolfe written upon it.

When she finally walked back to the house, a wagon drew up and another behind it. She quickened her step.

The wagons were filled with supplies. Emma could not help but feel excited, like a little girl again, her father home from London laden with dolls and dresses and tea sets. Except these baskets and boxes were filled with flour, tea, coffee. Chocolate—such an extravagance! How long had it been since she'd tasted a cup of chocolate? There were lemons and sugar and large joints of beef.

Mrs. Cobbett, who was trying to direct the unloading, told her Blakewell and Wolfe had gone into the village with Tolley to purchase supplies. They had not remained with the wagons, which pleased Emma. She was not ready to be grateful to them yet, even though the stores they brought her were more than she dreamed possible.

"Candles!" she exclaimed after opening yet another box. She sniffed. "Beeswax." A luxury unheard of.

Mr. Hale came to offer assistance, but Emma cautioned him to leave the heavy boxes to Tolley. Cook was beside herself with joy. Tolley kept repeating, "And we stopped at the inn for a pint of ale." His energy remained high even with hoisting box after box from the wagons.

It was not security, Emma reminded herself, but wonderful nonetheless. They would all eat well this night. And the next. And the next after that, and still without worry that food would run out.

Mrs. Cobbett opened a box tied with string. "Oh, how very nice." She handed the box to Emma. "This is for you, m'lady."

Inside was a paisley shawl in gentle swirls of aqua, red, and green. Emma lifted a corner. Its wool was so soft she thought it would disintegrate like a flake of ash in her hand.

She had seen the shawl in the village shop where gloves and hats and ribbon were sold, most brought in from London. She wished she could say such frivolity was not to her taste, but it would be a bald untruth. She loved such beautiful things. The only part of London she'd enjoyed in her brief time there had been the beautiful fashions. A lady could buy anything she fancied. Beaded reticules, glittering necklaces, buttery soft gloves.

Seeing the shawl in the shop had reminded her of London merchandise. It also reminded her how shabby her own clothes had become.

With a sigh of delight she lifted the shawl from the box and wrapped it around her. "It is lovely, is it not, Mrs. Cobbett?"

"Very lovely, m'lady." Mrs. Cobbett smiled. "It does my heart good to see you in it."

There was a mirror over the fireplace in the drawing room, and Emma wanted to run to look at the lovely drape of the shawl around her shoulders.

But there was also still too much to do, too many more items to be unloaded and put away. She refolded the shawl and returned it to its box, setting it aside. Tears stung her eyes. She was still angry with Blakewell and Wolfe, but it had been kind of them to buy her a gift, especially one so fine.

When dressing for dinner, she could not resist draping the shawl over her dress, even though it was warm enough to not need it. She hesitated self-consciously at the door of the drawing room, where the men waited until Mr. Hale announced the meal. She heard them conversing.

Spence would be there. She had not heard his voice, but she knew, because she'd peeked into his bedchamber before proceeding downstairs. As quietly as she could, she walked into the room.

The men were drinking some of the Madeira purchased that day. They stood at her entrance.

"Good evening, Lady Kellworth," Blakewell said, with his most charming smile.

Wolfe bowed.

Spence's approving gaze seemed to burn into her. Likely the others had informed him of their gift. It was a compliment to his friends for her to wear it. Even though her motivation had merely been because she relished its beauty.

"Would you like a glass of Madeira, Emma?" Spence asked as she crossed the room.

She accepted the glass Wolfe hastily poured for her, careful not to spill any on her lovely shawl. "Thank you."

Emma sat, as did Spence. She knew he had rested all the afternoon while Arjun looked in on him, but he still looked tired. Blakewell and Wolfe remained standing. Wolfe walked over to the window and gazed out.

She looked up at Blakewell. "Thank you for this lovely shawl."

He grinned at her. "It was not my gift, my lady. I fear I would have selected a pair of gloves." Cocking his head, he went on, "You have Wolfe to thank. It was he who insisted upon the shawl."

"Mr. Wolfe," Emma said, her voice conveying her surprise.

Wolfe turned to her.

She blinked. "I thank you, sir. It is quite the loveliest shawl I have ever seen."

His cheek twitched. "Spence charged us with buying it," he mumbled, giving her a bow.

She turned to Spence, just as surprised.

"I merely told them to purchase you something." Spence gave her another appraising look. "The shawl becomes you very well."

Emma felt herself blush. She ought not to be so pleased by his compliments, but it had been so long since any man but Reuben had admired her and he, somehow, did not count.

Their dinner was the most comfortable since the gentlemen arrived. The beef had been roasted to perfection and Spence happily announced he was abandoning Arjun's menu. For once, Emma felt she could eat her fill without a thought to what must be conserved for the following days. She even drank more than one glass of the barsac wine, enjoying the nice mellow feeling it gave her.

The men were in high spirits, Blake entertaining her with some of their exploits as boys. Their laughter—Spence's especially—was like a tonic.

It was a temporary reprieve, but a nice one. It was a bit late for him to act the concerned husband, but when they made their marriage bargain, he promised she would have all she needed and desired. Soon, when he was stronger, Emma would attempt another discussion about finances, insisting he ensure Kellworth always be provided with the funds it required. After he left, it would be too late. He was likely to forget her and Kellworth all over again.

But Emma wanted no worries crowding her head at the moment. She wanted only to feel the soft wool of her new shawl against her bare arms and savor the barsac on her tongue and the pleasant sensation of having eaten too much.

The men laughed about the time they managed to sneak a goat into the headmaster's office. They'd been caught and nearly ousted from the school, but the exploit finally earned them the respect of the older boys.

Emma smiled. Her memories of school were not quite as lively. She'd briefly attended a girls' school, but when typhus fever broke out, her father brought her home and hired a new governess.

When the laughter died down, Spence said, "Blake and Wolfe will be leaving tomorrow, Emma. They go to London on my behalf."

"Leaving?"

"They will look into my financial affairs for me. Try to discover what has happened."

Emma was halfway to believing Spence's assertion that he knew nothing of the decrease in funds. She glanced at Wolfe and Blake. "I thought you would stay until Spence was recovered."

Blake gestured to Spence with his fork. "He's well enough. In any event he will be in your good hands." He winked at her. "Wolfe and I shall have quite a lark, acting like Bow Street Runners."

"I doubt it will be as bad as all that," said Spence.

Blake feigned dismay. "I assure you, I am counting on danger and intrigue."

"I'll wager there is a lot to be discovered," Wolfe broke in. "I for one want to track down that Esmund fellow. He will come clean with me, I guarantee it."

"Oh, dear!" sighed Blake. "I suspect Wolfe will be much better at Bow Street 'running' than I."

"Who is Esmund?" Emma asked.

"The fellow from the duel," Spence replied.

The man who had been willing enough to shoot Spence dead—his only punishment, a trip to Paris.

"We shall have to chase him down, I suspect," said Wolfe.

"A wasted effort." Spence shook his head. "He's naught but a fool. I'd prefer you have it out with my man of business."

Blakewell raised his glass. "And so we shall."

Emma sipped her wine, surprised at this sudden flight to London, coming so soon after she rang a peal over Blakewell and Wolfe's heads. As much as she resented their presence, her feelings were confused at the prospect of them leaving, especially if she had caused it by her sharp words. How long would Spence last here without them? Possibly he would be in a great rush to join them as soon as he could tolerate the journey.

She said no more of it, and the evening progressed. The gentlemen did not tarry over their port after dinner, but joined her in the drawing room. The four of them even played at whist, until it was apparent Spence was fatigued. He was first to excuse himself. Emma watched his slow progress.

Alone with Blakewell and Wolfe, the awkward silence again descended, and it was not long before Emma bid them good night.

As she was walking from the room, she turned back. "Thank you again for my shawl."

Blakewell grinned. Wolfe merely nodded.

In her room Emma excused Susan, saying she would get herself ready for bed. After the elderly maid shuffled out, Emma hurried to the door connecting her room with Spence's. She opened it enough to see that a lamp was still lit. Spence, in his banyan, sat at the window, a glass in his hand.

The door creaked and his head turned.

"Emma?"

Chapter NINE

Spence thought his eyes deceived him, but there she was, the lamp in her room casting a glow around her. He'd been thinking of her, wanting her to come to him, but not daring to hope for her.

She still wore the shawl. Wolfe, of all people, had known what would please her—Wolfe, whose bitterness toward women was well-known to his friends, even though the reason was not.

The rich hues of the shawl had brought color to her cheeks and brightness to her hazel eyes, turning them green. He remembered how her eyes glowed in the candle-light at dinner. He'd been happy to see her almost relaxed, almost enjoying herself.

"Come, Emma," he said. "Come sit with me."

She walked toward him. "I was uncertain you would be awake."

He cocked his head toward the open window next to him. "I could not resist the night air." Holding up his glass, he said, "I would offer you brandy, but there is only one glass."

"There are more." She crossed over to the red lacquer cabinet in the corner of the room and took out another small-stemmed glass. Returning to his side, she extended it to him and waited for him to pour.

"Did you inform Arjun you have abandoned his menu and returned to strong spirits?"

He could not miss her disapproving tone, but answered agreeably, "I have indeed."

She accepted the brandy from him, but spoke crisply. "I wanted to speak to you."

This would not be a pleasant conversation, he surmised, but he was determined to show her goodwill. "I am here to listen, Emma."

She settled in the chair opposite him. "I will not keep you from your bed for long."

Her mention of bed made his senses flare. He'd been remembering the comfort of her warm body next to him when he had been in a panic of the dark. But he had no right to desire a husband's pleasure, not after failing her so thoroughly.

"What is it, Emma?" He took a sip of brandy.

She glanced out the window and twirled the stem of the glass in her fingers, the nut-colored liquid catching the dim light. Finally she turned to him and almost blurted out, "If you have required Lord Blakewell and Mr. Wolfe to leave on my account, I wish to tell you it is unnecessary."

"What do you mean?"

She took a sip of her brandy. "You made it clear you and your friends have been inseparable since childhood. I will not be the cause of dividing you."

Spence gave a low laugh. "I assure you, Emma, Blake and Wolfe and I go different ways when it suits us."

"Still." She continued to toy with her glass. "I have no right to dictate to you who stays at Kellworth."

"I should think you have every right," he countered. "Kellworth is more your home than mine."

She frowned. "I am not the earl, Spence. The property is yours."

He leaned forward. "I have brought you much unhappiness. I want to make it up to you, Emma. I want you to feel Kellworth is yours, that your wishes prevail here."

"I did not wish your friends to be sent away on my account," she stated firmly.

He put his hand over her fingers, stopping the twirling of her glass. "I need them to go to London for me, to find out what happened to the funds that were your due. I am still too much an invalid to attend to it myself."

This was half-truth at best. The other half was that he needed to set things right with her. That duty was his alone.

She lifted her glass to her lips and his hand slipped away. "You try to convince me," she murmured.

He attempted a smile. "Do you not realize I am determined to make up to you for the hardship you have endured?"

She blinked at him. "I realize you wish me to think as much."

He took the glass from her hand, set it on the table, and wrapped his fingers around hers. "I will do anything for you, Emma. I owe you my life, after all. While I am here I am determined to do whatever I can for you. Tell me what you want and I promise to give it to you."

"While you are here?" Her fingers tensed and she pulled them from his grasp. She stared at him a long time before standing and stepping over to the window, where the evening breeze blew a wisp of hair into her eyes.

"You made promises to me in the past, Spence." Her voice again turned as cool as the evening air. "How am I to believe in new promises?"

He rose to his feet with an ease that surprised him. He stood behind her, putting his hand on her shoulder and bringing his lips close to her ear. "I will convince you I am sincere," he murmured. "I will not hurt you again."

Her scent filled his nostrils and it seemed natural to wrap his arm across her chest, making her lean against him, her curves warm and soft through the thin fabric of his banyan. She did not pull away, and he slipped his other hand around her waist, pressing her harder against his growing arousal. He nuzzled her hair, and before he could make himself think again, his lips tasted her tender skin. At this moment he wanted nothing but to be with her, to savor the delight of holding her in his arms and tasting her with his lips.

She gave a small, surrendering cry, and his still-healing body suddenly demanded a man's pleasure. The thought of peeling off her threadbare dress and leading her to his bed drove all rational thought from his mind.

She released a long breath. "Am I to share your bed while you are here, my lord?" she whispered.

He gently turned her to face him. "You would be willing?"

She lifted her eyes to him and he felt her tremble beneath his hands. "If you require it."

He searched her face, but she quickly looked away.

He would be a scoundrel indeed if he *required* her to make love to him. He carefully released her. "I'll not force you, Emma. Have no fear of that."

He braced himself with a hand against the wall between the windows, feeling weak again.

She lifted her chin in a brave gesture. "Do you require any assistance?"

"Assistance?" His mind was not quite working yet.

"To help you into bed?"

His lingering arousal made it painfully clear he ought not trust himself near a bed with her. He wanted to give her a reassuring smile, but failed. "I can manage."

She took a step back and looked very much like the young, vulnerable girl he married. "I will bid you good night, then."

He nodded.

She wrapped her shawl more tightly around her shoulders and fled the room.

Emma made certain she was present to give Blakewell, Wolfe, and Arjun a cordial farewell. They left early, Arjun traveling in the carriage, the gentlemen's trunks strapped to the top, Blakewell and Wolfe, on horseback. Emma was glad to see the horses go. They consumed even more than the gentlemen did. Although she supposed she did not have to worry about such matters at the present moment.

Spence also saw them off, seemingly unfazed by their departure. She'd not spoken to him all the morning, but when she looked upon him, she remembered the previous night, the warmth of his breath, the low murmur of his voice, the tenderness of his lips. Remembering disturbed her.

It was as if she'd been suddenly made of wax, melting under the heat of his touch. If he had led her to his bed, she would have gone willingly. The knowledge that she could be so pliant when he was near had shaken her.

At such moments, why could she not retain memory of how many times she'd cursed him, how many disasters she'd faced alone without his even knowing of them?

The carriage and riders turned the corner at the end of the long lane, disappearing behind the trees. Emma turned to go inside the house, planning to tend to her garden before the whole morning disappeared.

"What might I do to assist you today?" Spence asked her, joining her as she crossed through the large arched doorway.

She preferred weeds to his disturbing company. "There is nothing."

"Help me learn of the estate, then," he persisted. "Show me some of the repairs necessary." He stood in the doorway so she could not easily pass without brushing against him.

She was impatient to make her way to the rear of the house, down the servants' stairway to the door leading to the kitchen garden. "Mr. Larkin had best show you."

She made the mistake of looking into his eyes, which crinkled slightly at the corners, as if she'd wounded him with her words. Why should she feel like the rag-mannered and churlish one?

His smile remained, though. "I shall ask Larkin, then."

She moved to enter the house, but he put a stilling hand on her arm. "A message arrived this morning. Did Tolley tell you? The dressmaker will call this afternoon."

"Dressmaker?"

"For new dresses, Emma. Order as many as you like."

Again he roused a disorder of feelings. Was she to have new clothes at last, to wear to church without trying to disguise where they were patched and mended?

Her excitement quickly plummeted. "It would be better to know she can be paid before ordering dresses. Or did you charge your friend Wolfe to pay her bill as well?"

His grip on her arm tightened; then he dropped his hand. "There is money enough for a few dresses, Emma."

She was not so certain.

They heard riders approaching and turned to see three men on horseback coming down the lane.

"Ah, the money from the bank at Maidstone," Spence said as he walked out to the lane to greet them.

Emma watched transfixed as he led one of the men to the doorway. She hurriedly stepped out of the way when they entered the house.

Spence said, "Come with us if you like, Emma."

She followed them into the library, where Spence completed the transaction and counted the money in the strongbox. He dipped a pen into ink and signed the messenger's receipt, thanked the man, and walked him out the door. As soon as the men left the room, Emma hurried over to the box to look inside.

It was filled with coin and banknotes. She gasped. The sums were princely compared to the contents of her little money pouch, all that was left until the next quarter's allotment.

Spence's voice came from the door. "The bank in Maidstone seems assured of our credit."

She looked up.

"Now will you cease your concern about my fortune?" He walked over to the desk and poured out one bag of coins.

Her worries were too much a part of daily life to be given up easily. "Bad tidings could still come from London."

He pursed his lips. "Less likely now. News of one's reversal of fortune travels quickly in the banking world, I expect. We shall proceed with some caution, but I believe it is safe to begin to set things to rights."

Emma looked into his face, wanting to allow the glimmer of hope to catch fire, but afraid it would burn her in the end. His smile was easy, his eyes full of reassurance. In spite of herself she was beginning to believe he had not gambled Kellworth's fortune away. She was beginning to believe he would restore it.

She glanced away, letting the coins run through her fingers. "We should pay the servants and workers their back wages first. Then the merchants in town. And the dressmaker would do better to measure Mrs. Cobbett and Susan and the maids for new clothes, before me."

"No, Emma," he said in a firm tone. "You shall be first in this."

Emma never did tend her garden that day. The rest of the morning was spent discussing the use of the money. She and Spence went over her lists, deciding in a most amiable way whom to pay first and what of the many areas of neglect were of primary importance. In the afternoon Spence met with Mr. Larkin while the dressmaker measured Emma and showed her silks and muslins in a rainbow of colors. They examined the dressmaker's fashion prints, and Emma could not help but be delighted with the pictures of pretty new styles. Perhaps she was more like her mother than she cared to admit, dazzled by the latest fashions. She could not deny her excitement at the idea of even one new dress.

She ordered three. A dress with matching spencer to wear to church. A new morning dress. A dinner dress. The dinner dress especially thrilled her, even though she felt frivolous to attach such importance to an item of clothing. She chose a deep rose silk to be trimmed with lace at the hem and neckline. The dressmaker promised the dresses in two weeks. It seemed an eternity to wait. What's more, she feared Spence would be gone by then and, against all reason, she wanted him to see her in her rose dinner dress.

That evening Spence was so clearly fatigued and in pain that she could have worn her oldest rag and she doubted he would have noticed. She claimed she wished to retire for the night immediately after the meal, so that he would not feel obliged to keep her company in the drawing room. She hurried ahead of him so she could fetch Tolley to assist him up the stairs. Emma was too ex-hilarated to be sleepy. Visions of fashion prints and her many lists flashed through her mind.

Two days later a messenger arrived from London with a letter from Blakewell. The Bank of England verified that the Kellworth capital was intact, still earning money in the 5 percents. The sum of ready cash staggered Emma, but Spence took it in stride.

Blake's letter went on to say that Ruddock had disap-peared. His older brother, the senior Ruddock of the firm taken over from their father, was as alarmed at the idea anyone would find his brother's dealings in question as he was at the man's disappearance. The senior Ruddock promised a close examination of his brother's Kellworth ledgers.

In the meantime it appeared money existed and could be spent, and spent it was. Spence lost no time in arrang-ing for repairs. The former servants were summoned back and workers were hired from far and wide to restore Kellworth to its glory. Emma felt as if a whirlwind had hit, but she surmised Spence would wish things done as quickly as possible so he could leave again.

By week's end the whirlwind had turned Emma's world topsy-turvy. Spence spent much of his day in the library closeted with Larkin or Gandy, the gamekeeper, or Boyd, the head groom. He interviewed stonemasons and carpenters and plasterers. The abundance of meat, fish, vegetables, even fruit, made choosing the day's menu a matter of a few minutes spent, rather than an hour going over with Cook and Mrs. Cobbett how to stretch a scarcity of food. As the former maids, laundresses, and milkmaids returned to Kellworth, Mrs. Cobbett had less need of Emma's guidance. Organizing the scrubbing, dusting, and laundry was an easy matter when there were workers aplenty.

With time on her hands, Emma donned her straw hat, half-boots, and gloves and walked out to the kitchen garden, only to discover three workers busily weeding and pruning. She wandered over to the farm buildings to check on her pigs. A farmhand was leading one of them away.

"Where are you taking him?" she asked, quickening her step to catch up to the man.

He stopped and tipped his hat. "Beg pardon, m'lady. Mr. Larkin said we could have this one for slaughter and for smoking."

It was one of the pigs she had been fattening up for market.

"Mr. Larkin said this?"

"He did, ma'am. Said we had need of more meat, ma'am, with all the new workers."

"You cannot take my pig!" She grabbed the rope from his hands.

With eyes bugging, he let go, and Emma pulled her precious pig back to the sty, the farmhand at her heels. She put her pig back into the enclosure, where the mother and father pigs snorted as they fed on kitchen scraps.

"Leave him in here!" she ordered.

She had seen Larkin enter the library earlier. Storming back to the house, she stopped only long enough to change her shoes and remove her hat and gloves.

She entered the library without knocking. Both Spence, who was seated behind the desk, and Larkin, standing in front of it, looked up in surprise.

She charged right up to the estate manager. "Mr. Larkin, did you order my pig slaughtered?"

He took a step backward at her onslaught. "Why, yes, I—"

"He is my pig. I was saving him for market. You knew I wished to sell him, and you acted expressly against my wishes."

"I—I—" he stuttered. "I did not think it mattered now we can buy more pigs."

"But this was my pig!" she cried. She sounded ridiculous, she knew. Of course there was enough money for more pigs, but it was the principle of the thing. The pigs were hers. He ought to have at least asked her permission.

Mr. Larkin gave a curt bow. "I beg pardon, my lady. His lordship and I had been discussing what was necessary to feed the new workers and . . ."

She swung on Spence. "You gave him permission to slaughter my pig?"

Spence looked dumbfounded. He turned to the estate manager. "Larkin, we are finished here. You may go."

Larkin bowed. "Very good, sir, but what shall I do about the pig?"

Spence said, "Leave the pig."

Larkin bowed again to Spence and to Emma and left the room with a very quick step. Emma turned to leave as well.

"Wait, Emma," Spence said.

She looked over her shoulder at him.

His expression was earnest. "Forgive me. I did not realize the pig was your pet."

Pet? She swung around. "You think I kept pets when I was hard-pressed to feed the people here? The pig was food. Or money for food. And even if I did have the leisure for a pet, it would not be a pig! I would have a dog or a kitten—"

He held up his hand. "Just tell me about the pig then."

"It was my pig." She marched to his desk and glared at him. "You had no right to order him slaughtered."

He nodded. "You have made me realize. What I do not understand is why *you* had a pig."

"I purchased a breeding pair of pigs," she explained, trying to use a patient tone. "The sow had her first litter, five piglets. This was the only one left. This pig was to go to market." She folded her arms over her chest. "Your friends ate the other one I wanted to sell."

He stood and walked around the desk to stand next to her. "Then I must apologize for my friends," he said using that warm, low voice that made her insides turn to butter. "You purchased the pigs to raise more pigs?"

She stepped away from him and averted her gaze, remembering where she had gotten the money to buy her pigs.

"It is more complicated than that." She faced him again.

He raised his brows and leaned against the desk.

She took a breath. "I did not have the money to buy the breeding pair, but I wanted them, because we could make some money from them, raising the piglets and selling them for profit."

"So how did you buy them?" he asked.

She raised her chin. "I sold a small Worcester bowl and a pair of Derby figurines and Sheffield candlesticks. I know they belonged to Kellworth—hence to you, not to me—but I sold them nonetheless."

He gave a serious nod. "I see. And how did you accomplish the selling of these items? Who bought them?"

She bit her lip. "I do not know who bought them. I had an . . . an intermediary to accomplish the sale."

"An intermediary?"

She hesitated, reluctant to divulge the identity of the person who helped her, but she also wanted Spence to know exactly what transpired in his absence.

"Reuben sold them for me in London, to get the best price. But you must not blame him for the scheme. It was my doing. He would not let me do it myself."

He gave a small laugh. "Reuben?"

"I had to depend upon someone. I confess Reuben was a great help to me. But you must not put any blame on him." She looked at him with defiance.

He walked over to her again and took her hand in his. "The blame is mine, is it not? I will not be angry at you for showing resourcefulness." He smiled and squeezed her hand. "What were you to do with the money from the piglets?"

She wished he would not touch her. It brought memories of his arms around her and his lips touching the tender skin of her neck, even though a whole week had passed since he'd held her.

She pulled her hand away. "I was going to buy food. What else?"

He reached out again, but she took a step back. "Oh, Emma," he murmured in low tones. "This is but more to make up to you."

That night after Spence retired, Emma was too restless to go to bed so early. She lingered in the drawing room, working on a piece of needlework she'd neglected for more than a year. It was to be a seat cover for a chair in the gallery, one of the rooms that had been closed with dustcovers draped over the furniture. When her eyes began to pain her from the strain of sewing by candlelight, she put it aside and went up to her bedchamber.

Susan dozed in her chair, so Emma tiptoed past her and quietly got herself ready for bed. Susan would be traveling to Dover to live with her sister within a few days, with a nice pension to keep her comfortable. Emma was too relieved that Susan would be settled so nicely to even think of missing her.

She gently touched the old lady's shoulder. "Time for bed, Susan."

The maid woke with a snort, blinking in disorientation, then gave Emma a smile. "Did I doze off?"

"Yes, you did," Emma said. "And I have managed to get myself ready, so there is nothing for you to do but go to your room."

The old lady nodded and rocked back and forth trying to get herself to her feet. Emma helped her.

"Shall I walk with you to your room?" she asked.

Susan patted her arm. "I can manage, my lady."

Still, Emma escorted her to the door and opened it for her.

A small cry, almost like a baby, sounded behind her. "What is that?"

Susan grinned, all her wrinkles visible. "Something from the earl, my lady." She shuffled out of the room.

Emma whirled around, wondering from where the sound had come. There was a basket on her bed. She hurried over to it and peeked inside.

A fluffy white kitten and an equally fluffy black one peeped up at her. The white kitten opened its pink mouth. *"Mew!"*

"Oh!" Emma exclaimed, reaching in to pick up the little creature.

They were merely kittens from one of the barn cats. Emma had seen the mother nursing them weeks ago, but so much had happened since then, she hadn't given the kittens another thought. Someone had cleaned up these two and tied yellow ribbons around their necks. The little black one yawned and licked his front paw.

Emma put the white one back in the basket, climbed on the bed, and, sitting cross-legged, picked them both up again and rubbed their soft fur against her cheeks.

Spence had given them to her, a gift of no monetary value, but one as precious as she could imagine.

They squirmed in her hands and she placed them in the circle of her legs, where they pounced on her nightdress when she wiggled her toes.

She laughed and rubbed her finger back and forth until they knocked into each other trying to reach it.

For all the time of Spence's absence, Emma had had plenty of people to provide for, to worry over, to take care of. But until this moment, she'd had no creature merely to love.

Tears moistened her cheeks. She picked up the kittens again, cuddled them against her face, and tried not to sob.

Chapter TEN

The next morning Spence woke when Tolley, cheerful as always, entered his room. After Tolley helped him dress and went out the door again, Spence checked the mirror, adjusted his neckcloth, straightened his coat, and again ran the comb through his hair, which now curled over his collar.

There was a rap at the door. "Enter."

He expected a chambermaid or someone to enter from the hallway, but the door connecting his room to Emma's opened. There she stood, wearing one of her threadbare dresses. Even so, his pulse quickened.

She carried the basket on her arm. "Thank you," she said in a tiny voice.

He walked over and peeked in at the two furry creatures peeping back at him. "Do you fancy them? Tolley brought me as many of the litter as he could find. I selected these two. I think they washed up rather well."

"They are lovely," she whispered.

He smiled, inordinately glad he had pleased her.

She petted the kittens with her finger. "I am taking them to the kitchen for some cream."

"I will walk with you."

He followed her all the way to the kitchen, where Cook broke into a big smile upon seeing him.

"My lord," she exclaimed. "It does my heart good to see you."

Cook had aged. All the old retainers had aged. Cook wiped her hands on her apron with the same vigor he recalled from his youth, and in the same voice he remembered as a boy, said, "I'll be making a special pudding for tonight, now that we have supplies aplenty. I made biscuits yesterday. Do you fancy one?"

"I do indeed." He could almost taste the buttery biscuits melting on his tongue, and was suddenly as eager for one as when he begged for them as a child. He had forgotten the pleasant times he sat dangling his legs at the long wooden table while Cook fussed over him and Stephen, fixing them a special meal or plying them with sweets.

The memory warmed him. "In fact, if breakfast has not yet been sent up, I would be delighted to eat right here."

At his words Emma glanced up from where she had been setting out cream for the kittens.

Cook's grin widened. "Like when you were a lad! You have a seat and I'll fix you a plate." She hustled him over to the same stool where he sat as a boy, although now his legs no longer dangled and the stool Stephen sat in was empty. Bustling to and fro, she set a plate of her biscuits before him. He took one eagerly and popped it whole into his mouth.

Emma stood. "I will breakfast here, too, Cook. There is no need to send food to the dining room for just me."

Cook caught one of the kitchen maids. "Run and tell Mr. Hale, girl, and be quick about it. Breakfast in the kitchen today!" She put Emma where Stephen would have sat, next to Spence. Soon they had plates laden with ham slices, baked eggs, mounds of butter and jam, and a pot full of tea.

Spence speared a piece of ham with his fork and lifted it to his mouth. Stopping himself, he looked to Emma. "Am I about to eat one of your pigs?"

She laughed, the sound as wonderful as Cook's clanging of pots and clinking of dishes. "No, you are not. My pig, the one your friends partook of, would not have had time to cure. I suspect this ham was one of Mr. Wolfe's purchases."

"I confess, I am relieved." He winked at her and bit into the piece of ham. "I feel some sort of kinship with your pigs."

She returned a serious look. "I was not attached to the pigs, Spence. They were raised for slaughter. I realize I need not concern myself with them anymore."

Their eyes caught, but she quickly glanced away.

The black kitten leaped onto Spence's leg and climbed it like a tree. When the little fellow reached his lap, Emma scooped him into her hands and put him back on the floor, where he promptly attacked the white one.

"They are frisky, are they not?" Spence said, hoping to recapture the ease between them. "Have you given them names?"

She did not look up at him, but reached over to pour their tea. "Tom and Puss."

"Oh, quite original, Emma." He flashed her a smile. "Do not tell me you have a male and female?"

She nodded. "The black one is male and the white a female."

He picked up the black one again and peered at it. "Indeed? How do you tell?"

She blushed, the color very becoming to her complexion. "You look on the other side."

He grinned and their eyes made contact again.

The kitten squirmed, driving needle-sharp claws into Spence's hand. "No doubt this fellow is the Tom. I'd have bet money on it."

She frowned at the reference to gambling and he felt like kicking himself for making it.

He placed the kitten back on the floor and tried to change the subject. "What will you do today, Emma?"

A line creased her forehead. "There is little for me to do of late, with all the new workers you have hired."

He placed his hand over hers. "You deserve some leisure."

Her fingers tensed and he let go.

Tolley lumbered in. "Here you are, my lord. I could not find you and I was looking. But here you are in the kitchen."

"I am indeed here," agreed Spence. "Did you have need of me?"

Tolley nodded. "Yes, indeed. You said I was to tell you if I heard the vicar was returned and I did hear it and he is."

"Did you send word that I wished him to call upon me?"

"No," admitted Tolley.

Spence opened his mouth to protest, but Tolley added, "Mr. Hale said I could go tell the vicar myself, and so I will go straight away."

"Excellent."

Emma turned to him. "You have need of Reuben?"

In all Spence's growing-up years, he never had need of Reuben. His cousin always preferred to stick his nose in a book rather than dash outdoors with Spence and Stephen. The two brothers would spend entire days exploring the vast property, coming home full of dirt. If Reuben accompanied them, he complained the whole time, tired quickly, or prattled on about some Latin translation he'd accomplished, or he made up acrostics and solved them when Spence and Stephen would not.

But Reuben had just spent time in London, had likely visited Uncle Keenan, and might now have information Spence needed. Like why Uncle Keenan would say Spence gambled away the family fortune. "I have some questions for him, yes."

Later that day Spence sat in the library examining Mr. Larkin's ledgers when Mr. Hale announced his cousin's arrival.

"Good day, Cousin," Reuben cried, walking toward Spence with hand extended. He shook Spence's hand so enthusiastically, pain shot through Spence's shoulder. "By God, you look well, very well indeed!"

"I am better." Spence rubbed his shoulder and motioned Reuben to a seat. "How was London?"

"Quite lively! The Season, you know. Everyone is in town. There were some excellent parties, I must say. Delicious food." Reuben's eyes brightened when Spence poured two glasses of port.

"You were there for the Season's entertainment?" For all Spence knew Reuben might have been searching the marriage mart for a wife, though his cousin would not be considered a highly desirable catch.

Reuben gave Spence a sheepish look. "Not for that, I assure you. I quite traveled there on your account."

"Mine?"

"I thought it best to directly explain these recent events to Father. Knowing him, he would get wind of it soon enough and would be very displeased if he had not heard of it first." Reuben took a sip of wine.

Spence's uncle, a Member of Parliament, was a politician of increasing influence in the House of Commons. He disliked being in the dark about any matter.

"Good of you," said Spence.

Reuben nodded approvingly of the wine. "I must say, Father did not seem unduly surprised. Perhaps he knew something of the matter already, although he denied it."

Reuben was distracted by two workmen passing by the window with a long ladder.

"I say, Spence, there is a grand amount of activity here! I am astonished! You have hired a score of workers."

"There is a great deal to be done." Spence sipped his wine.

"Quite. Little problems become big ones if not tended right away." Reuben covered this subtle gibe by rising from the chair and going to look out the window. "You must have had a run of very good luck. It is good of you to spend it on Kellworth."

"There was no run of luck," Spence snapped. "What is this talk of my gambling?"

His cousin turned back to him. "I do not get your meaning."

"You told Emma I gambled away the Kellworth fortune. I have done no such thing."

Reuben walked back to the chair and sat. He leaned toward Spence. "Do you mean it is not true?"

"Of course it is not true!" Spence shot back. "I do not gamble overmuch. Certainly no more than the next man. Why the devil has it been bandied about that I do?"

Reuben's brows knit. "But your debts have created much difficulty here, Cousin. I do not like to speak so plainly, but you have caused Emma . . . er . . . Lady Kellworth much suffering. If not for gambling, why did you cut the funds?"

Spence came to his feet, though he needed the cane to steady himself. "I did not cut the funds. I knew nothing of cutting the funds. Tell me what you know about it."

Reuben's eyes widened as he looked up at Spence. "Why, I know nothing about it, except what Emma . . . Lady Kellworth . . . told me. And Larkin. I did become concerned enough to speak to Larkin about it."

"Emma said you heard this rubbish about my gambling from your father."

Reuben nodded. "So I did. I had forgotten that. I sought Father's advice. I thought he might be . . . be of assistance to Kellworth, but he, as you might understand, was disinclined to help. He told me then that you were gambling heavily and drawing from Kellworth's assets to pay your debts."

"I had no debts. Why would my uncle say I did?" Spence sat down again.

Reuben rubbed his chin. "I had the impression someone had told him. He would not have invented such a tale, would he?"

Spence gave him a direct look. "Did none of you consider that I was soldiering? I had more to do than wager my fortune away, I assure you."

Reuben blinked. "Father told me about your debts. I certainly had no reason to doubt him. He has the ear of many in London, you know."

"Why did you not ask me, Reuben?" Spence challenged. "You could have sent word to me."

"I did!" exclaimed his cousin. "I wrote you many a letter."

More mail Spence did not receive. It was inconceivable that so many letters failed to get through to him. Spence had received Ruddock's correspondence well enough and an obligatory letter or two from his uncle. "Where the devil did you send your letters?" he asked. "I received nothing from you."

"Why, I sent the letters through Father, of course!" Reuben sputtered. "He could frank them, you know. And it did not cost me."

Spence leaned forward. "Did you send Emma's letters that way as well?"

"Some of them," admitted his cousin defensively. "But others she wanted sent to Ruddock's firm. Why do you ask?"

"I received no letters from you or from Emma."

"My God!" Reuben, struck speechless, leaned back in the chair. After a moment he said, "What could this mean?"

Spence stared into his cousin's face. "It means there are still funds aplenty for Kellworth. It means I shall make certain this never happens again. But how and why this happened, I do not know. I promise you, I intend to discover the cause. What else can you tell me?"

Reuben shook his head. "Nothing."

Reuben stared vacantly into the contents of his glass. Spence rose from his chair and turned away, frustrated that he could not mount his horse and ride straight to London to confront his uncle. The interview must wait until his health was fully restored, and then it promised to be difficult, an interview he could not cede to Blake and Wolfe. He and Uncle Keenan had barely spoken to each other since Spence married Emma. Their rare correspondence had been equally as terse.

Frowning, Spence returned to his seat and took a quelling sip of wine. "Emma told me you sold some things for her."

Reuben's head shot up. "I . . . I did not precisely sell them. I confess to telling her I sold them, but it was an untruth."

"Reuben, cease the roundaboutation."

Reuben tilted his head back and forth. "The pieces are at the vicarage. I gave her the money, but I never sold them."

"You kept them?"

"Oh, not for myself!" Reuben looked alarmed. "I always planned to return them to the estate. I will return them directly, I promise. It . . . it was a means to give her money. She would not accept money from me any other way."

Spence frowned, taking a sip of his wine. Here was another example of how he'd failed Emma, putting both her and Reuben in an uncomfortable position. "I will pay you back, of course."

"Yes. Yes. No need, really. I will return the items forthwith."

"Not yet." Matters were so tender with Emma, Spence had no wish to upset her further by showing how Reuben had deceived her. "Keep them until I ask for them."

"As you wish, Spence," replied Reuben.

There was a rap on the door and Emma entered. Both men stood.

"Will you join us, Emma?" Spence asked.

She hesitated, but shook her head. "I merely wanted to see if Reuben intended to dine with us this evening."

"I would be delighted, my dear." Reuben beamed. "I shall take my leave now and return properly dressed at the usual hour." He took a step or two toward the door, then halted. "That is, with your permission, Cousin."

"Of course," Spence said, although not eager for more of Reuben's company at dinner. Or rather, not happy to share Emma's. "Until dinner, then."

Reuben joined them for many dinners that week, and when Sunday arrived, Spence declared himself able to accompany Emma to church. The dressmaker had delivered her dresses and she wore a lovely sage muslin dress and a spencer trimmed in dark green ribbon. The dressmaker included a hat in the exact shade, trimmed with a dark green bow, and the shoemaker made a new pair of shoes as well. Emma felt self-conscious in the finery, so used to wearing her much-mended brown dress to which the villagers and neighbors were so accustomed.

Reuben gave a ponderous sermon on the Prodigal Son, ending it by exhorting everyone to give thanks that the Earl of Kellworth, who was present at the service, had returned to kill the fatted calf. The analogy was a backward one, but then Reuben's sermons often made little sense.

After the service the vicar was ebullient in greeting his cousin, the earl, and made a show of giving Spence and Emma the precedence to which Spence's position entitled them. After Reuben, the other members of the congregation gathered to greet Emma and Spence warmly. Emma wondered how they might have greeted Spence had he not already infused the village with new prosperity.

One of the tenant farmers stopped Spence to have a word with him. The man's wife spoke to Emma. "Lady Kellworth, I am sure you will be happy to know that my daughter gave birth to a fine baby boy not a fortnight ago." The woman beamed with pleasure.

"How lovely, Mrs. Oates." Emma had not seen the young expectant mother for over a month and had forgotten it was her time. "How is Mary faring? Did she have any difficulty?"

Mrs. Oates grinned. "Not a bit. She's a sturdy girl, my Mary. And the babe is a robust one, let me tell you."

"I am very glad to hear it. I shall send a basket for her." Emma squeezed the woman's hand.

"That is too good of you," exclaimed Mrs. Oates. "Now the earl is home, there is so much activity it takes my breath away. And you've fairly bought out the shops!"

The spending was as big a boon to everyone as Kellworth's poverty had been the cause of suffering. It relieved Emma that she no longer had to worry about the well-being of the whole valley—at least for the time being. "Yes, there is plenty now."

Mr. Oates finished his conversation with Spence and gave his wife an impatient glance.

She waved in acknowledgment. "I must go, my lady, but please come and look upon my new grandson, if you are able."

Emma might as well do so. She had nothing else to occupy her time. Mr. Larkin's reports on the crops and livestock now went to Spence, who passed on to her the briefest of summaries. Her kitchen garden was tended by others, so tidy no weed would dare take root there. She even gave up her pigs, now that there were workers to tend them and no need to use them for profit. She had given Mr. Larkin permission to slaughter the last of the litter.

Emma had nothing but time on her hands. "I should love to call upon Mary," she said to Mrs. Oates. "It will be a pleasure."

Mrs. Oates bobbed a quick curtsy. She took a couple of steps toward her toe-tapping husband, but hurried back to Emma. "Perhaps now the earl is back, you shall be next."

"Next?" Emma did not understand.

"You know," called the woman as she bustled away. "The next to be increasing! To get a fine heir, that is it!"

Emma kept her smile in place. In the early days of her marriage she had spun happy visions of holding an infant in her arms, Spence leaning over, a look of pride on his face. It was one of those many foolish dreams she'd learned to bury deep in her heart.

She tossed a quick look at Spence, chatting with Squire Benson whose property bordered Kellworth. Spence appeared as fit as the day she'd first seen him, though he'd become a bit winded at the end of the walk to church and he still carried the cane. The repairs to the house and outbuildings were progressing at a rapid pace, and, for all Emma knew, Spence might leave one day soon.

Spence concluded his conversation and returned to Emma, offering his arm. "Shall we walk back?"

She looped her arm through his, and they exchanged greetings with other folks as they started down the lane. Children, now free of church pews and Reuben's platitudinous sermon, ran and skipped ahead of their parents, shouting and chasing each other.

Children, Emma thought, an ache growing inside, one she had forgotten.

Spence's pace was slow, and when they came to the fork in the lane leading to Kellworth, she said, "If we take the path across the field, it will be a shorter walk."

He glanced at her feet. "You do not fear the ruin of your new shoes or to dirty your skirt?"

The truth was, she preferred to cross the field. One came upon Kellworth Hall from a high vantage point, and the grandeur of the house and grounds never failed to take her breath away. "The ground is dry enough."

Soon they could see no more than the spire of the church as Kellworth land surrounded them. The field was green with new grass and fragrant with spring. Pink lady's-smock, white clover, and wild pansies dotted the hillside. A flock of gray partridges darted into the hedgerows, while a lone sparrow hawk soared in a sky worthy of a Cozens landscape.

"I had forgotten." Spence spoke so low Emma was uncertain he meant her to hear.

"Forgotten?"

"How beautiful it is." He stopped and, leaning on his cane, seemed to drink in the sight of the verdant rolling field, the thick copse, the blue sky.

Emma sighed. "I think Kellworth the most beautiful place in the world."

He turned to her with an amused expression.

She felt herself blush. "You must think me ridiculous. I have hardly been anywhere else."

"I do not think you ridiculous." His eyes met hers with the same look of appreciation with which he'd viewed the scenery around them.

Her face grew warmer.

They resumed walking. "Paris is very beautiful," he went on conversationally. "Versailles, spectacular. There are views of the Alps that defy description, and in Spain, the villages that dot the Pyrenees look nothing like our villages here." He seemed now to be gazing at a more distant landscape. "There is a whole world of beautiful places." He turned to her. "Is there not some place in the world you pine to see, Emma?"

She shook her head.

He smiled and the faraway look in his eye returned. "I should like someday to visit the ancient ruins in Greece or Egypt. The Parthenon. The Pyramids. Would you not like to see such sights?"

Emma shuddered. It had taken a long time for Kellworth to become familiar to her. In the first days she would get turned around in the house and discover herself in the wrong corridor. When taking a walk, she took special care, lest she lose her way. Now that Kellworth felt as familiar as the land where she had grown up, she was loath to leave.

"I would prefer Kellworth," she said firmly.

"How do you know until you have seen Cairo first?" he asked in a teasing tone.

She answered quite seriously. "I should detest Cairo."

His smile faded and they began walking again. He barely used the cane over the uneven path.

Emma felt a sinking dismay. He was recovered. There was nothing to prevent him from traveling to Cairo, if that was what he wished. She would be alone again. The anger that burned within her during the three years of his absence sparked and rekindled.

They reached the crest of the hill, below which was Kellworth Hall. Its stone glowed golden in the sunlight. It looked timeless, as solid and secure as it had stood since the reign of Elizabeth.

Emma extended her hand toward the view. "Do you truly wish to leave all this?"

He put his hands on his hips. "Since I was a boy."

Her anger flared. "How could you?"

"This is not new to you, Emma," he countered. "We talked of this before our marriage. I have no wish to be a gentleman farmer. There is too much in the world to do and to see."

Though she'd been only seventeen at the time, she had perceived this talk as a young man's dreaming. Life was not so much about what one wished to do, but what one ought to do. And it was foolish to pine over what one could not have.

"That was three years ago," she replied.

"I have not changed." He looked back out to Kellworth Hall. "This was my brother's destiny, not mine."

Emma pursed her mouth. She could have argued that Kellworth *had* been his destiny. As it had been his brother's destiny to die tragically, leaving Spence to be earl. But she was in no mood for a metaphysical discussion.

Not waiting for the offer of his arm, she started down the hill in a hurry to be back within the walls of Kellworth Hall.

He caught up with her and grabbed her by the arm. "We made a bargain, you and I. Do you not remember? You would have the security of Kellworth and I would have my freedom."

She glared at him. "But Kellworth was not a place of security, was it? You broke your word to me."

He had the grace to look chagrined.

She did not relent. "You have repeatedly said you owe your life to me and that you will do anything to make up for Kellworth's neglect. But how can I believe anything you promise? You will leave. That will be the end of promises, will it not?"

His eyes flashed. "I did not know my promise was not kept, did I? And I am making it right now. Everything is being done that can be done."

"But you will leave again and forget us."

"I never forgot you!" he protested.

She pulled from his grasp and proceeded on down the hillside path almost at a run, not caring that she could hear him breathing hard as he tried to gain on her.

"Stop, Emma." His voice sounded strangled.

She turned. His hand clutched his side and he bent over. With effort she refrained from rushing over and lending him a supporting arm.

"I will not forget you," he said again, wincing. "But I cannot stay here. I cannot breathe here."

Nonsense, she thought. *You do not wish to stay here.*

"I want a new bargain." She met his eye, ignoring his grimace of pain.

"What?" he panted.

"I want an arrangement that will guarantee Kellworth's money will come to me in your absence, with permission to draw directly from the bank."

He nodded. "I never wished otherwise—"

She held up her hand. "There is more."

"Anything, Emma. I have told you I will give you anything you desire."

She turned toward Kellworth Hall and then back to him, holding her head high. "Give me a child."

Chapter ELEVEN

A *child?* Spence felt as if fingers of panic were firmly clamped around his neck. "A child?"

Emma's eyes shone as green as the field of grass. "A child. A baby. An heir. Or not. A daughter would be sufficient."

A child. His vision turned dark, his mind's eye seeing a lonely little boy, a boy like himself. "This was not in our bargain, Emma."

"Not in our *original* bargain," she countered. "But neither was all the hardship Kellworth endured."

He swung away, forcing himself to take long, even breaths, willing the darkness to recede.

A child.

The idea of bedding her flashed through his mind, the act that would create a new life inside her. Her wish to indulge that desire made it burn more hotly.

But he had no wish to create a child, no wish to be responsible for bringing a child into a world only to die again, as Stephen had died. Besides, a child would tie him to Kellworth and the old memories that lived in every corner. Spence craved new experiences, new lands, new people.

When they were schoolboys, Spence, Blake, and Wolfe made a pact to circle the globe like Sir Francis Drake, but even at that tender age, he knew his friends would renege. Blake and Wolfe needed to marry. Blake for fortune. Wolfe for status. Spence had been the only one who had no such need. He'd never planned to marry at all.

Until he met Emma.

He dared another glance at her. She glared back at him like a French cuirassier ready for battle. How different this Emma was from that doe-eyed girl he'd first seen in the London drawing room, who flinched under his uncle's frank admiration. How foolish he'd been, thinking he could rescue her and make her happy. Emma had been much too young to imagine a woman's desire to have children. And he had created the youthful illusion he could rescue her and leave her and still make her happy.

Instead she had rescued him.

They started back down the path past the copse, its elms thick with new green foliage.

"This is all I ask of you, Spence. A child and the financial means to rear him."

"Emma—" he began, but something zinged past his ear and the crack of a musket firing broke the air.

"Down!" He pushed her to the ground.

Daring to raise his head, he spied the shadowy figure of a man retreating through the trees.

Spence scrambled to his feet to chase the shooter, forgetting his cane and the need to use it. He managed no more than thirty feet before his legs gave out and he dropped to his knees.

Emma ran over to him. "Are you injured?"

"No strength," he panted, shaking his head. He looked in the direction the man had disappeared, and sat on the ground to catch his breath.

Emma sat down beside him. "He was after game, Spence. Gandy has turned a blind eye to poachers. No one abuses the privilege and only take what they need." She placed her hands against her cheeks. "I never sent word that the poaching should stop."

"He was a poacher?"

"He must have been. These years have been difficult. Some families were near starving. You cannot blame a man for hunting food."

No, Spence could not blame a man for hunting food, but Gandy had always taught him that the fowl and hares and deer must be protected or there would be no game left for future generations. Had the gamekeeper gone soft or had matters been that desperate?

Whichever it was, a poacher's shot could kill a passerby as effectively as it could kill a pheasant or hare, and this ball missed them by inches.

"I'll speak to Gandy." He struggled to his feet and extended his hand to help her rise.

Her delicate, gloved hand clasped his with surprising strength. "You might ask him if he wishes to be pensioned. He is very old."

Thinking of the strong, rugged Gandy, who always smelled of woods and earth, as an old pensioner depressed Spence, but he said, "I will."

He pulled her up, but she stumbled and almost collided with him. She regained her balance and stepped away.

They descended to the house and the subject of a child was lost for the moment, to Spence's relief. Still, he could not erase the picture of a little boy—his son—sitting alone in a huge dark room, as he had done when his parents were gone.

The house loomed more majestic with each step they took, making Spence feel small by comparison. Like it or not, he was responsible for this house, this land, and all the people who depended upon it. It had become his responsibility the moment he held his brother's limp body in his arms.

He suddenly felt as if he were a little boy again and the darkness closed in on him. He gulped for air, and his step faltered. Emma shot him a worried look, letting him lean on her while he concentrated on breathing in and out, repeating in his mind the word Arjun had given him.

They continued walking to the back entrance of the house. Emma did not call for Mr. Hale or Tolley, or one of the new footmen to attend them, but brushed off their clothes herself and cleaned their shoes. Her ministrations felt pleasant, soothing him as she'd once soothed his feverish panic.

But she did not dispel the feeling of being trapped by the walls of Kellworth.

Emma went through the motions of the day, swinging from rage to desolation, with no backbreaking, mind-numbing toil to distract her. The desire for a child, now voiced, grew inside her like a wild vine. Spence had not precisely said no, but his unwillingness to respond to her request was tantamount to a refusal.

They had breakfasted together after returning from church. She did not bring up the subject of a child during the meal, when a footman or Mr. Hale might at any moment enter the room. But in between their stilted, sparse attempts at conversation, she pondered her impulsive request, its truth more and more apparent. She needed a child. She needed someone to be hers, someone she could love wholeheartedly, someone who wouldn't leave her.

After breakfast she wandered into the library. Spence sat there reading the newspapers from London. She grabbed a book and retreated to her room, but the day was too fine to remain indoors. She gathered up her kittens and took them into the walled garden. Like the unused rooms in the house, it had been neglected and allowed to become overgrown. Now the space had been weeded and clipped and trimmed. She sat on the grass and teased the kittens into play with a flower she'd plucked. They lost interest quickly when a yellow butterfly fluttered nearby, jumping over each other in an effort to catch it.

The gate opened and Spence appeared. "I could not stay inside." His countenance was as gray as her mood.

He joined her on the grass, placing the black kitten in his lap. The little fur ball just as quickly jumped off and ran after the white one, who'd found a tiny toad to pounce upon. As the toad hopped away, both kittens scrambled in pursuit. The lines of stress in Spence's face eased as he laughed softly at their antics.

Emma found herself feeling sorry for him, which only made her more furious, this time at herself.

He sat so close his scent filled her nose and each rustle of his coat sounded in her ears. She remembered how he'd placed his lips so gently on her skin and how he'd held her in his arms, like some valued possession.

She knew little of men's desires. All those years ago, when she'd known instinctively that Spence's uncle had wanted to couple with her, it had frightened and repelled her. But it had never troubled her to think that Spence might want her in the same way. In his absence and neglect she'd given up such foolish notions, but perhaps now he was present, she could make him want her.

Growing up in a country house gave her some vague knowledge of how animals copulated, though she had always been scooted away before totally figuring it out. She used to listen to the maids giggling about what men and women did in bed, but she'd been too shy to ask them directly.

She looked at Spence again while he played a game of fisticuffs with furry little Tom, sparring fingers to paws. The shadow of his beard was visible on his jaw. One eyebrow danced as he laughed at the kitten. As when he kissed her, her body seemed to reveal its every nerve and come from dormancy to life.

She wanted to retain that giddy intensity for as long as she could.

She took a quick breath and turned her gaze from him, pretending to search for Puss, who had not wandered far. It was a child she wanted, not this visceral reaction. She'd brave it, though. She'd brave anything to make him want to copulate with her. Could she act the part of a seductress? She must, if she wanted what only he could give her.

His child.

When they finally walked back into the house, it was time to dress for dinner. Emma wore her new rose dinner dress and daringly fussed with the bodice and her corset so that the dress came as low as possible. From the entailed family jewelry, she chose a long ruby pendant, which dangled between her breasts, drawing the eye's attention to that tantalizing location. Dorrie, the fresh-faced, eager girl Mrs. Cobbett had recommended to be her new lady's maid, fashioned her hair so that her curls framed her face and cascaded to caress her neck. She draped her paisley shawl gracefully over her arms.

"By Jove, you look splendid, Emma, my dear!" Reuben said as she entered the drawing room. Spence eyed her, but did not speak.

Reuben repeated the compliment when they seated themselves at the dining-room table. She felt guilty for wishing the vicar to perdition—or rather to anywhere but here, when she wanted to be alone with Spence.

"The food is delicious," Reuben gushed as energetically as he'd admired Emma's appearance. He placed another slice of veal next to the broiled salmon on his plate.

Emma picked at her asparagus.

After an initial silence Spence played the gracious host, engaging his cousin to talk about old neighbors and families who lived in the village. Emma, who knew more about those people than the man who was responsible for their spiritual needs, chimed in here and there.

Spence watched her during the meal. It made her pulse quicken to feel his gaze upon her. It made her long for night to fall.

After dinner they retired to the drawing room, where the gentlemen drank their port. Emma barely refrained from pacing the room.

Finally the sky began to darken, and Reuben rose to leave. "Best I get back while I still have the light." It was what he always said upon leaving.

Emma walked him to the door, and Mr. Hale handed him his hat and coat. As he went out the door, he turned around, giving Emma one long but silent look.

Embarrassed, Emma glanced at the butler to see if he'd noticed Reuben's admiring gaze.

Mr. Hale looked so fatigued, she was surprised he could remain standing. "You look weary, Mr. Hale."

"I confess, I am a bit, my lady."

So wrapped up in herself, she had neglected to think of Mr. Hale, one of the people who had helped her through the most difficult times. "With all these young footmen, why have you not retired for the night?"

He gave her a wan smile. "Habit, I guess, my lady. I did not think to ask them."

She extended her hand to touch his arm, but caught herself. The very correct and proper servant would not appreciate such familiarity. "Has the earl spoken to you of a pension? You deserve some rest after all your years of service."

"I told him it would be best if I first saw to the new footmen." Mr. Hale straightened his normally curved spine. "There is much training to be done."

Emma worried that such a task would be too much for him, but she did not speak of it. "I do not know what I should have done without you, Mr. Hale."

His eyes darted uncomfortably, but she was still glad she had spoken.

She cleared her throat and spoke more like a countess. "We shall have no more need of you this evening, Mr. Hale."

He bowed. "Very good, my lady."

She started back to the drawing room, glancing over her shoulder to make sure Mr. Hale left the hall to seek his own rooms. She hesitated outside the door of the drawing room, knowing she and Spence would be alone.

When she gathered enough resolve to walk in, Spence stood by the window, fingering the keys of the pianoforte.

He looked up. "Do you play, Emma?"

"I used to play passably well."

In fact, for a while the pianoforte had filled many empty hours at Kellworth, the music nourishing her like rain on a rose.

"No longer?" he asked.

"It is broken." She walked over to the instrument and pressed down on middle C. It made no sound. "See?"

"That too," he said in dismal tones. He was so close to her she could smell the scent of his soap and could see where he'd been nicked shaving for dinner.

"We shall have to send to Maidstone for someone to repair it." His voice vibrated inside her like the instrument's bass keys.

They stared at each other. Emma felt the warmth of his body, heard each intake of breath.

She glanced away and nervously pecked out a melody until hitting another key that did not sound. She did not wish to be so affected by him. She had no desire to be like the naive girl she'd once been. It was a child she wanted. A child, that was all. A baby in her arms would be enough to fill her heart. She did not need him to intrude there.

Spence stepped up behind her and she thought for a moment he would touch her, kiss her as he'd done in his bedchamber, but he did not. "It shall be repaired, Emma."

He pressed down on the broken key. "Pigs, poachers, and now the pianoforte."

She turned to face him and his hand left the keyboard and rose.

He withdrew it. "Here is another sacrifice you made in my absence. Shall I discover more each day I remain?"

She froze. *Each day I remain, he'd said.*

He expelled a long breath and stepped away. "I believe I shall say good night, Emma."

She glanced at the window. There would be light at least another hour.

"Good night," she said stiffly.

He walked to the door but stopped. With one hand bracing himself on the doorjamb, he looked back at her, eyes boring into her with an intensity that made her breath catch. His dark hair looked mussed as if he'd run his fingers through it. She waited for him to speak.

He said nothing. He turned away and walked out.

Emma picked up his glass and almost flung it behind him. She waited a few minutes to try to calm herself. She had no idea how to compel him to stay with her, touch her, kiss her.

Novels were replete with men whose passion for ladies defied control. Even Spence's uncle averred a passion for her, but she never knew exactly what she'd done to elicit such emotions. She wished she could figure it out.

She hurried to the library and pulled from the shelves *Evelina* and one volume of Fielding's *Tom Jones* she'd hidden behind *Marmion*. Carrying the leather-bound volumes back to the drawing room, she sat by the window and leafed through them. It was no use. She could not decipher what Evelina did to attract her suitors, nor what attracted Jones to his Sophia. Her eyes started to strain with the reading.

She slammed the book shut and rested her chin on her hand. She must try in any event. She returned the books to the library, her pulse beating excitedly. Halfway up the stairs to the bedchamber, she froze. What if he turned her away? Could she bear it?

If she truly wanted his child, she should brave anything.

Except that this involved her heart, a heart once shattered and now held together by mere determination and anger. She clenched her fingers into a fist and walked the rest of the way to her bedchamber.

When she entered, her new maid, Dorrie, was busy rearranging her chest of drawers.

The girl bobbed a curtsy. "Oh, my lady. Beg pardon but I do not have your nightdress laid out. I did not expect you so early."

Emma felt her face grow hot. "I . . . I decided to retire early tonight." She suddenly thought everyone in the house knew what she was about to do. That was absurd, but the servants would know quick enough if she slept with Spence. Servants knew everything in a household.

Dorrie smiled, showing deep dimples that reminded Emma of Blakewell. "It'll take me no time a'tall to pull out your nightdress."

Emma started to reach behind her back to try to undo the mother-of-pearl buttons of her dress. The two kittens came out from under the bed, stretching and licking their paws. They quickly decided to play around the hem of Emma's dress.

"Shoo, rascals!" the maid said. "Those two have more liveliness than is good for them." She shooed them away with her foot. "They mustn't claw the hem."

Emma stepped out of her dress, and the maid quickly lifted the garment up high so the kittens could not reach it.

"Those rascals will not spoil this dress. Why, it is as grand as Lady Pullerton bought from London, it is."

Dorrie, who had been one of the upstairs maids at Kellworth three years earlier, had gone to work in Lord Pullerton's house near Tenterden, when Emma cut back on servants. She'd attended Lady Pullerton's daughters, who were all nearly of an age to make their come-out. A clever girl, she had learned quickly about fashions and hairstyles and ladies' accessories.

Still chattering about some of the dresses she'd seen, Dorrie helped Emma out of her corset, and busied herself elsewhere in the room while Emma poured water in the bowl and washed herself with a bar of lavender-scented soap, a rare luxury she'd made for herself last winter. After she dried herself off, Dorrie helped her into her white muslin nightdress. Soon she was removing pins from Emma's hair and brushing out the tangles before putting it in a plait down Emma's back. The kittens scampered away off to some new game.

"Will there be anything else, my lady?" Dorrie asked.

"No, that will be all."

Dorrie did a quick straightening up of the room, then left. Emma glanced in the mirror. Her eyes and lips were really too big for her too-round face. She looked like an owl. She fussed with the neckline of her nightdress, but there was no way to make it lower.

She held her breath and closed her eyes. She must think pragmatically, not like a besotted fool. This was not romance, but a calculated means to a goal.

She released her breath, rose from her chair, and walked toward the door connecting her room to Spence's. She put her ear to the door to see if she could hear Tolley still inside.

There was quiet. Trembling, she turned the knob and opened the door.

Spence was standing near the window, dressed in his banyan. "Emma," he said in some surprise.

She gave a nervous laugh, suddenly having no thought of how to entice him. "I . . . I figured you were not yet sleeping." She looked over to the table by the window where a decanter stood. "May I have some brandy?"

He stared at her, as if he'd not immediately understood her words, then he said, "Yes, yes, of course."

He walked over to the cabinet, where she'd fetched the glass before. She sauntered over to the table. Staring at her, he hesitated before filling her glass. The last time they'd drunk brandy together, he'd kissed her, she remembered, finishing the glass in one long sip. She thrust the glass toward him again.

He poured more. She wandered over to the window and sipped more slowly.

"What are you doing here, Emma?"

Turning to smile at him, she murmured, "I am drinking brandy."

He continued to stare at her. She put down her glass and sauntered over to stand very close to him. "Am I disturbing you?"

A sound came from deep in his throat, but he stepped back.

Emma felt her courage falter. What was she to do now? She stepped forward again.

This time he did not step back.

She reached up to stroke his cheek with the back of her hand.

He stood very still, staring at her, making her feel even more uncertain. She clasped his neck and eased his head to hers, standing on tiptoe to reach him. Tentatively she let her lips touch his, thrilling with their softness and the taste of brandy upon them. To her surprise and delight he put his arms around her and kissed her back, not softly, but in a way that sent sensation through every part of her.

It seemed as if she moved without will, pressing herself against him, very aware of how he felt beneath the thin layers of his banyan and her nightdress. He groaned.

He broke off the kiss. "What are you about, Emma?"

With his hands on her shoulders he moved her away, but did not release her. His breath came rapid and he would not look into her eyes.

She was more than confused. His grip on her shoulders maintained the contact she craved, but it was so much less than her body suddenly demanded. The intensity of sensation alarmed her as much as it had thrilled her. The loss of it would be desolating.

He slowly turned his head to look at her. His eyes were dark and searching. "You want a child so much?" His voice was deep, intense.

She could barely breathe. "I want many things, Spence. A child among them."

He was silent, one hand moving from her shoulder to

caress her cheek. She could hear the beating of her heart, the ticking of the clock upon his bureau.

Slowly he leaned down and touched his lips to hers. In a fluid motion his arms encircled her and she was again flush with his body, feeling every contour of muscle, including the male part of him.

What was to come would be new to her, but her customary trepidation was surpassed by an overwhelming need.

No longer in command of herself, her fingers played in his hair. She kissed him back, crushing her lips against his.

Chapter TWELVE

Spence felt her tremble against him as she returned his kiss with an unschooled ardor that filled him with tenderness. Through the thin fabric of her white nightdress, he felt each soft curve of her luscious body. He was hard with wanting her, madly hard.

His day had been spent in an agony of indecision. One moment he decided to refuse her request and leave Kellworth as soon as possible, the next he could not bear to disappoint her again. Most of all, he'd been consumed with the idea of making love with her, how smooth her skin would feel beneath his hand, how her lips would taste. He savored the taste of her now.

At this moment Kellworth did not feel like entrapment. It felt like a place of dreams, a place where everything he could ever want existed.

Emma.

He lifted her into his arms and carried her to the bed. Laying her gently on the bed linens, he climbed in after her.

Stroking her cheek with the back of his hand, he murmured, "Don't be afraid, Emma."

"I am not afraid," she murmured.

Her eyes were dark with passion, her breath eager. He reached around her, pulling the ribbon from her plait and loosening her thick and luxurious hair with his fingers. His senses quickened.

He was powerfully aroused, had been as soon as he'd seen her facing him in the doorway. He wanted to take her quick and ease the ache inside him. But she deserved more than some rough and hurried coupling. And he craved more as well.

"Emma," he whispered, sliding close to her, grazing his lips near her ear. "I will make this pleasant for you." He silently resolved this would be one promise to her he would keep.

Nuzzling the silky skin of her neck, he feathered her with light kisses. She smelled of lavender, a scent he knew would forever remind him of her, of this moment of making love with her.

She gasped, a tiny, vulnerable sound. He gently turned her head toward him and touched his lips to hers, barely grazing them at first. She met him with a gratifying fervor, and he rewarded the effort by deepening the kiss, coaxing her mouth open so he could fully taste her. She touched her tongue to his, mimicking his every move.

He admired her courage. She was not about to shirk from this experience, but showed herself willing to grasp for every part of it. He plied her with kisses and gradually intensified the pressure of his hand on her breasts, his fingers lightly circling until she made an urgent sound in the back of her throat.

No less urgent than he, for every muscle, sinew, and nerve in his body demanded he take her now, plunge into her and slake his desire. But there was so much more he could show her, wanted to show her, would show her.

"Let me see you," he murmured, urging her to sit up.

She kept her gaze locked on his as he pulled her nightdress over her head and tossed it aside. She was a vision, breasts high and swollen from his touch, waist narrow, skin glowing in the dim light. He shrugged out of his banyan and watched her look at him much more tentatively than he'd looked at her. He touched her face gently and slid his hand languidly to her breast. She closed her eyes and leaned into his touch. He laid her back down. Slowly he moved his lips from her neck to her breast, tasting the sweetness of her, feeling her nipple harden under his tongue.

She gasped.

"Do you dislike this?" he murmured, determined to cease if she was not ready.

"No." She groaned and pressed herself against him.

Again she would not retreat. She inflamed his senses anew and filled him with confidence that he would not disappoint her.

While he tasted her other breast and continued to explore her with his hands, she became more pliant under his touch. She showed only ease with each new touch, but he knew that he would soon have to hurt her. It made him feel he would betray her all over again.

"I must prepare you," he said, sliding his hand to the dark thatch of hair that had tantalized his vision. She stiffened and he felt as if he'd already injured her. "Be easy," he murmured as he fingered the opening. "This will make it less painful for you."

He hoped.

His own excitement mounting, he gently explored her secret places. She squirmed beneath him, flinging her arms back over her head to clutch at the pillows.

He stopped. "Am I hurting you?"

"No." She gasped. "No. Not hurting me."

"I will stop if you wish it." Though it might kill him to do so.

She shook her head. "Do not stop."

When his fingers gingerly entered her, she stiffened, clamping her legs against his hand. He started to withdraw, but she relaxed and opened herself to him.

It touched him that she trusted him with such an intimacy, making him rue the need to pierce her virginity, but her eyes turned glassy and unfocused. It was time.

He rose above her. "Are you ready, Emma?"

She closed her eyes and nodded. He dropped his head and kissed her, not carefully this time but hungrily. Feeling as if he would burst, he eased himself inside her, moving as slowly and gently as he could. She was so trusting, so willing. Her pain would be the only way to show her what her body craved and his demanded. With a deep intake of breath he thrust hard.

She cried out and clutched his back.

He stilled. "I'm sorry, Emma."

"Do not stop." Her voice was taut with emotion.

He obliged her. The moment had passed, and soon they moved in rhythmic unison, climbing to the peak. Nearer. Nearer. So close now.

Until pain shot through his shoulder. "Ah!" he cried, his arm unable to hold him up. It gave way and he collapsed against her and rolled to the side. He clasped his palm against the site of his wound.

"What happened?" she asked breathlessly.

"I can't hold myself up." The throbbing made it hard to speak. "I can't continue." He felt like smashing something. Or felt like he'd been smashed in two, one half pulsating with need, the other paralyzed with pain.

"Is it over?" Emma's voice was as taut as a string on a violin.

"No." He pressed hard against where he'd been wounded, trying to still the pain radiating all the way down his arm. "My shoulder gave out."

She rolled onto her side and sat up. "Your wound?"

She eased his hand away so she could inspect it, but the damage was internal. His injured muscle could not hold him over her any longer.

"It pains you?"

He nodded, damning his weakness, when he'd come so close to giving her the pleasure a man could give a woman.

"Did you . . . did you spill your seed?" she asked.

Spence squeezed his eyes shut, unreasonably wounded that she thought only of conceiving when he'd endeavored to show her so much more.

She could not guess at the pleasure, he reminded himself. He'd failed to show her. Failed her again.

"I did not spill my seed," he answered, rolling onto his back. "But I can show you another way."

He reached for her. "Come atop me."

Her eyes widened, but she hesitated only a moment before mounting him as a man would mount a horse. "Like this?"

He tried to smile. "Yes. Like that." The mere view of her above him aroused him again.

He lifted her at the hips and eased her onto him. She leaned down to kiss him as he had kissed her when their positions had been reversed. The gesture made him feel tender toward her. Guiding her hips, he set the rhythm. She caught on quickly and followed his lead. Then every thought left his head, and nothing in the world existed except Emma and the escalation of promised release. In unison their pace quickened. Nearly lost to the sensation, he watched her face reflect the same urgency, the same need.

She cried out, and he felt the spasm of her climax around him. No more need to hold back, he exploded within her and still she pulsed around him. They clutched each other as the pleasure rose, peaked, and plummeted, floating them into a haze of languor.

She lay atop him, her lips resting on his neck. He turned to kiss her one more time, a long, restful, leisurely kiss. She slipped off him, but he held her close to his side.

"I did not know it would be like that," she murmured.

He planted a kiss atop her head.

He held her for a long time, before getting out of bed and bringing her a damp towel. Moving the covers off her, he washed her as gently as he could. Her breath quickened with his touch. After drying her with a towel, he saw to himself as she watched. It was enough to arouse him again, but he feared making her sore if he took her again. He crawled into bed beside her, nestling her against him, petting her hair until her breathing slowed and she slept.

Emma woke when the first glimmers of dawn peeked in the window. For a moment she was disoriented; then she realized she was in Spence's bed, and Spence was warm and naked next to her. Just as shocking, she was naked herself.

He faced her, one arm flung over her body. In the growing light she examined his features. His strong brow, his sculpted lips. Lips she had kissed and had kissed her back. Nearly gasping aloud, she remembered all that had transpired the night before.

How could she have known it would be like that?

She had expected something pleasant. It would have to be pleasant for women to want to do it, as some seemed to. But nothing could have prepared her for how it actually felt. Her body sprang to life again from the mere memory.

Or from gazing at him.

He opened his eyes, as blue as the spring sky, and smiled at her, a knowing, intimate smile that made her feel he remembered the pleasure, too. He stroked her hair with a gentle hand. Suddenly, fiercely, she had need of him in a way she'd not known possible before.

She moved closer and dared to put her lips on his.

He groaned and rolled onto his back, pulling her on top of him. She could feel him hard beneath her. Now that she knew what to do, she was in a hurry to do it. She positioned herself so he could guide himself inside her. It hurt a little, then not at all, as she moved up and down, her body demanding release. The previous night had seemed like a lovely, leisurely walk, but this was a race, a wild, frenzied gallop that both exhilarated and left them damp with sweat.

They rode faster and faster, until it happened again, that magic, that spasm of pleasure, that shattering peak of sensation. How could she feel both scattered into tiny bits and glued fast to him as if they had become one person? In her waves of pleasure she felt him convulse and she knew his seed was inside her once more.

That had been all she thought she wanted—his seed inside her—but she had not reckoned on what went with it.

Her pleasure ebbed, her body relaxed, and she could think again. She would lose *this* when he left, as well as losing him. And she would lose a part of herself that now was part of him.

Forcing herself to smile, she blinked away tears. Her heart was lost to him and she must not show it.

He smiled back. "We ought to rise before Tolley bursts in and your maid goes searching for you."

"I suppose." She made no effort to move.

He cupped his hand around the back of her head and met her in one more, luxurious, soul-stealing kiss.

Heavy footsteps sounded in the hallway. "Tolley." Spence sat up.

Emma scrambled off the bed and grabbed her nightdress, not stopping to don it as she ran across the room to the connecting door.

As she was closing it behind her, she heard Tolley's cheerful voice. "G'morning, my lord."

It was silly to scurry away from the servants. The evidence of what they had done stained Spence's bed linens. If Tolley did not put two and two together, the laundry maids certainly would. Emma expected all the servants would know by midday.

She lifted the nightdress over her head and put her arms through its sleeves.

The servants would never speak directly to her about it. She need not talk of it to anyone. How could she? Words could never do justice to the experience. In a day, news would likely reach the village that the earl had finally bedded his wife. Soon every woman in the valley would be watching her for signs of increasing.

She wrapped her arms around her stomach as a thrill raced through her. Spence's child might be growing inside her right now.

Though if she were carrying a child, Spence would leave her.

Emma crawled into her own bed and buried herself beneath the covers, trying to escape this sudden plunge into desolation. How could she discover paradise, only to have it wrenched away?

Her kittens mewed from the little closet where their sandbox was kept. Dorrie had probably forgotten and closed them in as she was tidying up the previous night. Flinging off the covers, she hurried over to free them.

They came leaping out like reprieved prisoners. Immediately they crawled under her gown and rubbed against her legs, purring so loud she wondered if Spence could hear them.

"My poor little pusses," she murmured, reaching down to scoop them into her arms. "You are free now."

She carried them to her bed and petted them, while they kneaded the covers with their little paws.

"My darlings, what shall I do?" Her furry confidants blinked up at her. "What shall I do? He will leave again. I've done nothing more than delay him for a short time."

Little Tom cocked his black head as if he understood. He bumped his head against her leg and meowed.

She laughed, though swiping at tears. "I will not regret this," she said with resolve. "No matter what, I will not regret this glorious night."

She picked up Tom, and his nose touched her cheek. With a scratchy tongue, he licked her salty tears.

"I will spend every night with him, Tom," she said. "I will always have the memories, won't I?"

Fluffy white Puss tried to climb up Emma's nightdress to see what Tom was doing. Emma lifted the kitten onto her shoulder.

"I'll have a child, as well," she went on. "A part of Spence always."

Emma played with her kittens until Dorrie rapped at the door and came in to help her dress. She donned her new yellow morning dress, and Dorrie tied up her hair with yellow ribbon. When Emma looked in the mirror, her eyes were bright and her cheeks flushed pink. She hoped Spence would think her pretty.

By the time she was ready to leave the room, Tom and Puss were sound asleep on her bed.

Emma descended the stairs nearly breathless with the hope that he might still be at breakfast. She hurried into the dining room, but Spence was not there.

Mr. Hale attended her, looking much more rested and refreshed. "Lord Kellworth asked me to convey his regrets. Mr. Larkin had need of him."

"Are they in the library?" she asked.

"I believe they were to ride somewhere. My lord said he might be gone a good part of the day." Mr. Hale bowed and left the room.

Emma pounded her fist on the table, then scolded herself for the outburst. She buttered her toast, telling herself she could last a couple of hours before seeing him again.

But a "good part of the day" and more went by and Spence did not return. By the time Emma retired upstairs to prepare for dinner, worry nagged at her. What if he had tricked her? What if he had left, never to come home again?

While dressing her for dinner, a dinner she might eat alone, Dorrie grinned at her, obviously having heard of the stained sheets. When Emma descended the stairs, Reuben stood in the hall, chatting with Mr. Hale. Of all nights, she wished he'd not come this one. If Spence were indeed gone, she'd rather be alone in her misery.

The vicar appeared preoccupied, but that expression cleared when he caught sight of her. "Ah, Emma, my dear, you are in fine looks again tonight."

"Good evening, Reuben." Her eyes slipped to the door, hoping it would open and Spence would walk in.

Reuben offered his arm to escort her into the drawing room. "I hope you do not mind that I stopped by for dinner. When I saw my cousin and Larkin earlier, Spence extended the invitation."

Her hopes rose. Reuben had seen him! Perhaps he had not run to London, after all.

"You are always welcome, Reuben," she said, but her suddenly cheerful voice was not meant for him.

He squeezed her arm as if it had been, but she quickly stepped away, regretting having given him that impression. She poured him some wine. "Spence has not yet returned."

"That is so like him." Reuben looked up at her. "Do not tell me you are worried?"

Reuben was a friend, but she had never truly confided in him. "Well, he is not completely recovered, you know."

Reuben gave her a sympathetic look. "Fear not. Leave it in God's hands."

Everything that happened was in God's hands, Emma felt like saying. But she always believed God preferred a man to be responsible for his own behavior.

Instead she said, "I always do."

She sat on one of the chairs near the fireplace, and Reuben seated himself in the other, sipping his wine.

After a brief silence he spoke in a knowing way. "Mr. Hale seems to believe you and Spence are getting along splendidly."

"We have been managing."

He suddenly leaned toward her. "Forgive my impertinence, but has he . . . has he done his duty by you?"

Her cheeks burned, but she forced herself to give an ingenuous smile. "Spence has worked tirelessly. He has managed to remedy all of Kellworth's neglect."

Reuben shifted his chair closer to her. "I meant, has Spence performed his husbandly duty to you?"

She gave him a level stare. "You are crossing the bounds of propriety, Reuben. I beg you will cease doing so this instant."

He tapped his fingers on the arm of the chair and looked around the room, finally directing his gaze at her again. "You do not know him as I do, Emma. He will hurt you again. Do not put your trust in him, I beg you."

Emma's immediate impulse was to spring to Spence's defense, although Reuben only voiced her own fears. She opened her mouth to speak, but at that same moment the door opened.

Spence crossed the threshold, still dressed in his riding clothes.

Emma jumped to her feet, her heart beating wildly at the mere sight of him. "You have returned! I was beginning to fear something had happened."

His eyes were warm and seemed to savor her face. "Something did happen. I lost my stirrup and fell off the horse, which I daresay my friends would endlessly tease me about." He smiled at her. "I beg you will not tell them."

She reached out to touch his arm. "Are you hurt?"

He covered her hand with his own, but moved stiffly. "Not a scratch. But it was a long walk home."

"Where was Larkin?" Reuben piped up.

Only then did Spence seem to notice his cousin's presence. "We'd finished our task and he'd ridden on ahead, so I was alone." He turned back to Emma. "I will take but a moment to dress for dinner, but you may begin without me."

"We will wait for you," she said.

After he left and she walked back to her chair, Reuben gave her a pained look. "Be wary, Emma. Guard your heart."

Throughout dinner Reuben was unusually quiet. Emma suspected Spence did not notice, but she thought she understood how Reuben felt. He had discovered he was not as important as he hoped. She well knew that feeling.

Emma felt guilty for her dependence on him, which certainly fostered his *tendre* for her. Still, it was past time for him to abandon his attachment to her and search for a wife of his own.

After dinner they all retired again to the drawing room for more stilted conversation. At his usual time Reuben stood and said, "Best I get back while I still have the light."

Emma walked him to the door as usual. Before he took his hat and gloves from Mr. Hale, he leaned close to her ear. "Remember my caution, my dear."

"Do not concern yourself about me," she replied, as direct as politeness would allow.

She was eager to return to the drawing room and did not wait for Reuben to go out the door.

When she reentered the room, Spence rose to his feet. The mere fact of being alone with him roused her desire, leaving her trembling. She walked over to him as if drawn by a rope.

He searched her face. "I am sorry to have caused you worry, Emma."

She tried to compose herself, to rise above the flood of emotion roiling inside her. Her voice cracked. "I . . . I thought perhaps you had gone back to London."

Frown lines creased his brow. "I promised you I would stay to give you a child."

She wanted to be strong, to act as if she believed his promise and as if conceiving a child were still her only desire. It was impossible.

"Well . . . I . . . I thought perhaps . . . after last night . . . you . . . decided once was enough."

He put his fingers under her chin, raising her face to him. "Once was most definitely not enough."

"A baby might be inside me now." She touched her belly.

He placed a hand over hers. "It might not happen so easily, Emma."

She began to feel light as air, as if floating two inches above the ground. She took several deep breaths. "Then we must try again."

His eyes darkened. "Yes, we must." He lifted her hand and pressed his lips against her palm. "I think we must try again this very night."

Chapter THIRTEEN

Their second night together surpassed the first, but could not compare with succeeding nights as they learned more and more what pleased the other. As Spence's physical strength grew, his lovemaking became more inventive and more passionate. Emma responded more boldly than she ever thought she could. She delighted in exploring his body, willing herself to remember every inch of him with sight and smell and touch.

If her nights were the milk that nourished her, then her days were the cream. Kellworth's demands on Spence's time decreased and they spent a great portion of the day in each other's company. They rode in the morning, Spence helping her gain confidence on horseback. They romped with the kittens. Read books to each other. In the evening she played the newly repaired pianoforte for him.

His strength and stamina restored, he took her on walks and picnics and excursions to the village, where everyone smiled in greeting at them. Spence insisted upon buying her whatever treats the shops sold. He insisted she visit the dressmaker again, ordering more dresses, giving her the delight of having to decide what to wear each day. They explored the estate and took inventories of each room of the house. Sometimes a black mood would suddenly come over him as they came across a familiar object or a place he said he'd played as a child, making the pleasant memories seem painful. She'd wrap her arms around him to soothe whatever caused his pain, and often her attempts led to a poignant, urgent sort of lovemaking in places other than the bed. But he never spoke of what had upset him.

Four weeks passed, the happiest time Emma could ever imagine. She pretended this idyll would last forever.

The illusion succeeded most of the time.

This night they lay in each other's arms, satiated and languorous. She loved moments like this when they talked of little things, ordinary things that contrasted so sharply with the extraordinary pleasures of their coupling.

She shivered and he reached over her to search for her nightdress, helping her don it; then he snuggled her close to him again.

He planted a kiss on her forehead. "You've no wish to be naked?"

She cuddled closer to him. "What if a servant comes in?"

He laughed softly. "The devil with them." Tightening his arms around her, he asked, "What is your pleasure tomorrow? I beg to please you."

She turned her head and kissed where her lips reached at the edge of his chest. "I am content."

"Nonsense. We need a new adventure."

He said this lightheartedly, but any hint of his restlessness merely reminded her that he would leave her.

Her hand slid to her belly. Her monthly courses were more than a week late, and usually she was as regular as the moon's cycles. She might be carrying a child. His child.

She wanted it to be true. It thrilled her to think that a new life could be born from the passion they shared, from the joining of their bodies. She longed to hold his child in her arms, longed to feel his child suckling at her breast.

And yet, if a child were inside her, their new bargain would be fulfilled, and Spence was free to depart. So she did not tell him her courses were late. She would delay for as long as possible.

"I have it!" he said after a piece. "I will drive you to Maidstone and we will buy out the shops for you."

"I have never been there." Emma had no desire to go to Maidstone. Going farther than the village gave her a flutter of nerves.

"Then it is high time I took you. If tomorrow promises to be a fine day, I will drive you in the curricle."

She sat up on her elbow. "Are you able to handle the ribbons for so long a time?" He had taken her for short drives, but a trip of two hours or more over questionable roads was another matter entirely.

He pulled her down next to him again. "I am certain of it. I am good as new."

She was not so certain, but she allowed him to lull her to sleep, talking of the sights they would see on the way and all the treasures he would buy for her in the Maidstone stores.

By the time Spence joined Emma in the breakfast room the next morning, he was no longer convinced of the wisdom of this trip to Maidstone. The idea had grown out of a wish to escape Kellworth even for a brief time. He had not considered that it meant riding on the section of road where Stephen was killed.

Where he killed Stephen, he meant.

The bleak misery of regret he usually held at bay pressed in on him as it had done so often during this time with Emma. Memories were in every corner of Kellworth, over every hill, and into each thicket. Most were of Stephen, alive, vibrant, happy. Stephen laughing at their childhood games, crowing in triumph when they climbed to the top of a tree, slapping him on the back after they leapt over the stream and did not fall in. If that were not disturbing enough, there were also flashes of his parents, a wisp of his mother's laugh, the whiff of his father's snuff. They were like ghosts haunting him, popping up anywhere, when he least expected it.

He could never explain to Emma when the memories assaulted him, but she'd noticed his distress. Sometimes he just wanted to run, to escape Kellworth for any place else.

His best escape was Emma. When he made love to her, he felt transported. At the same time it was like coming home. Sometimes, when she lay in his arms, he decided that life with her would be adventure enough for him. Then the next day he would turn a corner and the ghosts would be waiting, and the urge to be on the road, in a carriage, on horseback, in a ship, returned.

With his arms wrapped around her in his bed, he'd thought a trip to Maidstone would content him. He wanted to spoil her, to lavish gifts upon her. Spending the day with her seemed irresistible.

"What concerns you, Spence?" Emma broke into his reverie and peered at him over her cup of chocolate.

"Why, nothing," he lied, attempting a reassuring smile.

She gave him a worried frown. "Are you not feeling up to this trip to Maidstone? I do not mind if we stay home."

She already wore a new carriage dress and looked so fetching he could only imagine how she would be admired in the town. He wanted to show her off.

If only he would not have to travel that haunted piece of road.

He reached over to clasp her hand. "I am perfectly well. We will not miss our little adventure."

She lowered her lashes. "I am not much made for adventure."

"We shall have a splendid time. You will see." Spence knew she felt most comfortable in the safe bosom of Kellworth, the same place that to him felt like being trapped in the coffin. She did not desire this trip, but he needed it.

If only he would not have to travel on that haunted piece of road.

Within the hour a groom brought the curricle to the front door. The horses harnessed to it were the same animals that seven years ago had been harnessed to the high-perched phaeton he'd badgered his brother to buy. Had no one rid Kellworth of them? He'd been too grief-stricken to think of it at the time, too much in a hurry to run off to war.

This day, cloudless and crisp, was as perfect as the day he'd held the phaeton's ribbons and uttered to his brother those fateful words, "Let me show you how fast it can go."

Spence helped her into her seat and climbed up beside her, taking the ribbons in his gloved hands. They started down the long lane on Kellworth land and soon enough reached the road, taking the fork with a sign pointing to Maidstone.

Neither of them spoke. Emma seemed lost in her own thoughts and Spence would just as soon heave up his breakfast than turn onto this road. Only the horses seemed cheerful. They were frisky and eager to run, just as they had been seven years ago. Spence set a brisk but sensible pace, feeling the horses strain against it in disappointment.

The haunted stretch of road came into view. Each twist and turn made Spence's head pound and his hands shake as he came closer to the spot. The memory of his excitement returned, of laughing as the phaeton rounded each bend, challenging his driving skill, and giving him the sensation of flying.

Now as he drove the curricle sedately around that same sharp turn, he could not help but remember how the phaeton started to tip, how he'd tried to pull the horses to compensate, how the speed was too fast. He could still hear Stephen's shout as the phaeton flipped over. Spence jumped up, laughing, without a scratch. But Stephen . . .

Stephen lay in a heap under the tree he'd been thrown against. He died in Spence's arms.

The curricle passed that tree while Spence felt the wrench of agony, the taste of bile in his throat. But as soon as it had been reached, they were past the spot, unscathed, merely scraped by a painful memory. The horses were as sprightly as when they had started, and Emma had relaxed her grip on the seat. Spence felt as if he had scaled the rocky face of an Alpine mountain. He exhaled a long, pent-up breath and glanced at Emma. She smiled back at him and a knot loosened inside him.

Everything would work out, he suddenly felt. The future was as bright as the sun shining down on them. First they would enjoy the shops at Maidstone and who knew what other adventures they could share. They had the rest of their lives to discover.

Spence took in the familiar countryside as if seeing it for the first time. He savored the glimpse of verdant hills, of lush foliage. He lifted his face to the sun.

As the horses turned down the next bend in the road, he heard a loud crack from the wheel on his side. The curricle tipped as the wheel shattered. He was in the air, hearing Emma scream as the sky turned upside down and back again. He landed hard on his wounded shoulder, through stars of pain glimpsing the horses dragging away the now one-wheeled vehicle.

"Emma!" he called, painfully struggling to his feet. He twisted around to search for her. "Emma!"

She did not answer.

He finally saw her at the bottom of the slope at the side of the road, looking like a rag doll tossed away. She didn't move.

"Emma!" he cried again as he slid down the embankment and limped to her side.

He untied the ribbons of her bonnet, searching her neck for her pulse, his shaking fingers frantic until finally he could feel its tiny beat.

She moaned, and he was grateful for another sign of life. He felt for her spine and checked her arms and legs. Nothing seemed broken. There was a tiny scrape near her hairline, but no other evidence of harm.

"Wake up, Emma," he demanded. "Talk to me."

But she made only unintelligible sounds.

He needed to get her back to Kellworth, to send for the surgeon. Reluctant to leave her, even for a second, he climbed back to the road. Through the trees he could see where the road doubled back. He caught sight of the horses galloping out of sight.

They were at least six miles from Kellworth. He could not carry her such a distance. No one would come looking for them until day's end, and even then they might assume they had stayed the night at Maidstone. This road was too untraveled to trust another carriage to happen by.

He hurried back to Emma's side and pulled her into a sitting position. "Wake up, Emma," he pleaded again.

"Mmmmm," she murmured, falling against him.

He did not have the strength to carry her up the embankment and was forced to drag her up the steep incline, her new dress tangling in a prickly vine and ripping. Once on the road, he lifted her over his good shoulder, as he had done many a time to carry wounded men off the battlefield.

His shoulder throbbed with pain and his legs felt weak, but he ignored the discomfort and headed toward Maidstone, toward the main road some two to three miles distant. Carriages and wagons and riders would use the road heading to the town. Someone would find them.

With luck one of Kellworth's tenant farmers came upon them, returning from Maidstone. He made room for them in the back of his wagon, and drove them all the way back to Kellworth, Spence holding Emma in his arms the whole way. She woke several times while he held her, but always slipped back into unconsciousness again.

It was well past noon when the farmer brought them directly to Kellworth's door and later still when Mr. Price attended her. Spence paced her room while the surgeon performed his examination. Mrs. Cobbett and the new lady's maid stood by her bedside.

All Spence could think was that she would not wake up, that he had killed her, as he had killed Stephen. She would draw one long, deep breath and release it slowly and life would leave her as it had left Stephen. Spence had seldom prayed since that day, except to ask God why his life had been spared and his brother's taken, why he walked off a battlefield when thousands of good men did not. He prayed now, for Emma. He prayed to God, who took from him his parents and his brother, not to take Emma as well.

He ought to have checked the curricle. It would have only taken a moment to examine the wheels and the undercarriage. Instead, he had been feeling sorry for himself because he would be forced to face Stephen's death once again.

Every person he had ever loved had died. His mother, his father, Stephen. He'd dared to fall in love with Emma and now she could die, too.

"Please, God," he silently prayed. "Let it not be so."

He ought to have checked the curricle.

Mr. Price stepped away from the bed and walked over to Spence, who steeled himself to hear the worst.

"She's had a nasty hit on the head, looks like," the surgeon began. "I expect you recall how that felt."

Spence nearly took the man by the collar and demanded he get on with it.

The surgeon took a long look over to where Emma lay on the bed. "She answers me, however. At least some of the time. With yes and no." He tapped his fingers against his lips and Spence clenched his hands into fists. "I daresay she will be fine in the morning. No reason to believe otherwise."

Spence collapsed in a nearby chair and dipped his head into his hands.

Mr. Price put a hand on his shoulder. "There, there, my lord. Nothing to fear. Have her remain abed for a day or two. That is all she will need."

Spence heard Price walk over to say the same to Mrs. Cobbett, who saw him to the door and returned to her lady's bedside. Spence finally looked over at Emma, staring at the delicacy of her profile, the luxury of her hair tumbling around her shoulders. Her maid tucked the bedcovers around her.

He'd escaped God's fate this time, but how soon before he caused another fatal accident? Or what if she died in childbirth? Women died bearing children. Reuben's mother had died giving birth to a dead baby. She'd been a silly woman but had filled in when Spence's mother accompanied his father on their travels. She'd done her lying-in at Kellworth while Uncle Keenan was in London. Spence remembered her screams.

He placed his hands over his ears now and rose, striding out of the room.

His heart beat in panic and he spun around in the room, helpless for what to do. Acknowledging his fear only made it more real to him, more inevitable.

When Tolley walked into his bedchamber a few minutes later, Spence was stuffing clothes into a valise. "What are you doing, m'lord?"

"Leaving."

"Leaving?" cried Tolley in a shocked voice.

"I . . . I have urgent business in London. I must be away." He walked to the bureau and dumped in his razor and hairbrush.

"While my lady is sick?" Tolley's eyes were wide with shock.

"I will pen her a note." He waved his hand at the footman. "Run get me ink and paper."

Tolley did not move.

"Do it!" Spence shouted.

Tolley dashed out of the room, but it was Mr. Hale who brought him the writing implements.

Mr. Hale gave him a puzzled look. "You are leaving, my lord?"

Spence grabbed the ink bottle, paper, and pen, making the mistake of looking into the faithful old retainer's concerned eyes. He nearly lost his tenuous control.

He glanced away, clearing his throat. "I do not belong here. I never did. I'm going back to London. Tell . . . tell Lady Kellworth she shall have all the money she needs, but I cannot stay."

"My lord—" began the butler.

Spence sat at the table and started writing. "That is all, Mr. Hale. You may go."

Spence did not look up from his pen, but heard Mr. Hale hesitate before finally leaving the room. Spence threw the pen down and crumpled his note into a ball. He could not think straight. All he knew was, he must leave.

He scribbled a note and blew the ink dry before folding it and writing her name on the back.

Then he grabbed the valise and ran from the room, down the stairway and out the door, heading toward the stables. If he rode hard, he would reach London by dawn. He could not think beyond that.

Several hours later, Spence sat on the floor outside the door of Blake's rooms in the Stephen's Hotel on Bond Street where he, Blake, and Wolfe always stayed in

London. The hotel clerk, surprised to see him arrive full of dirt from the road at such an hour, informed him that Mr. Wolfe was out of town and Lord Blakewell had not yet returned from his evening outing. Spence thanked the man, took the key to his room, and dumped his valise inside. Then he waited in the hallway for Blake so he would see him straightaway.

He fell asleep, his head resting against the wooden door, until whispering voices in the hall woke him.

Blake tiptoed down the hall leading the cloaked figure of a female, admonishing her to be quiet. Spence tried to stand as Blake caught sight of him and hurried over.

"Spence! What the devil—what are you doing here?" Blake gave him a hand and pulled him to his feet.

"I nearly killed her, Blake," he mumbled.

"Killed her!" cried the cloaked young woman.

"Shhhh." Blake shot the female a stern glance. He made sure Spence could remain standing and stuck his key in the door. "Come inside and sit."

Spence gestured to the girl. "No, it can wait. I will return to my rooms. Talk to you tomorrow."

"It is tomorrow," said Blake. "Come in and sit. I won't be but a moment."

Spence entered the room and found a chair, flopping down in it. Blake lit a lamp and whispered something to the girl.

"Naw," she cried. "T'isn't fair!"

Blake raised his voice to Spence. "Wait there for me. I shall be back directly."

He took the girl by the arm and led her protesting out the door. Spence rested his head on the back of the chair and started drifting off to sleep again.

When Blake returned he was alone.

"Forgive me." Spence rubbed his face. "I ruined your dalliance."

Blake laughed. "It was of no consequence. I promised her a bauble to appease her. I believe she was even happier for it."

"A bauble? You have so much money to spend?"

"Of course not." Blake winked. "It shall be a very cheap bauble and that will be the end of that."

Spence stretched out his legs. "Who was she?"

"An opera dancer." Blake opened a cabinet and took out a bottle, pouring for both of them. "Now talk, Spence. What are you doing here?"

Spence took the glass and brought it to his lips, smelling the brandy before tasting it. Its warmth eased the numbness inside. "I left."

"As I surmised." Blake sipped. "But why?"

After a second's hesitation, Spence blurted out the story, only leaving out his fears of Emma dying in childbirth.

At the end he said, "I ought to have checked the wheels. It is my fault." He looked at Blake. "I am cursed. All I need do is love somebody and they die."

Blake listened with that calm, placid expression that rarely left him. When Spence finished, his friend gave him an intent look. "You are daft. You do realize that, don't you?"

Spence scowled. "I agree I am less than coherent, but, I confess, I expected a bit more sensibility from you."

"Rubbish." Blake wore a half-smile that Spence suddenly wanted to punch off his face. "You need someone to kick you in the pants. All this talk of killing your brother and almost killing your wife, of making people die, it is rubbish."

Except that it did not feel like rubbish to Spence. It felt real.

Blake ignored him. "You were not the first foolish puppy to upset a phaeton, God knows. Which one of us has not raced at imprudent speeds? And I have yet to hear of another earl who must maintain his own carriages. You do hire a man for that work, do you not?"

Spence shot him a quick glance before looking away again. "Yes, but the man is new, an ex-soldier or someone. I do not know him. I ought to have checked up on him to make sure he did his work."

Blake was undaunted. "Is that not Larkin's responsibility? This talk of failing to check the vehicle? More rubbish."

Spence glared at him.

Blake leaned forward, staring him in the eyes. "Did you drive the curricle recklessly?"

"Of course I did not!" he shot back.

Emma had already been nervous about the excursion. He would not have frightened her by racing down the country lanes like a deranged man. The wheel broke. The wheel he ought to have checked.

"They were *accidents*, Spence. Nothing more."

Blake's words were beginning to sound reasonable. Spence gazed at his friend, wanting to believe.

Blake put a hand on his shoulder and spoke softly. "If your theory were correct, why, then, have Wolfe and I been able to get through an entire war without a scratch? Or do you have no fondness at all for the Ternion?"

Spence stared at him.

"Go home," Blake said.

Spence dropped his head in his hands. "If what you say is true . . ." Spence's panic had receded and rationality returned, but also the harsh reality of his actions. He had run out on Emma a second time.

Blake's brows rose. "Do you love her?"

Miserable, Spence downed the last of his brandy and nodded.

"Go home," Blake repeated.

Could it be that simple? Spence straightened in his chair. "I will do it. She will have lost trust in me again, but I'll fight to win it back."

Blake clapped him on the shoulder. "That's the spirit!" He poured Spence more brandy.

Spence leaned back in his chair, feeling a weight off his shoulders. "Where is Wolfe, by the way?"

"France. He insisted upon searching for Esmund, who is hiding out somewhere on the Continent. *Last seen in Paris.*" He spoke these last words with dramatic emphasis.

"Indeed? I thought you would have sent Esmund news of my recovery."

Blake laughed. "Of your resurrection, you mean?" He poured himself another glass. "We notified his family immediately and intended to send a dispatch directly to Esmund. His family would not tell us his whereabouts. They *forbade* us to do more. It was all very havey-cavey, as Wolfe would say, and it sent Wolfe jauntering off to find the twit. He suspects some sort of plot. You know how his mind works. Of course, we did discover Esmund's debts had been paid off shortly after the duel." He looked up at Spence. "I say, you must not have received my letter. I exerted myself to write all about it."

"I've had no letters from you for over two weeks, not that I am tabulating," Spence said.

Blake responded with a guileless look. "I sent the letter two days ago. Possibly you crossed paths with it on the road."

"Anything else you exerted yourself to write?"

"Yes . . ." Blake frowned. "We found Ruddock."

Spence sat up. "But that is splendid—"

Blake held up a hand. "Not so splendid. He was fished from the Thames. How his brother identified him, I shudder to think. The fellow had been in the water for weeks, apparently."

"Drowned?"

"That is correct," Blake said. "No money on him. His coat and shoes were gone. The victim of footpads. There has been an increase in crime apparently. Blamed on ex-soldiers with no work."

"Deuce!" Spence sank back in his chair.

Blake leaned forward. "I did not write this in the letter, but the senior Ruddock told us that his brother received a message from your uncle about a week before he disappeared."

Spence leaned forward. "My uncle?"

"Wolfe, as you may expect, perceives a connection between the two events, but they were a week apart." Blake took another sip of his brandy.

"Was the message found?" Spence asked.

Blake shook his head. "But"—he lifted his finger—"there were two men arrested for attempting to rob a fellow in that very neighborhood. The man fought them off and got the better of them."

"Did they admit to the crime?"

Blake laughed. "Of course they did not!"

Spence lowered his brows in thought. "My uncle may be involved in the embezzlement, however. He seems to have played a role in keeping Emma's letters from reaching me."

"That appears likely," Blake agreed.

Spence groaned. "I should clear up this mess once and for all."

There was much of a practical nature to accomplish. His affairs were still managed by Ruddock and Ruddock, and he certainly did not wish to continue there. He also wanted to fix things so Emma would feel secure about money, transfer a substantial amount to her name. If he returned to Kellworth bearing papers proving that, perhaps she might forgive him for running off in a panic.

The sky outside began to brighten.

"Do you have pen and ink?" he asked Blake.

Blake opened a drawer and placed the items on the table in front of Spence. "What are you doing?"

Spence dipped the pen in the ink. "Writing to Emma that I will return to her in three days' time." He glanced up at his friend. "I shall try to explain."

But he feared she would not believe a word of what he wrote. Putting money into her hands might be his only chance to make restitution.

Chapter FOURTEEN

The next morning Emma woke with a throbbing head. Too filled with pain to open her eyes, she groped for Spence, but he was not there. His absence made her feel adrift, a ship without a sail in an ocean of pain. She made herself lie very still, but it was of scant help.

She tried to lift her eyelids, but it felt like being speared with sunlight. Clamping them shut right away, she'd not seen a thing, but something did not feel right. More cautiously she peered through her lashes until her eyes grew accustomed to the light. She blinked several times.

She was in her own bedchamber, in her own bed, alone. Forcing her mind to work, she tried to remember why she was not in Spence's bed where she'd woken these past four weeks.

Memory returned. The crack of wood shattering. The curricle tipping. Flying through the air.

"Spence!" She sat up at once, then clutched at her head to stop the surge in pain.

Dorrie gave a surprised cry and jumped to her feet from the bedside chair. "There, there, my lady. You mustn't rise up like that. You are supposed to rest. You had a very nasty spill yesterday."

Emma gripped the girl's arm. "Spence?"

Dorrie patted her hand. "His lordship is hale and hearty, I assure you. It was he who brought you home."

Her maid eased Emma back against the pillows, and Emma closed her eyes again while her head throbbed. "I want to see him."

Dorrie ceased her fussing with the bedcovers and did not answer right away. "His lordship is not in the house, my lady."

"Have someone fetch him, Dorrie, if you please."

"I . . . I do not know—" Dorrie began.

"Please send for him," Emma cried. "Please, Dorrie."

She wanted to see for herself that he was unhurt. She wanted the comfort of his arms, the consolation of his low voice, because she truly felt wretched.

The maid hesitated again. "Yes, my lady."

Eyes still closed, Emma heard the swish of Dorrie's skirts and the sound of her footsteps as the maid left the room. Emma lay very still until the pain diminished and she dozed off.

The sound of the door opening woke her. She sat up, but it was not Spence who walked in, but Mrs. Cobbett with Dorrie behind her.

Wincing with the pain again, she asked, "Where is Lord Kellworth?"

Mrs. Cobbett bustled to the bedside bearing her usual kindly smile. "Now, just you rest, my lady. His lordship is not here."

"Where is he, Mrs. Cobbett?"

A sympathetic expression came over the housekeeper's face and Emma sensed the foreboding of bad news. Mrs. Cobbett fussed with her chatelaine, jingling her keys like a musical instrument.

Emma seized the woman's hand. "Where is he?"

Mrs. Cobbett glanced sideways before meeting Emma's intent gaze. "My lady," she began in a soft voice. "His lordship is gone—to London, my lady. He did not leave word when he will return."

"Gone?" Emma gasped, her voice thin and reedy.

Mrs. Cobbett nodded.

"Gone," she repeated again, this time more like a moan. She rose up on her knees, releasing her hold on Mrs. Cobbett. "No! It is not so! Say it is not so!" Tears stung her eyes and she pounded her fists against the mattress. She pulled at the bedcovers, twisting them in her hands. The two servants grabbed her arms, trying to calm her.

"No," she cried over and over, trying to escape their grasp. "No."

"You must calm yourself," Mrs. Cobbett said with alarm. "You must be quiet."

"He cannot have gone," she wailed. "He cannot. There is some mistake."

Her head pounded with pain, and she tried to grab it, but the two women would not release her. The stabbing pain exhausted her, and she fell back against the pillows in an agony of both body and spirit.

"There, there, now," Mrs. Cobbett murmured, petting her head.

Dorrie dampened a towel in water and placed it on Emma's forehead. Emma, despairing inside, could not move. Her breathing was ragged and tears streamed down her cheeks, pooling in the corners of her mouth. She could taste their saltiness.

Why had he left her? Why, when she lay ill in bed, after being insensible a full day? Was he so heartless? Why did he wait until she was most in need of him to flee from her again?

It pained her to think. The pain throbbing in her head made it impossible to make sense of anything.

Except that he had left her.

Her aching head kept her from moving, though she wanted to rage, to throw things, to shatter something as she herself felt shattered. Trying merely to bear the pain, she became aware of a sticky dampness between her legs. With a cry she rose up again, startling her servants. She flung off the covers and pulled up her nightdress.

Red droplets of blood stained the white bed linen.

"No!" wailed Emma. She thought more desolation impossible, but this cruelly proved her wrong.

Her courses had begun. She had not conceived. There would be no baby to hold, no piece of Spence to cling to.

She had nothing.

It was midday before Spence rose. He'd slept fitfully, his dreams filled with Emma. Emma laughing. Emma flushed with passion. Emma lying lifeless in the grass. His bed felt too empty, too cold.

He dressed quickly and hurried out to the street where he bought a Dutch biscuit from the basket of a girl hawking them. Her eyes were the same shade as Emma's, he noticed. She smiled pertly and curtsied, and he hurried away from her, gulping down the biscuit. He headed toward White's Club.

He hoped to encounter his uncle there. Uncle Keenan spent many an hour at the gentlemen's club, championing the cause nearest and dearest to his heart—his own power and influence. At White's, Uncle Keenan worked more diligently than when seated with his colleagues in Commons, where he could doze in his seat in St. Stephen's Chapel while debates droned on.

Bond Street was crowded in this height of the Season. It was impossible for Spence not to meet people he knew. He greeted them, other members of the *haut monde*, the Polite World, the upper ten thousand. He had grown up in this society, had been schooled with its sons, had fought next to its soldiers.

Had married one of its daughters.

At the time an announcement of his marriage had appeared in the *Morning Post*, and caused a flurry of gossip that the young earl had stolen the lady his powerful uncle had chosen for himself. Spence had no idea how long it had taken before a more compelling *on-dit* captured interest. He had traveled back to Spain to try to explain to Blake and Wolfe about making a bargain to marry in name only.

But then he had not realized what he now knew with every drop of blood within him. He married Emma because he had fallen in love with her, but he had been afraid, so afraid, of loving her, lest he lose her as he had everyone else—except the Ternion. Perhaps that had been why he'd convinced himself he could make Emma happy merely by giving her a country home, away from the society in which her mother reveled.

At this moment Spence missed Emma terribly. He felt as if one of his limbs had been severed from his body. He was surprised he could walk, surprised no one could notice a part of him was missing.

Spence turned down St. James Street and spied the bow window of White's Club, where Beau Brummell used to spend endless hours with his exclusive set. Spence heard Brummell was out of favor now, but had never troubled himself to learn the details. The man disdained army life, and Spence had no interest in him.

Spence had never spent much time in White's, preferring to explore London's more exciting and unsavory establishments with Blake and Wolfe, but it was a familiar enough place. Like Kellworth, it was a part of his heritage.

He chatted with a few acquaintances and soon learned his uncle was indeed present in the coffee room. Spence excused himself.

As he approached the room, he heard his uncle's laugh. Blake suggested he not confront his uncle about the embezzlement right away, to wait to see if they could unearth some definitive evidence when they went to Ruddock and Ruddock on the morrow. Spence paused, observing the man's behavior for himself. He had not called upon his uncle when previously in London, before his ill-fated duel. He had not seen the man since marrying Emma.

From the entryway, Spence spied Zachary Keenan seated at a table with another gentleman Spence recognized as Lord Castlereagh. He crossed the room to them.

His uncle glanced up in surprise, then his expression hardened.

Spence bowed. "Good day, Lord Castlereagh. Uncle."

"Kellworth, is it?" Castlereagh said, using his title. "You served in the 28th, as I recall. We heard good reports of you."

"I am complimented you should even remember me, sir," Spence said. Castlereagh, now Foreign Secretary, had once been Secretary of War.

His uncle gave him a stiff, unwelcoming smile. "I thought you were rusticating."

Spence deliberately made his expression affable. "I was, but business brought me back to town." He gave his uncle no sign that he was inclined to walk away from the table.

Castlereagh stood. "Well, I must be off. I have business to attend to, you know."

"It was an honor to see you, sir," Spence said.

His uncle shook Castlereagh's hand. "We shall speak more of that other matter."

"With pleasure," replied the secretary, who turned and sauntered away.

"You might as well sit." Uncle Keenan gestured to the chair Castlereagh had vacated.

Spence obliged, catching the attention of a servant, who took his request for coffee.

"No strong drink?" his uncle asked with sarcasm, lifting his glass of port.

Spence would not be baited. "Later, perhaps."

The servant brought a pot and cup to Spence.

"To what matter did you and Castlereagh refer?" Spence began conversationally.

"Take your seat in Lords and you will find out." Uncle Keenan sneered. "Or do you still pretend you are not earl?"

Spence momentarily gritted his teeth. This was an old, worn subject, the topic of many a shouting match with his uncle after Stephen's death. Spence had refused to sell the commission he had so recently purchased, and Uncle

Keenan blasted him for putting his life at risk, insisting his responsibility lay with Kellworth.

But Spence had thought himself clever enough to settle both the responsibilities of his unwanted title and his yearning for adventure. His uncle had scoffed at his plans.

Uncle Keenan had been correct, of course.

Had that been the point of the embezzlement? Had his uncle wanted to prove to Spence he could not cede responsibility of Kellworth to others?

Such reasoning did not make sense. Spence, the guilty party, had not suffered from it. The people of Kellworth had suffered.

Emma had suffered.

His uncle shrugged, not waiting for an answer. "I trust Lady Kellworth is well?" His tone was obligatory.

Spence closed his eyes for a moment, feeling guilt for leaving her pale and bedridden.

"She is." He hoped this was true. He hoped she woke this morning with no ill effects from the accident, as Mr. Price had promised.

His uncle stared down at the table, and uncomfortable silence descended.

Lifting his head, his uncle gave Spence a penetrating stare. "What is this tale your cousin told me?"

"That I was thought dead?"

"That you fought a duel." Keenan leaned closer and spoke in a fierce whisper. "What kind of stupidity was that?"

"An affair of honor." Spence spoke with sarcasm. "I am afraid you missed your opportunity to inherit. How unfortunate for you."

"It was indeed," Keenan answered in kind. "If your shot met its mark, I might also have had the pleasure of seeing you hanged for it."

Spence took a sip of coffee, regarding his uncle over the rim of the cup. Matters between them were as tense as always. He was struck anew at the depth of his uncle's anger toward him.

"Did you hear of Ruddock?" Spence asked, changing the subject, eager to skirt close to the topic of embezzlement.

"That he drowned?" His uncle nodded. "You can be grateful he managed that feat while you put in an appearance at your estate. Think of the difficulties of having no one in control of your affairs."

Spence looked carefully for signs that Uncle Keenan knew more than he let on, but he suspected his uncle was well practiced in deception after his many years in politics.

"Oh, I expect his brother would have taken over," Spence responded.

They fell into silence again. All Spence could sense was the same tension that had been between them for years, that had worsened since he'd married Emma.

His uncle broke the silence. "Where do you stay?"

Spence was caught off-guard. "Stephen's Hotel."

"I ought to have known. An army favorite, is it not?"

His uncle resided in the Kellworth London townhouse, had done so from the time Spence's parents died. No one else ever had need of the place.

There was another long, awkward pause.

Finally Keenan stood. "I must leave."

Without another word he walked swiftly away, not pausing to speak to anyone else, heading directly for the door.

By the afternoon it no longer felt to Emma that a hammer and anvil were pounding in her head. Not so her heart. Her heart was still broken and she did not think she would ever see it mended.

She asked for Mr. Hale and grilled him about what he knew of Spence's leaving. Reluctantly he handed her the note written before Spence's flight.

Mrs. Cobbett stood at her bedside looking worried as Emma broke the letter's seal.

She read:

Forgive me, Emma. I cannot stay here. I will put things to rights, I promise. Yours, etc. SK.

The word "promise" was underlined.

She flung the paper aside. This was no explanation. Did she not deserve some sort of explanation? What of her wish to have a child? Putting that part of their bargain "to rights" would be a neat trick, all the way from London.

She picked up the paper and read it again, with disgust. What made him think she could put faith in this latest promise?

She ought to have known not to trust him. Ought to have known she meant so little to him he would not bother with her convalescence. She had sat at *his* sickbed night after night, but he would not wait even one night beside hers.

She hated him. Hated him.

"My lady?" Mrs. Cobbett said uncertainly.

Emma had forgotten she and Mr. Hale were there. "It is nothing, Mrs. Cobbett," she replied in a dull voice. "Nothing at all. Thank you, Mr. Hale."

She reached over and finished the last drops of the tea Mrs. Cobbett had brought her. "You may remove the tray now. You may go, too, Mr. Hale."

Dorrie entered, carrying the two kittens. "I thought they might cheer you."

The maid put them on Emma's bed and they bounded over for a petting.

"Thank you, Dorrie." She picked up Tom and cuddled him against her cheek. "You may leave now. I do not need company."

"My lady, we do not think—" Mrs. Cobbett began.

Emma cut her off sharply. "I wish to be alone."

"Yes, my lady." Mrs. Cobbett wrung her hands worriedly.

She, Mr. Hale, and Dorrie left the room, but Emma could hear them whispering to each other as they walked out the door.

She put Tom back on the bed and leaned against her pillows. She ceased trying to reconcile the passionate and considerate lover with the man who could so abruptly abandon her. Instead, she focused on her rage. She could see it all happening again. He would forget about her and about Kellworth and the funds would stop again. He would be off exploring pyramids in Cairo or some such place and she would be tearing her hair out trying to contrive a way to feed everyone.

"I will not stand for it," she said aloud.

The two kittens cocked their heads.

"He made a bargain and he will keep it!"

She flung off the covers, and Tom and Puss scrambled away in fright. They peeked out from under the chair as she padded over to the basin and poured water into it. She pulled her nightdress over her head, washed herself, and tended to her feminine needs. Years of practice with the elderly Susan as her maid had taught her how to don her corset and manage the laces of her dress. She sat at her mirror to brush her hair, and the kittens poked their heads out and dared come sit at her feet.

She scooped them up. "We have work to do," she said, kissing them until they squirmed to escape.

By the dinner hour her plans were well in place. She sat in the drawing room thinking of what she was about to do, when Reuben walked in.

He rushed to her side. "Emma, my dear, I came to inquire of your health. Mr. Hale said you were here in the drawing room. Ought you not still be on your sickbed?"

Convenient that Reuben's godly good works of visiting the sick came at the dinner hour.

"I am well enough, Reuben." Without irony she added, "Would you care to stay for dinner?"

"I would be honored. If it is not an imposition."

"Not at all." In fact, she'd just as soon have the distraction.

He poured himself a glass of burgundy from the crystal decanter on the table. "I called upon you yesterday as soon as news reached me."

"That was good of you." She was certain a meal had been served during that visit as well.

He sat in a nearby chair and leaned toward her with a look of concern. "I know my cousin has left you."

The words were like jabbing spears. "Yes," she managed.

"I am so sorry, my dear. He has gone to London, has he?"

"Yes, London." She paused. Reuben's faithful friendship, annoying as it had been from time to time, entitled him to hear the news from her own lips. "I go to London as well. Tomorrow."

He spilled wine on his trousers and dabbed at the stain with his handkerchief. "Has Spencer sent for you?"

She laughed. "No, but he shall discover soon enough I am there."

Reuben grabbed her hand. "My dear lady, you must not go chasing after him. For one thing you cannot be enough recovered. I simply will not hear of this."

"You have no say in the matter, Reuben."

"You cannot go to the Kellworth townhouse," he said. "My father resides there."

"I sent word to my mother. She will be in London for the Season, of that you can depend. I daresay she will not be thrilled to have me as a guest, but how can she refuse?"

He took a deep breath before trying a different tactic. "The Kellworth carriage has not been used for years. After this terrible mishap of the curricle, you dare not ride in it until it is thoroughly checked."

"I have hired a post-chaise."

He sputtered. "You cannot go to London alone in a post-chaise."

She did not want him to know this part of her plan did frighten her, but she was not about to let fear stop her. "I shall have a groom accompany me."

He looked aghast. "You need a gentleman's protection."

She needed many things from a gentleman, but the gentleman in question had seen fit to abandon her. She was on her own. "I will manage."

Reuben stewed about the matter throughout the dinner, the pudding, and while they sat together with tea in the drawing room. No matter what he said, Emma would not be persuaded to change her mind. She was bound for London and would confront her husband. Somehow she would force him to fulfill his bargain to her. Get her with child and she would be done with him. Refuse and she would dog him to Land's End, if need be. Cairo, even.

"Very well," Reuben said in a defeated voice. "There is nothing for it, but I must accompany you. It is an easy drive over good roads. I will take you in my curricle."

"Your curricle," she repeated. Her heart raced at the prospect of riding in the same sort of vehicle that had so nearly taken her life.

"I assure you, *I* will not tip you over in it." He made her look at him. "Let me drive you, Emma."

Because she was more frightened of riding alone in a post-chaise all the way to London than climbing into a curricle again, Emma said, "Very well. You may drive me to London."

The next day Reuben arrived promptly, and they had an early start to the trip. Emma's small trunk containing her newest dresses was strapped to the back of the curricle next to Reuben's portmanteau. She was further relieved to see he had brought a groom with him, a new man he had hired, who would ride in the back as well.

Although initially breathless with anxiety at each bump in the road, she soon relaxed. Reuben kept a sedate pace and drove competently. Even better, he behaved in a very gentlemanly manner, as a family relation ought. At the posting inns the groom saw to the change in horses and Reuben ordered their refreshment. She was grateful to be spared attending to these details.

They reached London during the fashionable hour. On the roads of Mayfair, curricles and other fine vehicles clogged the streets on their way to or from Hyde Park. Emma's nerves grew raw, and the noise was enough to make her wish she could clamp her hands over her ears. Street hawkers called out their wares, horses' hooves clopped on the streets. Carriages rattled. Hack drivers shouted for slow vehicles to get out of the way. Splendidly dressed gentlemen escorted fashionably gowned ladies. Emma looked down at her own dress and spencer and felt like a dowd.

The last time she had been in London, Spence's uncle had driven her through the park. She remembered the other women of society seemed so sure of themselves, so practiced in flirtation, while she spent the whole time hoping Keenan would not touch her. He rarely missed an opportunity to do so. She imagined Spence atop one of the shiny vehicles, dressed in his finely tailored coat and buff pantaloons, his boots polished to a mirror finish. His strong gloved hands would expertly hold the ribbons while some expensively dressed woman simpered at his side. The mere thought of it made her vision turn red.

Had that been why he'd run to London? Engaging in dalliances was the way of men, her mother always said, although Emma never saw any sign of that in her father. She had carefully avoided thinking of Spence with other women during the years he left her alone. It had been too painful, and that was before she knew what it was like to make love to him. To think of his arms around another woman, his lips kissing her, his . . . Well, it drove her mad.

She did not truly believe Spence left her for another woman, but the idea helped fuel her anger. And it was anger that gave her the courage for this trip.

He would pay for trying to renege on the bargain he'd made with her. She would hold him to it no matter how noisy and busy and enormous London was.

She was determined.

Chapter FIFTEEN

Reuben pulled his curricle up to the front of her mother's townhouse on Hartford Street. While Reuben assisted Emma from the vehicle, the groom jumped off to sound the knocker. A footman admitted them and directed the groom to bring the trunk to the servant's entrance.

When the footman left to announce their arrival, Emma turned to Reuben. "I am grateful to you for transporting me, but you do not have to stay."

He looked wounded. "I must see you to your mother."

"I wish you would not," she said. "It is better for me to greet her alone."

Emma could not predict her mother's reaction to her presence. She might greet her with pleasure or become bored with her in an instant, but she certainly would ask some questions Emma did not wish to answer, especially in front of Reuben. Besides, if she were alone, her mother could not turn her away, another possibility.

The footman returned to say her mother would receive her. Emma gave Reuben a pleading look.

Finally he said, "Very well, but I shall call on you to make certain of your well-being. Tomorrow, if I may?"

"Yes. Thank you, Reuben." She pressed her hand into his. "Thank you for everything." She hurried to follow the footman.

In the sitting room on the first floor, her mother was lounging on a chaise. Another lady sat nearby.

The Baroness Holgrove remained seated but extended a hand to her daughter. "Emma, darling, what a surprise! I had no idea you were in town."

"Did you not receive my note?"

"Your note?" Her mother twisted around and pointed toward a table with a silver tray upon it. "Go see if it is there."

Emma crossed the room to the table, where several envelopes, notes, and invitations lay on the tray. Buried in the pile, its seal unbroken, was Emma's message. How typical of her mother. She held it up.

"Tell me what it says," commanded her mother.

Emma made no effort to open it. "It says I am to arrive today and beg to stay with you for a few days."

Her mother sat up. "I would never have guessed."

"May I, Mother?"

"May you what?"

"May I stay?" Emma's pulse accelerated with anxiety.

"Of course, she must stay." Lady Vellamy rose and extended her hand. "I suspect you do not recall me. I am Lady Vellamy."

Emma tried to give a cordial smile. "My lady. Yes, I do remember you. My mother's friend."

Lady Vellamy shook her hand. "Friends since we were girls. I was present at your wedding, you know."

One of the very few people present. Her mother and

her new husband, Lord Holgrove, Zachary Keenan, and Lady Vellamy. "Yes, I do recall."

Though she had barely perceived anyone else that day except Spence, looking so handsome in his regimentals.

"What brings you to London, Emma, dear?" Her mother broke in. "I had given up seeing you in town."

"I have business with my husband," Emma recited. She had practiced the answer to this question.

Her mother's brows rose. "He is here, too? Holgrove said he left London. There was a rumor of a duel—" Her mother broke off and stared her up and down. "Good gracious, Emma, what are you wearing? You look atrocious, like you just arrived from the country."

"I have just arrived from the country, Mother."

"But you must not look it!" Her mother's eyes were wide with alarm.

Lady Vellamy swept in. "Then we shall have to pretty her up." She regarded Emma with a critical eye. "I fancy there are some dresses of yours, Agatha, that would fit her until we can have a new wardrobe made."

"*My* dresses?" Her mother gasped.

"Last year's dresses will do."

"Oh, last year's dresses. That is different," her mother said, sounding much reassured.

Lady Vellamy put her arm around Emma and brought her over to sit next to her on a settee. "Now tell us, my dear. Is your husband expecting you in town?"

"He is not."

Lady Vellamy nodded knowingly. "Do you suppose he is with his friend Lord Blakewell? Because I have seen that young man around town lately."

Emma all but gritted her teeth. "Undoubtedly."

"Oh, this is famous!" The lady clapped and leaned very close to her. "Do you wish to surprise him with your presence?"

Emma took a deep breath, unused to such an assault on her privacy.

She had not considered surprising him. She thought more of sending him a note to call upon her at her mother's house, or if that failed, going to his place of residence. The only problem was, she did not know where he resided.

"What mischief are you hatching, Phoebe?" Emma's mother broke in, her eyes suddenly dancing with interest.

Lady Vellamy turned to her friend. "Agatha, do you not think it would be splendidly entertaining to see Lord Kellworth come face-to-face with the wife he virtually abandoned?"

Emma's cheeks burned with shame. Her mother had obviously informed her friend of Spence's neglect, though Emma had been careful not to confide the extent of her difficulties when she answered her mother's correspondence. Emma was glad they did not know Spence had returned to Kellworth. It was bad enough to be abandoned by a husband once, but too mortifying to have been abandoned a second time.

"Oh, ho!" her mother cried.

"But we shall have to transform her into a real beauty."

Her mother turned to Emma and gave her another unenthusiastic look-over. "And how shall we do it?"

The ladies seemed to forget she had not agreed to this scheme.

Lady Vellamy's eyes twinkled. "Here is what we do. Lady Douden is hosting a ball tonight. You know her, Agatha."

"Yes, and I do not like her. She looks down her nose at one unless one possesses a vast fortune, yet everyone knows the Doudens haven't a feather to fly with anymore. I declined the invitation!"

Lady Vellamy waved a dismissive hand. "As did I, but we shall send a message saying we will attend after all."

Emma's mother fussed with her sleeves. "And why should we do this?"

Lady Vellamy spoke patiently. "Because her son will attend. Her son is Viscount Blakewell, who is Kellworth's schoolboy chum. Inseparable, they say. Where one goes, the other will follow." She stopped and gave a worried frown. "Of course, that includes the nabob's son."

She meant Wolfe, Emma realized. As much animosity as she felt toward that gentleman, she had an impulse to defend him.

Lady Holgrove gave her friend a significant look. "I am sure that young man's wealth makes his presence very palatable to Lady Douden."

Both ladies broke into gales of laughter.

Lady Vellamy sighed and wiped her eyes with her handkerchief. She turned to Emma. "What say you, my dear? Will you agree?"

It had been on the tip of Emma's tongue to refuse. The mere suggestion of a society ball made her hands shake and she still felt quite unwell. But if she encountered Spence there, he could not escape talking to her.

She could count on her mother to outfit her in splendor, as her mother had done that first Season. Emma wanted to appear before Spence in all the finery of a fashionable town lady. She wanted him to rue the day he so brutally cast her away. And she wanted to stir his blood so he could not resist bedding her again.

"I will do it," she replied.

Blake and Spence walked out of the tidy office at Ruddock and Ruddock, where they had read through the deceased Ruddock's books until Spence's vision blurred. Once upon a time he would have fantasized about running to the docks to jump on the first ship out of port, but now he merely wished he were back at Kellworth with Emma.

The elder Ruddock, a balding, bespectacled man of at least sixty years, escorted them down the short hall. "I hope your examination of my brother's books proved satisfactory, my lords."

Spence had brought along the papers the deceased Ruddock had sent him over the years. The figures matched Ruddock's figures in his official record, but another unmarked book appeared to record the exact amounts Larkin said had been cut from Kellworth's quarterly portion and Emma's allowance. Wolfe had discovered that book hidden in a secret compartment in the man's desk, when he and Blake had searched the office earlier. No incriminating correspondence had been discovered, however.

"It was satisfactory, sir," Spence responded.

"I am certain I would have known if Mr. Keenan had conducted any business with my brother."

They had been over this topic with him when they arrived. It seemed to Spence that the elder Ruddock had known very little of his brother's dealings.

"I only knew of the one note and that was because my brother told me of it. 'It is from Keenan,' he said." Ruddock wrung his hands. "I did not see it."

The man had fallen all over himself to be helpful to them, and well he might. He had much to lose if his brother's embezzlement became known. Spence had no intention of it becoming public, at least not until he had discovered the whole story.

The elder Ruddock kept talking. "I have the privilege of managing Mr. Keenan's affairs myself. I would be honored to take over the management of your funds as well."

But trust once lost was almost impossible to restore, one of the reasons Spence knew Emma's trust would be hard won. He had spent the morning at the bank, arranging funds for her and transferring his business to the bank to manage. In a day or so, Ruddock would be served papers to that effect.

"We must bid you good day, sir." Spence shook the man's hand before he and Blake stepped outside onto the pavement.

"Well, that assures me that the younger Ruddock deliberately sent me false accounting," Spence remarked.

"Indeed," Blake agreed.

"It tells us little else, however," he added in frustration. "No hint of my uncle or another person in on the scheme with Ruddock."

They walked the block to Fleet Street and caught a hackney coach to convey them back to Mayfair.

Once inside the hack, Blake spoke. "Do tell me you will accompany me to my mother's ball tonight."

Spence scowled. They had been over this before. "I don't want to attend a ball."

"You cannot make me go alone!" Blake wore enough of his typically pleasant expression that Spence could not ascertain the seriousness of the request.

"Why not?"

His friend gave an exaggerated shiver. "My mother is bound to throw every eligible female directly in my path. I need you to protect me."

Spence shot back a skeptical look. "She will only throw in your path the wealthy ones, whom you will undoubtedly charm with your dimpled smile and wit. You will have each of them believing you are about to make them an offer, and then you will run off searching for some opera dancer."

Rather than be offended by such a characterization, Blake grinned. "Indeed, but I should still like your company."

Spence drummed the leather seat with his fingers. "What business does your mother have giving this ball anyway?" he asked. "You keep telling me your family is nearly in River Tick."

Blake rolled his eyes. "The way she and my dear father figure it, they must put on a show of wealth this Season, because my sister will have her come-out next Season, and she needs to attract a wealthy suitor. Wealth attracts wealth, my mother would say."

There was some logic in this, Spence had to admit. "Must you attend as well?"

"My presence has been commanded." Blake sighed.

Blake's father had lost much of the family fortune through his own mismanagement and a fondness for the faro table. There was great family pressure on Blake to marry well. Blake always insisted he would enjoy life a little before doing his duty.

Spence's evening plans were to bring a bottle of brandy to his rooms and drink it, hoping to make time pass quickly. Tomorrow he would return to Kellworth.

"I suspect your uncle will be there," Blake added.

His uncle? He would learn more from his uncle by a return to White's. Spence was about to refuse when he saw a hint of serious entreaty in Blake's countenance. Blake rarely made serious requests of his friends.

It was just one night. He could hob and nob with the *ton* for just one night.

"Very well, Blake," Spence said. "I shall accompany you."

Emma's mother and Lady Vellamy performed wonders, given they had only one afternoon to transform Emma into a fashionable town lady. Lady Vellamy took charge, and before Emma knew it, a hairdresser had arrived to cut her hair. He created soft tendrils to frame her face and to cover the tiny scrape suffered from the curricle accident. The rest of her hair was arranged into a cascade of curls adorned by a single white orchid.

Lady Holgrove had her maid pull out three ball gowns from the previous year, each more elegant than the next. Emma could not help but contrast these satin and silk confections with the mended dinner dresses she'd worn for three years, though she still favored the rose dinner dress made by her village dressmaker, the one that made Spence gaze in pleasure at her.

Lady Vellamy selected a gown made of sage satin with rows of lace at the low-cut bodice and at the hem. One of the maids, clever with a needle, altered the sleeves so it would not be obvious as her mother's discarded dress.

"A little rouge powder, I should think," her mother said, critically examining her.

"Not too much." Lady Vellamy frowned.

"Phoebe, I know how to apply rouge." Lady Holgrove dipped a rabbit's foot in the powder and lightly brushed it on Emma's cheeks. "Some kohl for her eyes as well," she added, taking a tiny brush and darkening Emma's eyelashes.

It was so artfully accomplished, Emma herself could not tell.

"Well done," approved Lady Vellamy.

Lady Vellamy dashed home to see to her own toilette, and Emma was left to sit very still and eat a light supper in her room. Her head still ached, and if she moved too quickly, she felt dizzy and her stomach unsettled, but she was not about to plead too ill to attend the ball, not when she might shock Spence with her appearance. By the time the maid came to help her into her gown, she was eager to get on with it.

Lady Vellamy's carriage arrived to carry them all to the Douden townhouse. Her mother's husband, Lord Holgrove, a man Emma barely knew, escorted them.

When they arrived, Emma felt faint, but she managed to enter the lovely townhouse decorated with flowers, candles in every corner giving a blaze of light.

They were announced, but in the din few people heard the countess of Kellworth's name. Emma was glad. If Spence were in the crowd, she did not want him to realize she was present before he saw her.

Earl Douden and his wife stood to receive their guests. Emma's mother presented Emma to them.

Lady Douden, a tall woman with dramatic streaks of gray through her dark hair, and Blakewell's dimpled cheeks, made no comment about being presented to the wife of her son's friend. Perhaps she knew as little of her son's life as Emma's mother knew of hers.

"I am a little acquainted with your son, my lady," Emma said.

Blake's mother showed little interest. "So are all the young ladies, my dear."

She turned to greet the next guests and Emma moved on. Lord Holgrove made a dash for the card room, and Lady Vellamy craned her neck to look about the room. "I cannot see Kellworth. Come, let us promenade a bit."

Emma's mother wandered off to speak to friends, and Lady Vellamy led Emma to a place in the room that afforded a good view of the doorway. The musicians had taken their places, but had not yet begun to play. The tuning of their instruments and the numbers of people talking roared in Emma's ears. Her head pounded.

Summoned by another lady, Lady Vellamy stepped away, leaving Emma to stand alone. Emma felt utterly discomfited, certain people were staring at her, the gentlemen especially. Worried that her hair was askew or her face smudged, she noticed two ladies glancing at her and whispering behind their fans.

This is what she most detested about London. She felt out of place, like a china cup stored with the silver. What she detested more was the feeling that she wanted to cry, the worst possible thing she could do in such exalted company.

She tried to cover her nerves by forcing her chin up and looking about the room. A tall gray-haired gentleman turned at the same moment she glanced in his direction. He froze.

It was Zachary Keenan.

He crossed the room to her. "Lady Kellworth," he said, bowing.

"Mr. Keenan," she replied, her voice reedy.

"I did not realize you were in town, my lady." He stared at her, the expression on his face like a mask.

"I . . . I have only just arrived."

Foolish of her, Emma had not considered that she might see Spence's uncle here.

She forced herself to speak. "Is Reuben attending the ball, sir?"

He looked puzzled for a moment, but then his mask returned. "Reuben is somewhere about." His eyes narrowed slightly. "Did Reuben know you were in London? He did not inform me."

She wished she had not spoken. "Yes, he knew."

She always said the wrong thing in these situations.

"Well!" said Lady Vellamy, coming over to where they stood. "You have seen our little surprise, Zachary."

He bowed to her. "Good evening, Phoebe."

"Is your nephew here?" Lady Vellamy asked.

He looked puzzled again. "I have not seen him." There was a silent pause that made Emma even more uncomfortable. Finally he took a breath. "I must bid you ladies adieu."

He bowed, turned, and walked away.

Lady Vellamy laughed and gave Emma's arm a squeeze. "I think he was almost as shocked as his nephew will be."

She took another sweep of the crowd of guests. "Let us take a turn around the room. I want everyone to see you."

Emma would rather have hidden behind the jardinière of flowers. Once she had been presented to the fellow guests, there was even more whispering. The doors between the drawing room and another spacious room had been opened to create a spacious area for dancing, and it seemed she was to walk around the whole perimeter of it with Lady Vellamy.

When they happened upon Reuben, his mouth dropped open. "Emma, I am astonished! I never expected you to be here." He, too, perused her as the other gentlemen had done. "And in such finery!"

Lady Vellamy, showing no interest in the vicar, turned to chat with some other people nearby, and Reuben took the opportunity to step closer to Emma in what she felt was an excess of familiarity. "Are you well enough to be out and about after your injury and the long journey?"

It was more of a scold than concern. "Most certainly. You are acquainted with Lady Vellamy?" Emma asked, pulling the lady back into her conversation.

"Indeed." He gave a fawning smile. "How are you, my lady?"

Before she could answer, the first dance was announced, a country dance, and couples began to take their places in the line.

Reuben turned to Emma. "Would you honor me with this dance, Emma, my dear?"

"I have not danced in three years, Reuben. I must watch first."

His mouth drooped in disappointment. "As you wish."

Lady Vellamy had again been drawn away. Though Emma felt a pang of guilt for turning down Reuben, she dreaded more to be left standing alone.

"But stay with me," she said to him. "I would be grateful for your company."

He brightened. "Shall I find you a chair and get some refreshment?"

"No, just stand with me until Lady Vellamy comes back."

As the dancers moved up and down the line in graceful symmetry, Reuben continued to make stabs at conversation. Emma answered in monosyllables, unable to keep her eyes off the doorway where new arrivals entered the room.

The set had not yet been completed when Reuben suddenly said, "Bless me!"

"What is it?" Emma's heart jumped.

Reuben chewed on his lip. "My father signals me. I must attend him."

Emma glanced at Mr. Keenan. The man quickly looked away.

"I dare not refuse him," Reuben fretted. "But I would not be so ungentlemanly as to leave you alone."

Emma did not wish to take the chance that Keenan would come over to where she stood with Reuben. "I see my mother. I shall join her."

"Capital idea," muttered Reuben, still looking distressed. He gave a quick bow. "Best I go."

Her mother was laughing gaily with a foreign-looking gentleman with many medals and decorations on his chest. Emma started toward her, taking care not to interfere with the dancers. She had to step aside and wait for a space to move, when, through the couples performing their figures, she saw two tall young gentlemen enter the room.

Spence and Blakewell.

Spence looked splendid in formal attire, a dark blue coat, under which a blue patterned waistcoat could be seen. His breeches and stockings were as snowy white as his elegantly tied neckcloth.

At the sight of him her senses flared as strongly as if she stared at him across a bed. She averted her gaze, not wanting to feel this breathlessness, not wanting him to affect her so much.

But she could not keep her eyes away from him, so she peeked through the dancers, watching him nod at something Blake said, watching him enter the room, watching him greet people familiar to him. His ease and grace set him off from all the other men, though she wished she could think otherwise.

The music stopped and the dancers left the floor, ladies on the gentlemen's arms. It was like a curtain opening with Emma left onstage.

Spence turned his head and saw her.

Chapter SIXTEEN

E*mma.*
    At first he thought she was an illusion, his eyes playing tricks on him, turning some other lady into a vision of her, the one who lived in his thoughts. But she returned his gaze and there was no mistake.

Emma.

The room blurred and all he could see was Emma, looking resplendent in a dusty green gown, her hair a tousle of curls. She stood alone, no part of any group, and something tender ached inside him.

He crossed the room, barely hearing Blake's "Spence?" Not one more moment could keep him away from her.

As he neared her, he saw her breath quicken, her color heighten. A bit closer revealed the glitter of anger in her eyes.

"Emma."

"Spence," she countered as if facing him *en garde*. "I see you are enjoying London's entertainments."

"What are you doing here, Emma?" He could not even attend to her sarcasm, nor her anger. "By God, you were so ill—" All he could picture was her pale face against the pillow of her bed the last he had seen her, and the surgeon's statement that she should remain there.

"Thank you for your touching concern." Her lip curled. "I am quite recovered."

He shook his head, unable to comprehend. "Emma, I . . ." he began, wanting to explain.

Her eyes flared and he realized he could not speak with her here, not without creating a scene, something she would detest.

He took a breath. "Where are you staying?"

She glared. "Where are *you* staying, Spence?"

"Stephen's Hotel." He tossed off his answer quickly, his concern focused on her. "Did you bring Mr. Hale with you? Or Tolley? Or your maid?"

Before she could answer, he noticed people casting curious glances their way. The music had started again, a waltz, and couples were taking their positions.

"Dance with me." He extended his hand.

She hesitated, but with a tiny shrug, put her hand in his.

He brought her onto the dance floor and put his hand at her waist. She rested hers on his arm. Holding her, inhaling the lavender scent of her, awakened memories of lovemaking, of savoring her silky skin next to his. Almost forgetting to move, he forced himself to attend to the three-quarter time, and to lead them into the dance.

"Do you wish me to answer your questions?" Her expression was like a cannon about to be fired.

He had forgotten his questions, distracted by her eyes, perfectly matched to the color of her dress, and the feel of her in his arms as they twirled to the music.

She answered in clipped tones. "I am a guest in my mother's house, no servants accompanied me, and your cousin was good enough to transport me."

Spence winced, dismayed his foolish cousin would transport Emma so soon after her injury. He peered at her. She was pale and tiny lines of pain etched the corners of her mouth.

"But why, Emma? My letter—"

She laughed. "Your letter. Now *that* was edifying." Her voice and eyes became steely. "I came to London to hold you to our bargain."

"But I wrote you I would return."

Her brows knit, then rose. "Indeed?" she said sarcastically. "I read only that you 'could not stay.'"

His insides sank in dismay. She did not receive his London letter. She knew only that he had deserted her—again.

They circled the floor, twirling in time to the music, the other dancers a blur. In spite of the tension between them, they moved as one.

"Emma, I fear I cannot explain to you—"

She cut him off. "I fear that as well. How can you explain why you broke your word to me?" She missed a step. Spence tightened his hold, clutching her against him for an instant to keep them both from tripping. When they recovered their balance and their rhythm, a tinge of color touched her cheeks.

"I—"

"—Do not even try to concoct a story now. I have more to say to you than can be said on a dance floor."

He accepted her anger. All he could do was fight to get beyond it. "Let us find a room here where we can talk."

She shot more daggers with her eyes. "Certainly not. I have been the object of curiosity ever since I stepped in this house. I will not cause more talk by disappearing with you."

He closed his eyes, realizing he was putting his need to throw himself on her mercy ahead of what her desires would be.

"Tell me what I must do, Emma," he murmured.

He thought he saw her countenance fleetingly soften, but she answered him in a frosty voice. "You may call upon me at my mother's townhouse tomorrow. I beg you to come early. Eleven o'clock?"

He nodded, trying to meet her eyes to show his sincerity. "I shall be there, Emma."

They completed the dance in silence. And when it was over, he conveyed her to her mother, who was seated in a chair next to her friend Lady Vellamy, whom Spence remembered from their wedding. The two ladies looked as if they'd just won a bundle backing Cavendish's Nectar at the Newmarket Races.

"Good evening, Lady Holgrove. Lady Vellamy." He bowed and Emma released her hand from his arm.

"Good evening, sir," Lady Holgrove chirped.

"Do you like our surprise?" Lady Vellamy asked with a grin.

He directed his gaze at Emma. "I like it very well."

Emma turned away from him and made as if to straighten her skirt.

"I did not think Emma well enough for such a trip," he added.

Her mother looked puzzled. "Oh? Were you ill, dear?"

"No, Mother." Emma darted a glance to Spence before taking the seat next to Lady Vellamy.

"What did he mean then?"

Emma flashed Spence a warning look, which he interpreted as a request to keep his mouth shut. "I do not know, Mother," she replied. "Thank you for the dance, my lord."

"Emma—" he began, but she averted her gaze and he knew she wished him to leave.

"I will come beg another dance," he said to her.

She replied with an uninterested look.

He bowed to all three ladies and walked away.

Blake, who was lurking nearby, grabbed him almost immediately and dragged him to a quiet corner. "Emma is here? What is this, Spence?"

"She is furious at me, Blake, and rightfully so," he said with gloom. "She did not receive my letter."

"Oh, dear." frowned Blake. "This is a coil. What is her purpose in coming here? I thought she was ill."

"She is ill, I fear." He avoided the other part of Blake's question. His arrangement with Emma was a matter even too private for the Ternion.

Blake did not press him. "I must keep moving. I am dodging my mother, but I will certainly give my regards to your wife."

"Do so." Spence rubbed his brow. "Forgive me, Blake. I will see you directly." Spence walked out of the room and ducked into the library nearby, dark except for the glow of a fireplace. He closed the door and placed his hand on his brow, trying to quiet the tumult of emotions inside.

"I take it you have seen your wife." His uncle's voice came from a wingchair in the corner. Spence looked over to see him hold a glass of wine to his lips. "I take it you were as ill-prepared to see her as I."

Spence crossed over to him. "I was indeed, sir."

His uncle signaled him to sit, but Spence shook his head.

His uncle shrugged. "Reuben tells me she stays at her mother's house. Why is she here, Spence?"

Spence hesitated a moment before answering, weighing how prudent it was to talk with his uncle about Emma. "I will call upon her tomorrow. Perhaps she will tell me."

"Do you plan to leave her at her mother's house?" his uncle asked.

Spence kept his expression steady, although he felt anything but steady inside.

"I had not considered the matter."

"It will cause talk if she stays there and you at your hotel. The room in there is already buzzing with speculaton." His uncle stared into his glass of wine before looking back at Spence. "You should relocate to the townhouse."

He did not wish to tell his uncle he planned to take her back to Kellworth right away. "I would not displace you, sir."

His uncle responded, "You ought to take residence. I can have your rooms ready with a moment's notice."

Spence regarded the man. If he had more time, perhaps he could uncover the truth of his uncle's involvement with Ruddock. But Emma came first.

"I shall think on it," he prevaricated.

"Your wife." His uncle's voice turned low. "The last person I expected . . ."

His uncle fell silent and Spence took his leave. He returned to the rooms where the festivities continued, in time to see Blake escort Emma to the dance floor. He could not help but watch her. When the supper was announced, he attended her, fixing her plate and bringing her a glass of champagne, but she had little to say to him. He later asked her for one other dance, another waltz, but they danced in silence. When Ladies Vellamy and Holgrove decided to quit the ball, he accompanied Emma to their carriage.

"I will call upon you tomorrow," he said, but she barely looked at him.

Emma slept fitfully that night, her dreams of Spence waking her, and the disorder of her feelings about him keeping her awake.

She'd thought her anger would protect her from her senses, but he affected her as always. She wanted to hate him—*did* hate him—for not loving her enough to stay with her, but all it took was a glimpse of him and her body forgot.

Lady Vellamy arrived early for breakfast so that she and Emma's mother could supervise her toilette. Lady Vellamy chose a morning dress of palest blush and Lady Holgrove's maid dressed Emma's hair in a simple knot atop her head. A light touch of rouge put some needed color in her otherwise pale face.

The ladies pronounced her ravishing and were nearly giddy with excitement that her husband would see her in such fine looks. Her mother assured her she would finally make a real conquest of him and come into all the deserved privileges of her rank.

The only privilege Emma wanted was to produce the heir—or a daughter—any baby to love.

Spence arrived promptly, but her mother insisted she keep him waiting.

"Shall we receive him with her, Phoebe?" her mother asked, clapping her hands in excitement.

"I beg you would not," Emma piped up. "I must see him alone, without interruptions."

Her mother gave a moue of disappointment, but Lady Vellamy said, "Oh, let them be private, Agatha."

Spence waited for her in the drawing room. She opened the door to see him staring out the window onto Hartford Street.

He turned. "Emma." He crossed the room to her with his hands extended, but, rather than clasp them, she wrapped her arms across her chest.

Spence regarded her. "You are still pale, Emma. Are you feeling ill?"

Her pallor probably disappeared because she felt her face flush. "I am perfectly well. Say your piece, Spence."

She wanted to sustain her anger toward him, to not be seduced by his tall good looks or his spoken solicitude.

His eyes looked remarkably tormented. "I do not know what to say."

She glared at him. "Begin by telling me why you left."

He swung away from her and walked to the window to stare outside. He turned back. "I beg you to listen to the whole of what I say."

She gave an acquiescing nod.

"Will you sit?" he asked.

"No," she said.

He bowed his head for a moment, then lifted his eyes to hers. "I panicked," he said. "I ran from Kellworth because I had nearly killed you in the exact place I killed my brother, in nearly the same manner." His gaze seemed to bore into her. "I know it defies understanding, Emma, but that is the reason. I had the notion you would die like Stephen, like my parents, if I stayed one more minute at your side."

She felt the tug of sincerity in his little speech, so seductive. She swept it away with a ruthless vow to remain rational and leveled a skeptical glare at him. "You left me because you feared I would die?"

His gaze remained steady. "I knew you were not seriously injured. Mr. Price said so."

She laughed dryly. "So you left because you knew I would *not* die?"

He glanced away, his lips stretched into a grim line. When he looked back, his eyes looked bleak. "I left because I panicked."

She turned away, walking over to a small table and fiddling with a porcelain figure of an Arcadian maiden.

He continued to explain. "As soon as I arrived in London, I realized my folly. I dispatched a letter to you immediately, saying I would return. I planned to return to Kellworth today."

"A letter I did not receive," she scoffed. "Another missing letter."

Her anger flared. Dare she believe anything this man told her? Each word strengthened the notion that all he told her, even the purported embezzlement, had been a lie.

She swung back to him. "Give me one reason I should believe any of this!"

He bowed his head. "I can think of no reason you should believe me, Emma." His voice was so low, she could barely hear him, yet it plucked a chord inside her that threatened to unleash the very emotions she fought to control.

His eyes rose to pierce her again. "I have wronged you from the beginning, Emma. Married you and left you and told myself I was acting the gallant. I told myself I must go fight for my country and my king, when all I really wanted was to escape Kellworth. Then what did I do? Trapped you there and near starved you as well"—his eyes filled with what looked like remorse—"You are right. There is no reason you should believe me."

In spite of her resolve, she was shaken, almost feeling his pain resonating inside her.

She shook her head. She simply must not allow herself to fall under his spell.

"I am pleased we agree on something." Her voice came out churlish, but she hated the sound of it.

He reached into his pocket and pulled out some papers, handing them to her. "I was able to accomplish one useful task while here."

She stared at the words "Bank of England." The papers seemed to document a large sum of money in her name. She gasped at the amount and shot a glance at Spence.

"Part of our bargain." He gave a wan smile. "Financial security for you."

She stared back at the figures, not able to believe that there had ever been that much money in his fortune. What sort of man would give his wife such a sum? She shook her head. It was inconceivable. A wife's money belonged to her husband, did it not? This might be all a hum, an effort to fool her again.

"One part of our bargain," she repeated, giving him a hard look. "And what of the other part of our bargain?"

His eyes darkened and his expression filled her with memories of their lovemaking. "Let us return to Kellworth," he said. "I will give you a child."

She swung away, her heart pounding. *No! No!* she screamed inside. Could she bear filling Kellworth with more memories of him? Pretending at marital bliss? She had never dreamed he would return with her.

She shook her head. "If I allow you to take me back to Kellworth, how can I know you will not simply leave me there and run off to your pyramids or some such place?"

He looked stunned. "What else would you suggest?"

"We stay here," she declared, surprising herself as much as she did him. "In London."

She ignored the change in his countenance, to that soft expression she used to revel in across the pillows. "Emma, I could leave you in London, too, if I wished."

She straightened. "But if you do leave me in London, there are other men who might be willing to bed me." She glared at him. "I can find another man to father a child. I do not need you. Now that we have cohabited, the baby can be passed off as yours."

He strode over to her and put his hand on her arms, but his voice was gentle. "You cannot mean this, Emma."

Of course she did not. The mere thought of sharing with another man the intimacies she'd shared with him made bile rise in her throat.

He continued, speaking gently. "Perhaps you are with child now—"

She pulled away. "Then you would be free to leave, but I assure you I am not." Her voice betrayed too much emotion. She spilled her words in a rush to disguise the trembling of her chin. "Stay in London until it is certain I am increasing. Then I do not care where you go. Go anywhere but Kellworth!"

His face lost all expression, but he still spoke quietly. "As you wish, Emma. My uncle offers to vacate the townhouse.

I would desire to give him one or two days to settle himself elsewhere."

She'd pushed her anger to the fore and felt a grim satisfaction that he had acceded to her wishes—what she thought were her wishes. "He can remain in the house. I do not intend to stay there long."

He peered at her uncertainly. "Are you certain you wish him to stay there?"

"I do not care one way or the other." Pretending to feel strong was almost making her believe she could do anything. "Let him do as *he* wishes." She narrowed her eyes. "Or is it you who wish a delay? Perhaps so you can plan an escape?"

He shook his head and leveled a gaze at her that almost shook her newly won courage. "I'll not leave you, Emma."

"Then I will move in tomorrow." She could not believe she was speaking this way.

"Tomorrow," he agreed. "I will call for you at noon."

"Very well."

He bowed. "Until tomorrow, then."

When he opened the drawing-room door and walked into the hall, Emma heard the voices of her mother and Lady Vellamy, and it occurred to her that they may have been trying to listen. She marched out to see what the ladies were doing.

"Oh, how delightful to see you," her mother chirped to Spence. "We were hoping to catch you before you left."

The older ladies had each grasped hold of his arms and were walking him to the door.

Lady Vellamy said, "We wanted to insist you come with us to the musicale this evening at Lady Bolton's. Everyone will be there. We simply cannot allow our Emma to miss it."

He looked over his shoulder and saw Emma watching. "Emma?" he said. "Do you wish me to escort you?"

She had no more wish to attend the musicale than she had the ball, but at least she would know he was not on some boat to the Americas or something. "Yes," she said firmly. "Come with us to the musicale."

After he left, her mother and Lady Vellamy skipped up to her, demanding all the details. At least that assured Emma they had not heard the true course of the conversation.

"I am to take up residence with him at the Kellworth townhouse tomorrow," she said.

"Just think, at last you will be mistress of that grand townhouse," her mother cried.

"I am more in the nature of a temporary guest," Emma insisted. "I intend to return to Kellworth before long." *As soon as I've conceived,* she added silently.

"Oh, but first you must wrap the earl around your little finger." Her mother laughed. "And I will wager you will enjoy London's delights. Why, the Season is almost over and the biggest event is passed. The wedding of Princess Charlotte to her Leopold!"

Emma was taken aback. "You were invited to those festivities?"

"How I wish!" Her mother sighed. "But there were many other lovely parties in her honor."

"Enough chitchat," broke in Lady Vellamy. "We must get busy and devise a wardrobe for you."

"Oh yes," agreed Emma's mother. "Let us hurry and see what I have packed away that might do."

That evening, Spence appeared at the Holgrove townhouse, as commanded. He was admitted and asked to wait in the hall, since the ladies were ready to depart. A minute later Emma appeared in a gown of a fabric so light it seemed to float around her. She carried the paisley shawl.

Lady Vellamy and Lady Holgrove were right behind her, but Spence could not take his eyes off Emma. He stepped forward to drape her shawl across her shoulders.

"My carriage is waiting," Lady Vellamy said. "Let us not tarry."

He played escort to all three ladies, freeing Lord Holgrove from the task. The musicale was the social event of the evening. Even his uncle and Reuben attended. The program included a piece by Cherubini for string quartet. Cherubini had come to London the year before to conduct his new symphony and had never left. Emma, declaring she had never heard his music before, listened with an expression of delight on her face.

The night was over too quickly for Spence. Before he left Emma at her mother's door, he kissed her hand.

"Until tomorrow," he murmured.

When he stepped back to the pavement, Lady Vellamy leaned out of her carriage door. "Shall my coachman drop you off somewhere, Lord Kellworth?"

The night was crisp and fine and he wanted to be alone with his thoughts. "Thank you, no, my lady. I will enjoy the walk."

"Good night." She waved as the coach pulled away.

He headed toward Bond Street, wondering if Emma would have that same expression of delight if he introduced her to the singing energy of the Spanish guitar, or the bagpipe-like drone of the French *vielle à roue*.

But he reminded himself that there was much restitution to be done before he could propose even a minor adventure to her.

He neared Henrietta Street and heard a sound behind him. He halted, but the sound had gone away.

As he turned down Henrietta Street, he spied movement out of the corner of his eye. He whipped around, but the street was quiet and dark. He walked on, but now his soldier's senses were on alert.

All of a sudden two ruffians jumped out from the shadows. One man grabbed him from behind, his hat went flying, and beefy arms held him like a vise. Spence tried to twist from the man's grasp. The other man came at him, wielding a club. Spence elbowed his captor hard in the ribs and managed to wrest himself away right as the other man swung. The club struck his companion and sent him flying. Spence rushed the attacker, grabbing the arm holding the club and forcing it backward until the man screamed in pain. The club clattered to the pavement.

"Get the bugger!" shouted the other one, now rising to his feet.

They both charged, but Spence ducked and rolled to the ground, groping for the club. His fingers closed around it and he jumped to his feet, swinging as he advanced.

The two ruffians backed away.

"Be gone, if you know what is good for you," shouted Spence.

"Let's be out of here." The one man pulled on his companion's coat.

A door to a nearby house opened and someone called out, "What goes there?"

Spence dropped the club as the ruffians fled.

"Footpads," Spence answered. "They are gone."

"In this neighborhood?" The man stood in the doorway shaking his head. "I've never heard of such. Are you injured, sir?"

Spence dusted himself off and retrieved his hat. "No, I'm all in one piece. Good night, sir." But his wound ached from the exertion. He realized how easy it must have been for Ruddock to wind up in the Thames.

He started back toward Bond Street, limping slightly.

Chapter SEVENTEEN

Emma's trunk, packed with her mother's castaway gowns, was sent to the Kellworth townhouse. Lady Vellamy and her mother had seen to everything she would need, including an experienced lady's maid to attend her in her new home and prevent her from making any fashion faux pas.

Emma, her mother, and Lady Vellamy waited in the drawing room for Spence to arrive. The two ladies, full of advice, rattled on about how she ought to run the household, what invitations to accept, what sort of parties she might host.

"I do not think I shall be entertaining," Emma said.

"Oh, but you must!" cried her mother. "At least have an at-home or a dinner party."

The idea made her head hurt all over again, but she chose not to argue the point. Her nerves were not fluttering at the idea of giving parties. They were fluttering in anticipation of seeing Spence, and she was angry at herself for feeling like a besotted schoolgirl when all she wanted was to be enraged at him.

The clock on the mantel showed ten minutes past noon. Not enough time to panic, but enough to prick the worry that he would not come at all.

It would be like him to seduce her with promises and then vanish. She told herself not to be surprised if he never came. She worked herself into a fine lather in anticipation of it. Better anger than that vulnerable, fluttery feeling.

She glanced again at the clock, and watched the hand count off another minute until finally the butler announced, "Lord Kellworth."

Her mother tittered excitedly as Spence entered the room. Emma's emotions reeled and she placed her hand on her chest in a vain attempt to quiet them and summon her wrathful demeanor. Unable to breathe, she watched him cross the room.

Something was wrong. His gait was stiff, careful, exactly as it had been after his injury.

"Good morning, ladies." He bowed to Lady Vellamy and Lady Holgrove. He turned to Emma. "Emma."

"I am ready," she said, but a line of worry creased her brow.

Her mother bid her good-bye with a flurry of tears and hugs, as if she might expire from missing a daughter she so rarely thought about and would likely forget again when Emma was no longer in sight. Lady Vellamy assured Emma they would call upon her soon and would see her at the various entertainments to which she and Spence were sure to be invited.

Emma kissed both their cheeks and thanked them. She was truly grateful to them for giving her the little launch into society that had put her in Spence's path. And grateful that they had dressed her so she need not be embarrassed to be seen.

Spence offered his arm and escorted her out the door. She managed a careful look at him. "What is wrong?"

"Wrong?" He looked puzzled.

"You are limping."

A corner of his mouth turned up. "Am I?"

A carriage bearing the Kellworth crest waited. He helped her into it and climbed in after her, wincing as he did so.

As soon as he was seated next to her and the carriage on its way, she pushed the brim of his hat back from his forehead to reveal a bruise on his temple.

"What happened to you?"

He repositioned his hat. "Nothing so extraordinary. A brush with a couple of footpads."

"Footpads!"

"Last night after I left you. I am a bit sore, and my shoulder pains me, but I was not injured." He leaned back in the seat.

Worrying over his health had become something of a reflex. "Was your wound reopened?"

He shook his head. "Merely made sore."

Even a return to the familiarity of discussing his health was not enough to keep her nerves quiet. It took no time at all for the carriage to travel the few blocks to Charles Street, to the Kellworth townhouse. Emma's heart raced as Spence took her hand to help her out and gave her his arm as they walked up to the door and were admitted.

Reuben greeted them. "My father sends his apologies, but he will be all day in Commons. He instructed me to welcome you." He spoke in a formal voice. "The house is, of course, yours. He bade me tell you that your wishes must prevail here. He willingly cedes to your precedence."

Emma had no wish to displease Zachary Keenan and no intention of changing a thing. This stay would only last as long as it would take to conceive a baby.

The Kellworth servants in pristine livery lined up to be presented. Following Spence down the line, Emma greeted the butler, two footmen, three housemaids, two kitchen maids, Cook, housekeeper, Mr. Keenan's valet, her new lady's maid, and Spence's new valet. She wondered they all did not bump into each other. She had managed a large country house with fewer servants than this. Her new maid, Tippet, assured her that her trunk had arrived and her dresses had already been unpacked.

"Your rooms are ready for you," the housekeeper said. "And Mr. Keenan took the liberty of planning this night's menu, but, my lady, he said to defer to your wishes after today."

"My father will not be dining with us tonight, however," interjected Reuben. "He is engaged to dine at the club."

"Let me show you your rooms," the housekeeper said. "You may inform me if they are satisfactory."

The housekeeper led them up the staircase to the bedchambers intended for the earl and his countess. Not as spacious as those at Kellworth, they felt oddly familiar. They also had a connecting door.

As soon as she could, Emma dismissed the housekeeper and sat upon her new bed, removing her bonnet. Closing her eyes, she wished herself back at Kellworth, wished for the days when life had been a simple case of scraping enough money to pay the workers or purchase food, when she felt nothing but anger toward Spence.

"Is everything to your liking, Emma?"

Her eyes flew open. Spence stood in the doorway, leaning against the doorjamb.

"It will do," she snapped, then took a breath. She ought to be more cordial. "It feels a bit like Kellworth."

He stepped inside the room and looked around. "It does, doesn't it? I don't believe this room has changed since my mother was alive. Or your bedchamber in Kellworth, come to think of it. You did not change that room, did you?"

She drew her brows together, trying to remember one single other time he had spoken of his mother. "I saw no need."

In the early days at Kellworth she'd liked thinking that Spence as a little boy had bounced into that identical room, perhaps to receive a motherly hug. Later the money was too tight for frivolous changes. In any event, now the room was so familiar she had no desire for changes.

She wished she were back there. "This room is only temporary."

He strolled over to the window that looked out on the street. "Do you have any plans today?"

She laughed dryly. "I have not been in London long enough to have plans."

He returned a half smile. "Within three days you have attended a ball, a musicale, and taken over as hostess of a London townhouse. I would deem that quite impressive."

Her brow furrowed. "I have no intention of taking over this house."

"Like it or not, it is yours," he said quietly.

Emma had great difficulty thinking of herself as a London hostess, a role that had terrified her when her mother all but arranged the marriage to Mr. Keenan.

She brought the subject back to schedules. "Do not feel compelled to change your schedule because of me."

"I am here to do as you wish, Emma."

The expression on his face was so soft and gentle that she turned away and rearranged the items on her dressing table. "Don't gentlemen go to their clubs or Tattersall's or something?"

He chuckled. "Are you trying to get rid of me?"

His laugh was as affecting as his eyes. She wished he would not play this part with her.

Emma kept her back to him. "You know I am not. Not until our bargain is fulfilled."

He fell silent and still for so long, her hand started to shake. She heard him move toward the window and she dared look over at him. He was leaning on the back of a chair as if needing it to hold him up.

"Are you in pain?"

He tilted his head. "It is of no consequence."

They fell silent again. Emma picked up her bonnet and worried the ribbon until it was in wrinkles.

With a mild groan Spence released his grip on the chair. "I suppose we ought to go downstairs. Reuben will be waiting to entertain us." He took a stiff step toward the door.

Emma did not move.

He paused and turned back to her. "Forgive me, Emma. I did not mean to say what you must do. Remain here, if you like."

She stood and straightened her skirt. "I will accompany you." What else was she to do?

They walked together to the drawing room, the same room where she had first made his acquaintance three years earlier. Reuben sat in the room, staring into space.

When he saw them, he jumped to his feet, and his typically agreeable expression returned. "There you are."

The afternoon produced such excruciating boredom, Emma wished she'd arranged to accompany her mother and Lady Vellamy on their morning calls, a task she'd once dreaded. She looked out the window, tinkled notes on the pianoforte, searched the library, which contained no book to interest a lady.

Spence spent his time pacing, even though it looked painful for him. Pacing, then sitting and drumming his fingers against the arm of the chair. Reuben buried his nose in the newspaper, then announced he would work on an idea for a sermon, so even his conversation was no diversion.

Nearing four o'clock, Spence vaulted from his chair and asked Reuben, "Are you in need of your curricle?"

Reuben looked up in surprise. "Why, no."

"May I have use of it?"

"If you like." Reuben returned to his writing.

Spence walked over to Emma. "Come ride with me in the park."

She did not relish sitting so close to him, or being alone with him when they had nothing to say to each other—or too much to say—but she would have gone with the very devil himself for relief of this tedium.

"Give me a moment to change."

A few minutes later they were pulling into the park behind a line of other curricles, carriages, and phaetons. There was much to look at and little conversation required. Emma occupied herself with an examination of the ladies' fashions, deciding her mother's borrowed clothes compared nicely, even if her mother thought they were "hopelessly outmoded."

Out of the blue, Spence said, "What you are wearing looks very well on you, Emma."

She glanced down at the light brown pelisse and pale yellow dress. "It is my mother's."

His eyes flicked over her, feeling like a gentle touch she did not want. "It becomes you."

She averted her gaze.

Inside the park they passed other carriages and were greeted by people Emma remembered meeting at the ball and musicale. At age seventeen she had been intimidated by such people. Now she noticed that they smiled at her and at Spence as if happy to see them. In an odd way they reminded her of Kellworth's villagers. When she and Spence had ventured to the village, the villagers had greeted them with similar good cheer.

But she dared not think of those times when she had been so happy to be at his side, when they talked so easily together. Those times had been illusions, and she would make every effort to keep clearheaded from now on.

Late that night Spence dutifully sat with his uncle and Reuben, sharing brandy. Emma had retired early. Spence had intended to follow her, but his cousin kept so constant a stream of conversation, he could not find an easy escape. Then his uncle arrived home. Spence wanted Uncle Keenan to believe he wished to be on good terms, so he drank another glass of brandy with him.

Spence had been surprised when Emma had not accepted Uncle Keenan's offer to vacate the house. She had been so frightened of him years ago. But, then, she had gained much courage since those days. Leaving her sickbed and pursuing him to London had been very brave of her. He could admire her tenacity even while lamenting that his actions had driven her to it.

Spence glanced at his uncle, who was gazing into the fireplace. Uncle Keenan had always been a man who stopped at nothing to get what he wanted—and he had wanted Emma. Spence remembered the look in Uncle Keenan's eyes when he had gazed upon Emma—like a hungry lion stalking a deer. Spence thought Emma—as she was now—could have dealt with the pressure to marry his uncle, without any need for Spence's youthful brand of chivalry. As it was, Uncle Keenan had never forgiven Spence for stealing Emma from him. He'd barely been able to tolerate speaking to Spence since.

But how did these old events play into the embezzlement? It still made no sense that Uncle Keenan would embezzle money. Money had never been important to him.

Had all this been about Emma?

Spence needed to have a more pointed conversation with his uncle about this very soon, but he was much too weary and sore to keep his wits about him at this moment. He detected something disturbing beneath his uncle's distracted demeanor this evening. Spence would not tarry in settling this matter, once and for all. In the meantime he would make certain not to leave Emma alone with his uncle. Just to be safe.

Spence rose from his chair. "I believe I shall retire, Uncle. I bid you good night. To you as well, Reuben."

Reuben merely muttered, "Mmmmm." His uncle nodded.

Spence left the room and climbed the stairs. His muscles and shoulder were so painfully stiff, he felt like an old man.

Emma probably thought he'd plotted to avoid a liaison this night by retiring so late. Would she be abed at this moment, believing he had disappointed her once more?

Worse than the pain in his legs and shoulder was the gut-wrenching pain of knowing he had made it so impossible for Emma to believe he wanted to be with her. He longed to tell her he loved her, had discovered the truth of loving her at the same moment panic drove him from her.

She would never believe him. He must be patient. He must show her.

Spence entered his bedchamber, where his new valet stood like a soldier at attention. Quickly and efficiently the gentleman's gentleman assisted Spence out of his clothes, making the process less painful than had he undressed himself. Blake had talked him into hiring a man for himself, and now Spence was glad of it. Blake somehow knew where to find a valet on short notice, although how he knew was anyone's guess.

The valet bowed himself out of the room, and Spence swung around to the connecting door.

Spence gladly would defer making love to Emma until he'd proven himself to her. He had made a bargain with her, however, one that now convinced her she must force what ought to be natural between them. He could not imagine making love to her while she despised him.

At the same time he could barely look upon her without feeling aroused. He longed to reexperience the ecstasy they had shared, longed to see her flushed with passion, to hear her cries of pleasure.

He took a resolute step to the door. If she expected him to come to her this night, he would do so. If she turned him away, he would accept it. If she wanted him in her bed, he would do his damnedest to make it pleasurable for her. He'd do anything to keep from disappointing her again.

Taking a breath, he tested the doorknob. It turned. He opened the door ever so quietly. A candle burned near her bed, but she did not move. He stole closer and gazed down at her.

She slept on her side, her arms tucked close to her chest. The candle illuminated her flawless complexion, her pink lips, her thick lashes twitching ever so slightly.

"Emma?" He kept his voice just above a whisper.

She opened her eyes and stared back at him, almost as if he were a dream.

"Shall I join you?" He suddenly did not want her to refuse him.

She did not speak, but moved over to make room for him. He shed his banyan and climbed in, aroused already by the scent of her, the warmth of her body.

"Do you wish to make love?" he murmured, wanting, needing her to say yes.

Her gaze did not waver. "I want to make a baby."

He accepted that blow. "I am aching too much to hold myself over you."

"Then I will do it." Without removing her nightdress she climbed atop him. Without kissing him she positioned herself over him. He feared hurting her if she were not ready for him, but he feared any hesitation as well, lest she feel he was disappointing her again.

For a moment he was poised in indecision, but ultimately his body was too greedy to wait. He entered her. At first she moved against him like an automaton, and it grieved him more than he could bear. Still, every stroke accelerated his need. He did not want to take his pleasure at the expense of hers. He gripped her waist and forced her to slow down, to move slow and easy. Slow and easy. He finally felt her relax, accepting the leisurely pace, giving herself over to his direction. He watched her face and saw the hardness of her expression ease, then fill with passion. Still, he was careful to move slow, knowing her pleasure depended upon drawing out the moment, intensifying her need.

She felt delicious around him. He savored her lavender scent, the tickle of her hair as it swept his chest. She made small sounds from the back of her throat, urgent sounds that gratified him. Quickening their rhythm, he was reminded of waltzing with her in his arms, twirling faster and faster.

A moment later his thoughts were no longer coherent. Sensation took over, but still he bided his time, the instinct to please her even deeper than pleasing himself.

Then he felt it, felt her spasm around him, heard her cry out. He let go, giving himself over to his own shattering climax.

She collapsed on him, her breath gradually slowing to a normal rate. Then she slipped off and turned her back upon him. Her shoulders shook.

"Emma?" he whispered.

She did not answer, and he was left to endure the torture of her silent weeping until she finally fell asleep.

Emma woke the next morning to her maid entering the room. "Did I wake you, my lady? I will come back later if you wish."

She was alone in her bed, and it almost seemed like a dream that Spence had come to her in the night. She again felt him touching her, making love to her, so much like that transcendent experience they had once shared, a cruel mockery of what she once fancied to be love.

"I will rise now." She made herself throw off the covers and climb out of bed.

"Do you wish to dress, m'lady?"

She might as well force herself into the day. "Yes. Pick out a morning dress. Any will do."

Tippet selected the pale blush muslin, as delicate as Emma's emotions. Skilled at her job, the maid dressed her, arranged her hair, and made her all ready to go downstairs in no time at all.

When Emma walked out of her room, she glanced at Spence's door, wondering if he were abed or if she would face him over breakfast. She did not know how she would feel. Ashamed? Or aroused? She had been so easily aroused the night before.

Reuben sat in the dining parlor, breakfasting alone.

"Good morning, Reuben," she managed, with some effort at cheer.

His lower lip jutted out. "Good morning."

She fixed a plate for herself and sat opposite him, pouring herself some tea.

"What is it, Reuben?" He was so obviously sullen.

He did not answer right away, darting glances at her. She waited.

He worked his mouth before speaking. "I cannot like what transpires between you and my cousin, Emma. I fear this attempt at reconciliation will wound you even more."

Emma lowered her eyes. "That is none of your affair, Reuben."

He leaned over the table. "I disagree, I am your spiritual adviser, after all, and I believe that gives me some right to warn you when the devil is at your door."

Her eyes shot up at him. "The devil?"

He fussed with his fork. "My cousin. You know what I mean. You are leaving yourself open for heartbreak by returning to his bed."

"Reuben!" she cried, horrified.

He stared back at her and crossed his arms over his chest.

With blood rushing to her face, she fought to control her temper. "That is quite enough. You have been my dearest friend, but neither that nor your vicar's collar gives you leave to intrude upon my private matters, especially regarding my husband."

"You have confided in me about Spence in the past." He huffed.

"I have done no such thing." She straightened in her chair. "I lamented my lack of money with you, and begged your help contacting Spence, but never did I discuss my marriage with you."

He pursed his lips. "I am well able to read between the lines."

She felt her eyes flash with anger. "Do not credit such imaginings, and never speak to me like this again."

The door opened and Zachary Keenan entered, breaking his stride when he saw Emma. His brows furrowed. "Have you found everything to your liking, Lady Kellworth?"

Still angry at Reuben, her words caught in her throat. "Yes. Thank you."

He nodded curtly and proceeded to the sideboard.

She had forgotten about Keenan this morning. His appearance ought to have rattled her, but at the moment, he merely looked like a grim old man, not the lecher she so feared when she'd been seventeen.

He sat and glanced at his son. "What the devil is wrong with you?"

"Not a blessed thing." Reuben sulked.

Spence walked in. "Good morning," he said, favoring her with a warm look.

She felt her cheeks grow hot.

Reuben set his teacup noisily in its saucer and stood. "I beg your leave."

At the same time his father said, "Go," Spence said, "Very well."

Reuben did not move.

Keenan coughed. "I beg your pardon, Spence. I misspoke."

Spence turned from the sideboard. "Good God, Uncle. I do not care about precedence here. Give your son permission to leave the room."

His uncle glared at him. "Perhaps you ought to care about precedence."

Spence shook his head. "Let us not discuss that now."

"I will say what I think as I have always done," Keenan snapped.

Emma glanced at them all. She suddenly felt as if she were in charge of a nursery instead of sharing a meal with an earl, a Member of Parliament, and a vicar.

"Shall we have a peaceful breakfast, gentlemen?" she broke in.

All three gaped at her.

"Of course, Emma," said Spence. "I do apologize."

"Your forgiveness, my lady," Keenan added.

Reuben merely glared at her.

Spence placed his plate next to hers and sat down. "Do you have plans today, Emma? If not, I would like to take you to the shops."

She spread jam on her toast. "I have no need to go to the shops." He'd once offered to buy out the shops in Maidstone for her. She now had no intention of being seduced by gifts.

"Then some other place. Something novel." He tapped his knife against the tablecloth as if thinking. "The Egyptian Hall, perhaps. Have you been there?"

She shook her head, but was unhappy at this reference to Egypt, knowing he pined to travel there, as far away from her as she could imagine.

She glanced up to see both Reuben and his father watching to see how she would respond. After Reuben's outburst she dared not appear churlish toward her husband.

"I believe I must meet with the housekeeper, but I am at liberty to accompany you after that."

"That is excellent." Spence smiled at her, but she turned her attention to her toast.

"Do I have your leave or not?" Reuben still stood looking like a petulant schoolboy.

Spence did not even glance up at him. "Of course you do."

Reuben walked out with a dramatic flourish.

"What the deuce is the matter with him?" Spence said to nobody in particular.

His uncle answered, "Devil if I know."

Emma was not likely to tell either of them. At least the moment of greatest tension in the room had passed.

"Sir?" Spence looked at his uncle, "I need to speak with you at some length. Can you give me some time—while Emma meets with the housekeeper perhaps?"

Keenan stiffened, glancing from her to his nephew and back again. Emma felt the tension rise once more.

Finally his uncle answered, "I am engaged all day, but I will be available to you tomorrow morning."

"That will do." Spence nodded.

Emma's meeting with the housekeeper was brief. She needed only to direct the woman to continue as she was. The menus Emma selected were copied from Keenan's past ones.

No more than two hours had passed before she and Spence were walking the streets of Mayfair toward Bond Street. They took a hack to the Egyptian Hall on Piccadilly. The outside of the building, with its huge columns, hieroglyphics, and statues of Isis and Osiris, looked as if it had been transported straight from that exotic ancient land.

But inside was nothing of what Emma had imagined. There was only one room filled with the antiquities she expected to see. Another was packed with naturalist specimens, animals that had been stuffed to appear as they had in life. For the first time Emma realized the size of an elephant, marveled at the stripes of a zebra, and the ferocity of a polar bear. Another room was transformed into a tropical jungle, complete with an Indian hut. In spite of herself, Emma was fascinated by these things.

Next they waited to get into the most crowded of the exhibits, where Napoleon's carriage, captured at Waterloo, was on display. When they finally pushed to the head of the crowd, Emily stared at the blue vehicle trimmed in gold, thinking it looked much like any other gentleman's carriage.

"It looks so ordinary," she remarked.

"Not ordinary on the inside," Spence responded.

They were able to get close enough to see the clever compartments inside the carriage, where wine and food and weapons were stored. There was even an emperor's bed that could be made up.

Emma knew Spence had been at Waterloo that day. After news of the battle reached Kellworth, Emma had pored over the lists of officers killed and officers wounded, name after name after name, for fear of finding Spence listed there.

As they walked out of the room, she asked, "Did you see the carriage that day?"

"I glimpsed it, I think." His face turned bleak. "There was much I witnessed that day."

She felt a surge of sympathy. "I am certain."

She also felt companionable, sharing this new experience with him. How easy it was to be seduced into believing this gentlemanly escort, this interesting conversationalist, this excellent guide, was not also a man who could so easily walk away from her.

They left the Egyptian Hall soon after and rode back to Bond Street. Spence had the hack drop them at Berkeley Square, where he treated her to an ice at Gunter's, taking her to eat it in the square under the shade of an old maple tree. They could easily walk to the townhouse from there. The day was sunny and not too chilly, though eating the ice made Emma shiver, even as she enjoyed its fruity sweetness. Spence engaged her in conversation about what they had seen and the time was pleasantly spent.

When they had finished their ices, they crossed over to Charles Street. Suddenly the sound of hooves thundered in Emma's ears. From out of nowhere, a horse and rider charged straight for them.

Emma screamed.

Spence grabbed her and dived for the pavement, rolling them both away. The horse's hoof landed inches from her face, spattering stone chips against her cheeks.

She landed on her back, the wind knocked out of her. Spence knelt over her. "Are you injured, Emma? Are you hurt?" He felt her arms, her neck, her legs.

Other people who had been lounging in the square ran over.

"By Jove," one man said. "That fellow meant to run you down."

Emma sat up. "I am not hurt."

"Can you stand?" Spence's voice was as taut as a string.

"I believe so."

As soon as her words were spoken, he lifted her to her feet. She dusted herself off, still shaking. Spence pressed a hand against his wounded shoulder.

"But you are injured!" she cried.

"It is nothing." He turned to the onlookers. "Did anyone see the man? Did you recognize him?"

"He had a hat covering his face," one said. "His clothes were plain. Brown coat, I think."

"Brown coat," another agreed.

He turned his attention back to Emma. "Let us leave this place."

He thanked the people and hurried her away, holding her close against his side. When they turned the corner out of sight, he suddenly threw his arms around her, pressing her close.

"Emma, Emma," he rasped. "I almost got you killed. I almost got you killed again."

Her emotions, all raw to begin with, swirled into confusion. She embraced him in return, unmindful of the public street, heedless of propriety.

"I am not hurt," she repeated, clinging to him. "Do not fear. I am not hurt."

He finally released her. His eyes glittered with emotion. "It was deliberate. I am sure of it. We were meant to be run down."

"Deliberate?" Her heart pounded.

He wrapped her in his arms again and held her so tightly she could barely breathe. "I'll not have any harm come to you, Emma. I cannot risk it. You must go back to Kellworth in the morning. You must go back."

Chapter EIGHTEEN

She pulled away, looking as if Spence had run a blade through her heart.

"No," she cried, the sound coming from deep in her throat.

Spence could not heed her dismay. This time he really could get her killed. "Let us hurry home." If the horse and rider returned, they might not be so lucky a second time.

He set a brisk pace back to the townhouse. Once inside, Emma broke away from him and ran up the stairway to her bedchamber, slamming the door behind her.

He followed, entering her room without knocking. Her maid was present, looking at both of them in alarm. They must have appeared a sight, clothes wrinkled and soiled, emotions high.

"I beg your pardon, miss," he said to the maid, but directed his gaze at Emma. "I need a moment with Lady Kellworth."

The maid hurried out.

Emma tore off her bonnet and pulled at her gloves.

He threw his hat and gloves onto a table and ran a hand through his hair. "You must return to Kellworth, Emma. I would send you today, if it were not too late to get you there in daylight."

She returned a mutinous look. "Why?"

Taking two strides toward her, he lightly touched her arms. "Someone tried to run us down. You could have been killed."

She glared at him. "So could you."

He tightened his fingers around her arm. "Emma, don't you see? Someone is trying to kill me. Two nights ago it was footpads. Today a horseman. It is too dangerous for you here."

Her eyes narrowed. "Why would anyone wish to kill you?"

"I don't know." He shifted his position, realizing he was not telling her the whole truth, not telling her he feared his uncle was the one. He tried again. "At least I am not certain."

He walked a few paces away from her, his hand rubbing the back of his neck. "Ruddock is dead."

She still looked puzzled. "Ruddock?"

"We now know for certain he embezzled your funds from Kellworth. There are indications that another person is involved, but we have been unable to discover who."

"How did Mr. Ruddock die?" she asked in a trembling voice.

"Drowned. I presumed he was the victim of a robbery—there had been many robberies thereabouts—but now I question it."

She blinked. "Well, this is shocking, but I do not see what this has to do with me, why I have to leave."

He turned toward her. "Whoever is trying to kill me does not seem to mind if you get in the way."

"Then you must return to Kellworth, too." Her voice shook.

He held her gaze. "I cannot. The danger follows me."

"I want to stay." Her eyes entreated him.

He made a helpless gesture. "Emma, you must remain safe. I cannot have you remain here."

She swung away. A moment later she straightened and turned back to him, her face the picture of indignation. "What of our bargain?"

"We must postpone." He said this as gently as he could.

She stared at him a long time. Finally she spoke. "You are breaking your promise to me."

"I must, Emma." He reached a hand to her, but she waved it away. "I will come to you as soon as I have sorted this out."

Her eyes, kindled with anger, did not waver. "I have heard such promises too often."

He came over to her again and lifted her chin with his fingers. "Believe me this once, I beg you, Emma. I will return to you, but I cannot both protect you and discover what treachery is afoot. Go to Kellworth and wait for me."

She shook her head.

He stepped away again, desperate to figure out a way to convince her.

He folded his arms over his chest and used the tone of voice that had once made his soldiers quake in their boots. "I am ordering you to leave, Emma. And I will brook no more disagreement. I will arrange for Reuben to drive you. You will not stay here."

She turned pale.

Sick with fear that he had put the final nail in the coffin of their marriage, Spence walked out of her bedchamber.

Emma turned around in a helpless circle, hugging herself. She did not know if she should be angry, hurt, or terrified. She felt all three emotions at once.

She was furious at Spence for ordering her away, and hurt that his first thought was to be rid of her. But most of all, she was terrified. Terrified he would be killed, that same deadly fear that had never left her all the years he was at war. Even though she'd despised him, cursed him for impoverishing Kellworth—or so she'd thought—she always felt that leaden knot of dread whenever lists of the war dead had made the newspapers. After that dreadful battle at Waterloo the lists had gone on and on. She'd read them a dozen times to be certain he truly was not listed. Napoleon's carriage had brought it all back to her. Did Spence think she could again stand to be miles away wondering if he lived or died?

She walked over to the bed and hugged one of the posts, pressing her cheek against the cool carved wood.

There was no denying that she loved him. She scrunched her eyes closed and willed herself not to cry. She loved him. Had loved him from the day he smiled at her in the drawing room of this house.

The idea that someone wanted him dead brought a wave of nausea. Perhaps if he had not returned to Kellworth, he would never have discovered the embezzlement. Perhaps he would be safe if he had not returned to her.

She pressed her hand against her throat, wishing he had never returned. She could have gone on telling herself she hated him. And he would have gone on to explore the ends of the earth—alive.

She plopped down on the bed, remorseful for bringing their bargain into the argument. She merely had hoped to make him feel guilty enough to agree for her to stay. The ploy had not worked.

Her maid walked in. "I hope I am not disturbing you, my lady."

"I have the headache, Tippet," she said. "I need to rest."

The maid wore a forlorn frown. "The earl told me I must pack your trunk."

He'd begun arranging her departure so quickly? Emma felt a stab of pain.

"You may do as he wishes." She would not give up trying to change his mind, however. A trunk could be unpacked as easily as it was packed.

"Am I to be dismissed, my lady?" the maid asked, her expression wounded.

Emma wished she could reassure her. "You must ask Lord Kellworth."

"He went out, ma'am."

Emma felt her skin grow cold. She sprang off the bed and hurried over to the window, looking out onto the street. It was empty, but she pulled a chair close so she could keep a vigil.

Tippet packed her trunk. Emma did not bother to tell her the dresses ought to go back to her mother's house. She would arrange that later. When Tippet completed her task, Emma asked her to send word that she would have dinner in her room.

An hour later there was a knock on the door.

"Who is it?" Her hopes rose, even though she had not seen Spence return.

"It is Reuben," came the answer. "I am concerned for you, Emma."

She did not wish to speak with Reuben. "Has Spence spoken to you?"

"He has," Reuben called through the closed door. "I gather I am to take you back to Kellworth tomorrow."

She did not answer right away. "That is so."

"Emma?"

"Do not concern yourself, Reuben. I merely have a bit of a headache."

"Shall I fetch a physician?"

As if a physician could help what ailed her. "No, indeed," she said. "I want only to rest and it will go away."

"As you wish." His voice trailed off, and she heard his footsteps retreating.

She sat at the window watching for another hour before Spence's unmistakable tall figure appeared on the street. She watched until he entered the townhouse, disappearing into the door below her window. With a relieved sigh, she rose from the chair and stretched her legs. Later her dinner was brought to her, but she only picked at it. She called for Tippet to ready her for bed early.

Then she waited again. Waited until she heard Spence's voice in the next bedchamber. Waited until she heard his valet leave.

Then she opened the connecting door without knocking. He was sitting on the bed, his face in his hands. He stood at her entrance and walked toward her.

She hurled herself into his arms, and he had no choice but to hold her.

"Emma," he groaned.

She reached her hands up behind his neck and pulled his head down to her lips. He returned her kiss like a starving man at a feast. She tasted the brandy on his lips, felt the warmth of his breath, and ached for what might be their last time to make love.

All day she had planned this, hoping that making love to him might change his mind about sending her away, but, if he remained resolute, needing to taste and feel him one more time. If he thought her only interest was to conceive a child, he would be wrong. She prayed a child would come of this, but if not, she still wanted him with every inch of her being.

Their lips broke apart, and he crushed her to him, burying his face in the hair she'd left unbound. "Emma," he murmured against her ear so that her name tickled and thrilled.

He backed up to the bed, still holding her. She defied him to forget her now, to forget this. She knew she would never forget.

She pulled away enough to hold his face in her hands and gaze into his eyes, so dark in the candlelight. "Make love to me, Spence."

He gazed back, searching, pleading, but she did not know for what. Then, as if he had allowed something to come loose, his eyes filled with need, and he lifted her chin to kiss her so gently on her lips that she thought she might weep.

She loosened his banyan and pulled it down so the sleeves slipped off his arms and the garment fell to the floor. His naked body was glorious, and she was halfway ashamed by the pleasure she took in it. Averting her eyes and stepping back, she loosened the ribbons of her nightdress so that it glided down her body to pool at her feet. Daring only a glance at him, she saw admiration in his eyes.

Like a gentleman asking a lady to dance, he extended his hand to her. She took it, savoring its rough texture, its strength. He scooped her up in his arms and placed her upon the bed linens.

Joining her, rising over her, she felt enveloped by him. Bracing himself above, he bent his neck to kiss her, this kiss long and languid and as tender as before.

She would never willingly give this up. She would fight for it as if her life depended upon it. Rubbing her hands over his back, his shoulders, his arms, she reveled in the feel of his muscles beneath her fingers.

"Does your shoulder pain you?" she asked.

He shook his head. "Let me stay atop you, make love to you like a man."

She knew from the strain in his face that he lied about not being in pain, but she would do as he wished, for both their pleasures. She tried desperately to tell herself this was not the last time, but each touch seemed to ring with finality. She vowed to savor every second of loving him. She willed every part of her body to retain the imprint of his hands. She willed her hands to recall each ridge of muscle, each texture of his skin.

As she tried to prolong this poignant interlude, her body, like a cruel taskmaster, demanded release. When he entered her, she shuddered with both need and regret. With each synchrony of movement, the promise of pleasure and the fear of loss increased. Blessedly, her senses quickly took over, escalating with need until the shattering pleasure of her release came the moment he convulsed inside her.

Cradled next to him, feeling sated and loved, Emma fought despair.

This will not be the last time.

She made love to him again and again until they both fell into exhausted sleep.

With the light of dawn, Spence opened his eyes to the sight of Emma sleeping so trustingly next to him. He drank in her features. It was so difficult to send her away.

But still he could see the horse galloping straight for them, and its hoof landing inches from her face. He could not risk her life a third time.

He decided to confront his uncle, to directly accuse him of being an accomplice to Ruddock and the man's murder, to threaten to take his accusations to the magistrate. To threaten a public accusation would be enough to force his uncle's hand. This time Spence would be prepared for the attempt on his life. This time he'd apprehend the culprit and make sure the man spilled the name of his employer.

He watched Emma's lips move in her sleep and dared to caress a lock of her hair without disturbing her. Had they made a baby the previous night? The idea suddenly filled him with pride. To have a child who was part Emma, who had begun life in her womb, created from their lovemaking, seemed more of an adventure than any voyage to a distant land could be. No adventure was without risk, but he told himself not all women die in childbirth. Emma was young and healthy and strong.

He gazed at her again. Even if she did not believe him, he would return to her. He would clear up this nasty business and ride hell-for-leather for Kellworth and Emma. With Emma he would make new memories to counteract the ghosts of the past.

He heard a scratching at the door. Tucking the bedcovers around Emma, he slipped out of bed and grabbed his banyan, wincing as he put his sore arm in the sleeve. He opened the door a crack and saw his valet.

Spence put his finger to his lips to keep the man silent. "I will forgo your services," he whispered.

The man nodded and Spence closed the door. As quietly as possible, he shaved and dressed.

He had nearly finished when Emma woke. "Spence?"

He crossed to the side of the bed. "I am here."

She looked disappointed to see him dressed. Seeing her all warm and sleep-tousled, he felt disappointed as well.

She sat up, holding the bedcovers around her. "Where are you going?"

He combed her hair away from her face with his fingers. "Downstairs."

She rubbed her eyes. "I wanted to speak with you."

He drew his hand away.

She lifted her face to him. "After last night you cannot want me to leave—"

"Emma—" he warned.

"No, listen to me," she begged. "I am staying."

He held up a hand. "No, you will leave, and that is all there is to say on the subject. Reuben's curricle will be waiting outside in two hours' time, and he will be ready to drive you back." And she would be miles away before Spence had finished confronting his uncle.

Her eyes filled with tears. "And if I refuse?"

He looked at her with all the love and pleading in his heart. "Do not refuse, Emma." He took a breath. "I do not want you here, Emma. Do you understand that?"

He turned his back on her so that his face would not betray him. "Get dressed for the carriage now, and come down for breakfast."

"You order me?" Her voice trembled.

He swung around, knowing he could make his features look resolute for a moment or two. "I order you."

Emma stared at him, the vision of a woman betrayed.

"Go now, Emma!" he barked.

Holding herself regally, she climbed out of the bed, letting the covers fall away from her, revealing her naked beauty, so illuminated by the morning sun that her skin seemed to glow. Spence could not help but stare at her.

Slow and graceful, she picked her nightdress off the floor and, still meeting his eye, she stepped into it, pulling it inch by inch over her body, until Spence thought he would groan aloud. She was more erotic than any other woman could be undressing. Once her arms were in the sleeves of her nightdress, she left the ribbons untied so that he could still glimpse the creamy fullness of her breasts.

She approached him, as slinky as a snake, passing by so close his nostrils filled with the scent of her. Still keeping her eyes on him while she passed, but without changing her pace, she walked to the door.

Feeling that his insides had been wrenched from his body, Spence watched her open the door and cross the threshold. A moment later she closed the door behind her.

Emma was sick to death with achieving ecstasy one minute and plunging to the depths the next.

As they made love over and over during the night, she'd convinced herself he would not be able to part from her, but still he'd ordered her away. Doubt planted itself in her mind. What if he had contrived the horse's attack as a way to convince her to leave?

She shook her head as a wave of nausea hit her. He would not do such a thing, would he? But once the seeds of doubt were sown, they began to grow. Was this all an elaborate ruse to be rid of her?

If he did not want her, perhaps she could show him how well she could live without him—even if she despaired she could not.

A grim-faced Tippet came in to help her dress.

"My lord has paid me the quarter's wages and left me with a letter of reference," Tippet told her. "But one wishes for employment."

Emma placed a consoling hand on the maid's arm. "I am sorry, Tippet. I fancy I know how you feel."

"He is sending you away, too, isn't he, m'lady?" Tippet dared to ask.

"Indeed." Emma gave her a determined look. "But he cannot keep me away."

When Emma descended the stairs, she formulated a new plan. She would allow Reuben to return her to Kellworth, but the next day she would send for a post-chaise to bring her back to London, with Tolley to accompany her, perhaps. She would again beg to stay at her mother's house, until finding accommodations of her own with the money he'd banked in her name. Spence would see her at every society event he attended.

When she entered the dining parlor, three gentlemen stood. Reuben, Spence, and Blakewell. Emma's eyes narrowed when she saw her husband's friend.

Spence barely looked at her. Reuben seemed almost cheerful.

Blakewell bowed slightly and gave her a dimpled smile. "Lady Kellworth, I am delighted to see you."

"Lord Blakewell," she responded in a flat voice. "What a surprise to see you here."

"Indeed," he said, with a brightness of mood she found most suspicious and irritating. "But I understand you are to be leaving us."

"Indeed," she said.

She tolerated Blakewell's friendly conversation as best she could. A few minutes later, Keenan entered the room and Spence presented him to Blakewell.

Keenan gave Emma a direct look, before turning to glare at Spence. "I hear you are sending your wife back to Kellworth."

"I am, sir," Spence replied, without apparent emotion.

Keenan did not address her or anyone else in the room, but ate in silence, looking very disturbed.

Soon Reuben's groom pulled the curricle up to the front of the townhouse, and Emma's trunk was strapped in. Reuben ran upstairs for something he had forgotten. Emma, with her pelisse, bonnet, and gloves on, was ready to depart. Spence did not speak to her. Keenan stood in the hall looking just as grim.

When Reuben came rushing down the stairs, it was Blakewell who walked her to the door and out to the waiting carriage. Taking the ribbons from his groom's hands, Reuben climbed into the driver's seat.

Before lifting her into the curricle, Blakewell spoke quietly, "Do not worry, my lady. All will be well."

She peered at him. His face was sober.

She settled herself next to Reuben. His groom jumped on the back and they were off. Emma looked over her shoulder as they pulled away. There in the doorway of the townhouse was Spence, watching. He remained there until Reuben turned the corner at Berkeley Square and Emma could no longer see him.

Chapter NINETEEN

Blake walked back from the street to where Spence still stood watching, though the curricle was now out of sight.

"I hope you know what you are doing," Blake said.

"She needed to be out of harm's way," Spence responded.

Blake watched the empty street with him. "You told her everything?"

"Everything except the name of the man we suspect." Spence could not bring himself to tell Emma that fact. The man she might have married, the man who now shared Spence's house, who shared his blood, might be the one trying to kill him.

Spence and Blake entered the townhouse. Spence's uncle stood in the hall, a stony look on his face. "If you still wish to speak with me, I will be available in one hour. I have some correspondence to attend to first. Meet me in the library."

Keenan turned his back and walked away. Spence glanced at Blake. Spence had sought out his friend the previous day after he'd left Emma, needing the familiar support of the Ternion. Together they planned how to confront his uncle. Blake insisted upon being present, even though doing so would place him in danger as well, because the Ternion were stronger together.

At the appointed time, Spence, flanked by his friend, entered the library.

Keenan sat behind the large desk, still writing. Without speaking, he finished, sprinkling sand on the ink to dry it. He tapped off the sand and, in a quick movement, half rose, leaning across the desk. "What the devil are you about, sending your wife away within days of reuniting with her? You trifle with her feelings."

Spence took an involuntary step back, surprised at this onslaught. If his uncle intended diversion, this was skillfully done.

He recovered and faced his uncle with the straight back and steely voice of the officer he'd once been. "That, sir, we will not discuss."

Sitting back in the chair, Keenan poured himself a glass of port without offering any to Spence or Blake. He gave no heed to Spence's command. "You have treated that woman shabbily from the moment you married her, leaving her alone at Kellworth all those years."

Spence used the barb to turn the focus back on his uncle. "What do you know of it, Uncle? Exactly how much do you know of my affairs? Of Emma's years at Kellworth? That is what I am here to discover. Tell me all you have done and, most of all, why?"

"Done?" Keenan took a sip of his port. "I have no idea what you are talking about."

Blake stepped forward. "Sir, we have recently discovered evidence that while Spence was stationed abroad, Ruddock was embezzling funds from Kellworth—"

Keenan pointed a finger at Spence. "See! I warned you that an estate's business could not be delegated. If the man stole your money, it serves you right."

Spence felt his body tense.

Blake went on. "There is also reason to believe Ruddock did not act alone."

Keenan grunted. "Of course he did not act alone." He glared at Spence. "The man was an idiot. His brother is well enough, but, even so"—he pointed at Spence again—"it was your responsibility to know precisely every detail of the management of the Kellworth fortune. How much did you lose?"

Again Spence forced himself not to become defensive. And to hold his temper in check. "It is not the amount I lost that I credit but how much Emma suffered."

His uncle's eyes widened. "Emma suffered?"

"Ruddock cut funds to Kellworth and to Lady Kellworth's allowance," Blake explained. "Lady Kellworth was forced to make severe economies."

Keenan shot Spence a venomous look, before narrowing his eyes. "What has all this to do with me?"

Spence gave him a level stare. "Explain that to us, if you please."

The man's eyes did not waver. "I cannot explain what I do not know."

Spence leaned into his uncle's face. "Here is what we know, Uncle. You failed to forward Emma's letters to me, which would have alerted me to the situation at Kellworth. You sent Ruddock a message a week before he was killed. You knew my whereabouts on both attempts on my life—"

"Attempts on your life?" Keenan's brows shot up.

Spence scoffed. "You knew where I would be walking the night of the musicale. You knew Emma and I would be returning from Piccadilly." He lowered his voice to a dangerous level. "It was not well done of you to put her in jeopardy."

His uncle shook his head, the very picture of confusion. "I know nothing of this. Nothing."

"Nothing?" Spence tried to scrutinize the man's expression, which seemed real enough at first glance. "You sent footpads to attack me the first time. Then you sent a horse and rider to try to run me down with Emma at my side. She missed being trampled by mere inches."

"My God." Keenan was barely audible. "I would never do such a thing. Why would I?"

"The obvious reason is to succeed to the title," Blake interjected, maintaining a didactic tone. "The embezzlement is more difficult to understand, because, in effect, you were stealing from what would be yours. Unless your intent was to cause Lady Kellworth hardship."

"Cause her hardship?" Keenan rose from his chair with such energy Spence took another involuntary step back. "Cease this nonsense at once! I'll have you say no more!" Keenan charged around the desk to where Spence stood. Blake stepped forward, shoulder to shoulder with his friend.

But Keenan did not attack. Instead, he looked as if his insides had been twisted into knots. "You understand nothing. Do you not know I would never do any of this?"

"We merely present the information we have gathered," Blake put in, in a pragmatic tone.

Keenan looked at Blake as if he were some new species of insect. "You insolent cur." He turned back to Spence and the lines at the corners of his eyes deepened. "Do you not realize?" he whispered. "I would never hurt her. Never."

Blake again said, "You are the logical suspect—"

Spence put a restraining hand on Blake's arm. He met his uncle's eye with a searching glance. "Why would you never hurt her?"

His uncle's eyes reddened. "I love her."

"You . . ." Spence began, but could not finish the sentence. He swallowed and tried again. "You wanted her—I knew that. But . . . ?"

His uncle averted his eyes. "She was so fresh and beautiful. It made me feel young just to look at her." He glanced back at Spence. "But seeing her now . . . Now I merely feel very old."

Spence murmured, "But, if not you, who?"

His uncle backed away and paced in front of them. "If she had given me letters for you, I would have forwarded them. I would have done anything for her. I would have given her money if she needed it. By God, why did she not ask me? All I wanted was her happiness, and you"—he turned on Spence again—"you thought nothing of her."

But Spence felt a new dread, more insidious than his own guilt. "Who, then?"

At that moment the butler rapped at the door. Opening it a crack, he said, "Lord Kellworth, a gentleman insists upon seeing you. Two gentlemen, actually. And another person."

Before Spence could reply, Wolfe burst through the door, knocking it against the wall with a bang. He dragged Lord Esmund, Devlin's former dueling partner, with him. Arjun followed.

The butler looked horrified.

Spence walked over to him and said, "It is all right. Leave us, if you please." He closed the door.

"I had the very devil of a time finding you," Wolfe said. "You could not leave word at the hotel of your whereabouts? I think I have been all over London trying to locate you. I daresay they were not happy at White's—"

He released Esmund, but Arjun stepped up to take hold of the red-haired young man's arm. Esmund looked both frightened out of his wits and as angry as a bear.

Blake gave Wolfe an appreciative look. "You dragged the fellow all the way from France?"

Wolfe nodded. "Easier than you would think." He noticed Keenan. His brows rose, a question in his expression.

Spence stepped forward. "May I present my friend Mr. Wolfe to you, Uncle Keenan."

"Keenan!" cried Wolfe, pointing at him. "That's the man! I told you the duel was a setup. Keenan was the man behind it. Hired Esmund to kill you in exchange for paying off his debts."

"See here." Keenan's face was flushed in anger. "This is absurd."

"No," wailed Esmund, trying to pull from Arjun's grasp.

Arjun tightened his grip.

Spence swung toward his uncle. "You almost had me fooled. Was this about Emma, then? Were you trying to punish her and me, as well? Or was that all a hum and only the title you desired? I suspect you would like sitting in the House of Lords."

"You insufferable prig!" shouted Keenan.

"Perhaps it is time to send for the magistrate," Blake suggested.

"Send for the magistrate, then." Keenan shot daggers at his nephew. "It was not enough for you to tempt Emma away with your title and estate. Now you mean to ruin me."

"No!" wailed Esmund again. "You have it all wrong!"

He finally received their attention.

His red hair fell over his forehead, and he swiped at it with his free hand. "I have never had the pleasure of this gentleman's acquaintance." He tried again to twist out of Arjun's grasp. "Though I have heard of you, sir," he added cordially.

Spence strode toward him. "Cut line, Esmund. What the devil are you trying to say?"

Arjun released him.

Esmund brushed off his sleeves and straightened his jacket before answering Spence. "It was not *this* Keenan who held my debts and made me fight the duel—I do beg your pardon, sir."

"Never mind that," Spence snapped. "Who put you up to it?"

"Not *this* Keenan," retorted Esmund. "The other one. You know, the vicar. Reverend Keenan."

"Reuben," Spence moaned.

Blake's eyes widened and Keenan's face turned white.

"Reuben!" Spence shouted. He looked from one man to the other, the horror becoming all too real. "My God, I sent her off with him!"

By the time Spence was on the road, he figured to be at least two hours behind Reuben. Leaving Blake and Wolfe to sort things out in London, he'd ordered his horse saddled and changed into riding clothes, all the while chafing at how much time ticked by. The streets of London were even more congested than when Reuben's curricle had pulled away, and Spence needed to thread his way through carriages and wagons and pedestrians before reaching the open road. He changed horses frequently, asking at each posting inn if they'd remembered seeing a curricle of Reuben's description. Each time they said yes, and he'd known Emma had been safe that much longer.

It began to rain, just enough to make the road a muddy mess, slowing travel but not halting it. He'd not bothered with a great coat, and it took no time at all for his clothing to soak through. He hoped Emma had remained dry. The rain caused him to fall farther behind. They'd had two hours' driving on good road before the rains began, two more hours than he'd had.

He prayed Reuben had taken Emma back to Kellworth. He prayed no harm had come to her. He feared his prayers were too late.

The long hours in the saddle gave him plenty of time to think. He remembered the poacher's shot, his curricle's shattered wheel. Had Reuben masterminded those events? If so, he'd been heedless of Emma's safety then, too. What of the other mishaps that occurred at Kellworth? The medicine making Tolley ill? The stirrup breaking? It all seemed patently clear now that these were manufactured events.

What motive could his cousin have for all this treachery? Did he desire the title? It seemed far-fetched, since his father was next in line. Or did he mean to kill his father, too? Had Reuben, professing all through childhood that he was called to the Church, broken the command-ment, *thou shalt not kill*? Had Reuben coveted Kellworth so much as to damn his soul?

Rain trickled into Spence's boots as he rode, but he ig-nored the discomfort. Spain in winter had been much worse.

Why would Reuben wish to harm Emma? Spence could not figure it. Reuben seemed devoted to her, and she was no threat to him.

Unless she produced an heir.

Spence groaned. Reuben would have known he and Emma shared a bed. There were no secrets in houses full of servants. Emma had been safe only when it was certain she would not bear an heir.

Daylight waned by the time Spence entered the famil-iar countryside surrounding Kellworth. The rain had ceased, and try as he might to urge the horse into a gallop, its hooves stuck to the still-muddy road. When Kellworth Hall finally came into view, it looked like an apparition through the still-misty air. Spence shouted as he ap-proached the main entrance. He dismounted and burst into the hall.

A stunned Mr. Hale stood there. "Lord Kellworth! What a surprise."

Tracking mud from his boots and dripping water onto the floor, Spence lost no more time. "Where is Lady Kell-worth?"

Mr. Hale's brows rose. "Why, I do not know, my lord."

Mrs. Cobbett swished into the hall, her chatelaine jan-gling. "I heard some shouting." She halted, spying Spence. "Oh my goodness!"

"Is Emma here?" he asked again, too impatient to credit their surprise.

"She is in London, my lord," Mrs. Cobbett replied, curtsying.

"Not here?" he repeated, his fear escalating.

"No, my lord," they answered in unison.

He could waste no time explaining. "I need a dry greatcoat immediately. Bring it here to the hall."

He raced to the gun room, unlocking a cabinet and removing a pistol and a pouch of cartridges. He checked the flint of the pistol and bit open a cartridge, pouring in the powder and packing the ball with skilled efficiency. He wrapped the loaded pistol in an oilskin against the damp and slung the pouch across his shoulder. His eyes lit on a dagger in an elaborately tooled leather sheath, a relic from one of his father's foreign trips. He strapped it on and hurried back to the hall.

Tolley waited with the caped coat. "What else can I do, sir?"

"Wait for my friends to arrive," Spence told him. "Blakewell and Wolfe. Tell them to come straight to the vicarage."

Tolley helped him into the greatcoat. Spence tucked the pistol into a pocket and dashed out the door to where the horse now munched on a patch of grass nearby. Spence mounted the beast again and set as fast a pace as he could toward the vicarage.

Not more than ten minutes later, he dismounted in front of the two-story house that had been home to Kellworth's vicars for three generations. Almost slipping in the mud as he hurried to the door, he paused a moment to unwrap the pistol and place it back in the pocket. He then hammered on the door until Reuben's housekeeper answered.

"Where is he?" he demanded.

The stunned woman said, "In the drawing room, my lord."

Spence burst into Reuben's drawing room, where his cousin sat comfortably in a chair sipping a glass of wine. Spence rushed at him, seized him by the front of his coat, and pulled him to his feet. The glass flew out of Reuben's hand, spraying wine on Reuben's coat, the chair, the carpet.

"What have you done with her?" Spence growled.

"With—with whom?" stammered his cousin.

Spence lifted the shorter man until they were nose to nose and Reuben could not miss the fury on Spence's face. "You know damned well who. Where is Emma?"

"Put me down and I will tell you!" Reuben cried.

Spence let Reuben's feet touch the floor, but he did not let go.

"She did not come with me, Spence." Reuben's expression was the picture of sincerity. "She made me drop her at her mother's townhouse. She never left London. I came on alone."

Spence put one hand around Reuben's neck. "Do not take me for a fool. I asked at the posting houses. You were seen. You are a dead man unless you take me to her."

Reuben's eyes flashed with panic as Spence tightened his grip on Reuben's throat. His face red, Reuben tried to pry away Spence's hand, to no avail.

Finally he nodded and Spence let go.

"I will lead you to her." Reuben coughed and rubbed his neck. "Let me fetch my hat and an overcoat."

"Bugger the hat and coat!" Spence said, pushing him out of the room. The housekeeper still stood in the hall wringing her hands.

He pushed Reuben past her and out the door. "Where to?"

"Follow me." Reuben walked with mincing steps, turning around to Spence. "She's come to no harm. You'll see, Spence! This is all a terrible mistake."

He sounded as forthright as his father, acting as if Emma were lounging in some comfortable haven. In the church, perhaps. Spence tried to hope that was true.

But instead of entering the church, Reuben led him around to the back.

"Where the devil are you taking me?" Spence placed his hand inside his pocket and removed the pistol.

"Not far now," his cousin responded.

Reuben walked to the gate of the church's cemetery and opened it. Spence felt the hairs on the back of his neck stand on end.

Daylight had all but disappeared, leaching the area of any color. They passed tombstones standing like ghostly sentinels. They kept walking until, at the far end of the cemetery, set off in a copse of white willows, the stone edifice of the Kellworth mausoleum loomed a somber gray. Reuben headed straight for it.

Cold fingers of panic raced up Spence's spine. He pushed at Reuben's back with the barrel of the gun. "Make haste."

Reuben tossed Spence a wounded look from over his shoulder.

Once reaching the door, Reuben spent a great deal of time searching his pockets, finally removing the key and turning it in the lock. Reuben pulled the door open.

Spence peered inside, straining to see in the gloomy interior. The scent of blood reached his nostrils. Just within the doorway there was the dark outline of a body lying on the stone floor.

"No!" Spence cried, pushing Reuben inside.

As Spence made his way over to the body and crouched down, Reuben sprang away and dashed to the doorway.

"Bugger!" Spence jumped to his feet, but the door slammed shut as he reached it, plunging him in darkness.

He dropped the pistol and flung himself against the door, banging on the thick wood. "Reuben! You bloody viper! You worthless cur! Open this door!"

He heard the key turn in the lock, echoing loud against the stone walls. "Reuben!" he shouted again, but no sound could be heard. Spence groped in the blackness and felt his boots step in something sticky. Blood.

Dear God. Emma.

"Spence?" A spectral voice drifted from the recesses of the gloomy interior.

He froze. "Emma?"

"I'm over here," she said, raising her voice.

She was real. Alive. He nearly collapsed with relief. He cast about in the darkness, trying to follow the sound. "Emma!"

"Here!" she cried. "I did not want to sit near that man."

Not caring what obstacles might lie in his path, Spence took bold steps toward the sound of her voice, until he bumped into a sarcophagus, one of the first of his ancestors to claim a final resting place here. Later relations lined the walls.

"I am right here." Her voice was very near. "I'm sitting on top."

He lurched toward her, hearing her crawling toward him. His hand suddenly caught hers, and he grabbed her, pulling her off the sarcophagus and crushing her against him.

"I thought you were dead." He buried his face in her hair, loose around her shoulders. "I saw that body and I thought you were dead."

"Oh, Spence!" she cried. "You came for me."

He kissed her and held her close. "Emma, my love."

Emma clung to him, rubbing her cheek against the wool of his coat. Hardly able to believe he was here, she thrilled at his words. She returned his kiss, almost missing his lips. If she could not see him, at least she could feel his arms around her.

She eventually felt able to speak. "Reuben said he would leave me to die here. He said he would kill you, too, Spence, as soon as a decent interval passed."

"Emma," he moaned. "Why here? Why did he bring you to this god-awful place?"

His body warmed her. The scent of him filled her nostrils, taking away the smell of dank stone and death. "No one would hear my cries for help, he said. It served me right, he said, because I was the one who kept you from being buried here."

"Now he means for us both to be buried alive."

She shuddered.

She felt his body tense. He released her. "The cursed viper. I am not going to let you die here. I promise I am not."

As he embraced her again, Emma smiled at the irony. This was another promise Spence was likely to break, but she would not fault him for it. She was only sorry he was with her to suffer the same fate.

"Blake and Wolfe will come, Emma," he said. "They are on to him."

Would it matter? Reuben would steer them away from this place, if he did not kill them, too. Reuben had told her of killing Ruddock. She'd seen him kill the groom, could still hear the shot of his pistol and its echo against the stone walls. She could still hear Reuben calmly discuss his intent to kill Spence and, later on, his own father if the man did not oblige him by dying of natural causes soon enough. Reuben would be earl and the people would love him because he would take much better care of the estate than Spence had.

Reuben had counted on Spence dying in battle, he'd said. When Spence had not obliged him, he'd arranged for him to be killed in a duel. Emma had ruined it all. If only she would have let Spence die, she could have married Reuben and been *his* Lady Kellworth.

The idea made her ill.

There was a skittering sound.

"What was that?" Spence asked.

"Mice," Emma replied. "That is why I climbed on top of this." She patted the sarcophagus.

"Let us get back on it." He lifted her onto it and climbed on after her. The stone cover was carved into the sleeping figure of some long-departed Keenan. They sat on the legs.

Spence tucked her close to his side and cocooned her inside his greatcoat.

She rested her head against him. "The dead man is Reuben's groom."

"Dear God." His words came from deep in his chest and she felt as well as heard them. "Emma, I failed to protect you. I put you right into his hands."

His clothing was damp against her cheek. "It is not your fault."

"No," he said fiercely. "I am at fault. If only—"

She found his lips and covered them with her fingers. "Shh, do not blame yourself. He fooled me, too. He fooled everyone." She melted back in the comfort of his arms, until the hopelessness of their situation struck her anew. "I wish you were not here! I wish you were safe in London."

"No." His voice was deep and firm. "I belong here with you. I will not leave you this time. You will not be alone."

When Reuben shut the door on her, she'd screamed and railed until almost too weak to stand. She'd crawled on the floor, trying to get as far away from the dead groom as she could, feeling the mice run over her fingers and get caught in her skirt. When she finally climbed atop the sarcophagus, she forced herself to think, to review her life. Rescue seemed impossible.

"I was not as afraid as I thought I would be," she told Spence. It was incredible but true. "And this is even more frightening than getting lost in Cairo."

"Cairo?"

She laughed softly. "Never mind." She turned, still unable to see him, but she put her hands on his face. "Spence, I want to tell you—I had much time to think—you must know that I have regretted nothing. *Nothing*. I do not regret marrying you, or struggling alone at Kellworth, or making you try to give me a baby. I do not regret loving you."

He cradled her again, his arms tightening around her. "I have many regrets, Emma. So many regrets."

"Remember, you rescued me from your uncle and gave me your home." She wrapped her arms around his neck. "Besides, if you had not left me, how would I ever have discovered I could raise pigs?"

He found her lips again and kissed her with a desperation only exceeded by their desperate circumstances.

His arms were strong, and they sat quietly until he began to speak. "Emma, I know why I never wanted to return to Kellworth."

"Why?" She liked listening to him. It made the darkness brighter.

"It was filled with memories of Stephen, my brother." His voice was hushed and sad.

"The one who died in an accident?"

"The brother I killed by my recklessness," he responded more harshly. "When my parents died, it was somehow bearable to be at Kellworth because Stephen was there. He was three years older and looked after me." He became quiet for a moment. "Stephen is buried here. You would think his ghost would haunt me here, now, instead of around every corner of Kellworth."

"Haunt you?"

He gave a soft laugh. "The memories haunted me, I should say. The worst was driving by the same stretch of road where Stephen died. Then to have you thrown from the curricle just as he had been—"

She placed her fingers on his lips. "Reuben said it was the groom who cut through the curricle wheel. He said no one would discover it now because that man was dead, too." Reuben's voice had been cold as he held her wrists and told her everything. She'd been unable to twist out of his grasp. "It was not your doing at all."

"I know that now." He expelled a breath. "No matter what happens, one thing I want you to believe, if you believe nothing else."

"What?"

He bent his head down so his lips touched her ear. "I was coming back, Emma. And I was coming back to stay."

She thought she'd shed enough tears in this place of horror, but more sprang to her eyes.

"I believe you," she whispered.

The claws of the mice skittered noisily on the stone floor. Spence must have heard them as well, because he tightened his arms around her.

Emma refused to think what they might be doing, but the harder she tried to forget them, the louder they became, scampering and squeaking and scuffling. Even though she could not see them, she squeezed her eyes shut and wished they would go away, just go away, from wherever they came.

Suddenly Spence released her. Her eyes flew open.

"Emma!" His voice was breathless. "They come from the outside. The mice come from the outside. From a hole somewhere in this structure."

"Yes?" she said, puzzled.

"If they can get in, we can get out!"

Chapter TWENTY

"The hole would be tiny," she said. "A little crack."

Spence did not care. "Holes can be made bigger."

He forced himself to think, to plan. "There might be a place where the mortar is crumbling, like the loose stones at Kellworth. If we could remove a stone or two here . . ." He vaulted off the sarcophagus.

"What are you doing?"

He heard her move as if to follow him. "Stay where you are. I'm going to look for my pistol. I dropped it when Reuben locked me in."

He crawled around on the stone floor, trying to remember where the groom's body was and hoping his pistol had not landed in the man's blood.

"What are you going to do with the pistol?" she asked.

It helped to hear her voice, giving him an idea of where he was in the room. "I need something to serve as a torch. Something to burn."

"I could tear cloth from my shift," she suggested.

"That will do." He inched his way, crawling on the floor, sweeping his hands ahead of him. "Long strips, Emma."

He heard the sound of fabric tearing.

Tiny, clawed feet scampered over his gloved hand, squeaking as he reflexively shook it away. He paused a moment for his heartbeat to return to normal.

"Keep talking to me, Emma," he said. "It helps me keep my bearings." *And my sanity,* he added silently.

She talked. Talked of how she had fallen in love with him all those years ago. Talked of her girlish fears and how, because of all that happened to her, she now felt she could face anything. She talked of wanting a baby, of wanting to keep a piece of him with her always.

Her words both filled him with melancholy and with hope. He still deeply regretted causing her suffering by not being with her. He supposed he would regret leaving her for as long as he lived.

Which might not be very many more days unless he could find the pistol. He inched his way across the floor, hoping he would not just miss it in his blind sweep.

Finally his hand hit something solid. "Got it!" he cried, stuffing it into a pocket.

"Bravo!" She clapped.

He groped his way back to Emma, feeling for her. "The cloth."

Her hand cast about for him and finally put the cloth in his hand. He stood and walked several paces from her to what he thought was the center of the room.

"Now what are you doing?" she asked.

"I am going to make a torch," he responded. "Or try to."

Working by feel alone, he laid the cloth on the floor and bit off the end of one cartridge, scattering the gunpowder onto the cloth by feel. He unsheathed the dagger and wrapped the cloth around its blade, carefully laying it on the floor nearby. Then he fumbled in the coat pocket for the pistol. Tapping the barrel to remove the ball, he heard it clink against the stone floor and roll away. Breaking open another cartridge, he poured more gunpowder into the barrel, and took the patch from the ball, packing it alone against the powder. Feeling the floor for the dagger, he pointed the barrel of the pistol right near the cloth.

"Emma, take heed," he said. "I have to fire my pistol to light the cloth. I am afraid it will be loud." He also hoped he would not set fire to himself in the process.

He squeezed the trigger and the pistol created a flash of light that illuminated the room for a scant moment before the pistol's report bounced off the walls. The mice screeched, and in the brief moment of illumination, he caught a glimpse of them scampering toward the wall to his right. Blinking his eyes to recover from the flash, he checked his makeshift torch. It burned, igniting small patches of gunpowder scattered on the floor. Smoke wafted toward the ceiling.

Spence pulled off one of his gloves and wrapped it around the enameled handle for extra insulation. He could already feel the metal growing hotter. He lifted the torch and turned toward Emma.

"It worked," she said. He could see her smile.

He stole a moment to gaze at her, to see she was truly in one piece, to savor the sight of her perched on one of four sarcophaguses lining one end of the room. He turned slowly. One wall was honeycombed with six empty compartments, waiting for some Keenan to die to fill them. Two were checkered with the sealed markings of those already deceased Keenans. The last contained the bodies of his aunt, the baby who had died with her, and Stephen.

Next to the space where his brother rested was the space intended for him.

"Spence! There are rushlights!" Emma slipped off her perch and hurried over to him, pointing to the corners.

He strode to one corner and lit the thin rush poking out of its wrought-iron holder. "I'll not light them all," he said. "We may need them later."

His hand felt seared from the torch handle's heat even through his glove. The cloth was burning rapidly. He had little time left, but took a few moments to examine the body of the groom. Emma remained at a distance, her hand covering her mouth. As best he could with one hand, he searched the man's pockets, but found nothing of use to them. He then walked to the wall where the mice had run, the wall where he would have been buried next to his brother. There was nothing to see but blackness.

"I can see nothing. We had better wait until morning. With luck some sunlight will peek through." If there was enough light. If the hole led directly to the outside.

The torch sputtered and went out, leaving only the dim illumination of the rushlight. Spence scraped the remains of the cloth from the dagger and returned it to its sheath, feeling the still-hot metal warm him where it lay against his hip. He led Emma to the wall where the light burned, and sat on the stone floor with his back resting against the wall, nestling her against him so his coat and his arms could keep her warm.

He relished the feel of her against his chest, vowing he would tear the building down, stone by stone, with his fingernails, if necessary to get her out.

She was very quiet, but he suspected she did not sleep. "Emma?"

"Mmm-hmm," she murmured.

"I will get you out."

"I know." She snuggled closer.

He soon heard the even sounds of her breathing and was glad she slept. He meant to stay awake, to tend the light and chase off any mice brave enough to return, but his eyes, too, became heavy.

He dreamed of light, of a brightness that enveloped like a blanket, familiar, a place he had been before. From the light a figure emerged.

Stephen.

His brother approached, that aura of peace encircling him, emanating from him. Spence remembered then, the other dream when he begged Stephen to take him with him into the light.

This time Spence called out, "Do not take me, Stephen. I'm not ready to go with you."

His brother smiled, the whiteness of his teeth as bright as the light. Stephen's voice came to him like a soft echo. "I know. I will come for you later, little brother. Much later."

Stephen began to fade, and Spence already felt the wrenching ache of missing him.

As Stephen disappeared, his voice wafted through the light reaching Spence's ear. "Name your son for me."

Spence jolted awake, his heart pounding. No more light. Only darkness. The rushlight had gone out while he slept.

"Spence?" He'd woken Emma. "Did I sleep long?"

He swore to himself. "I dozed off. I let the rushlight burn out. Who knows how long we slept?"

"Maybe it is morning." She sounded hopeful.

With luck, maybe it was morning. "Stay here. I'm going to look for light." Removing his greatcoat, he wrapped it around her and felt his way down the wall toward where the mice had run, the wall where Stephen was buried.

He hoped the mice entered through one of the three empty compartments he remembered seeing there. By feel, he climbed inside the first one, examining the wall up close, but there was no break in the relentless darkness, just the choking feeling of being entombed in stone. He edged out as quickly as he could. Fighting the vestiges of panic, his brother's words came back to him: *I will come for you later. Much later.*

He would live a long life and he would have a son.

In the second compartment there was nothing but blackness as well, not even a crack to feel under his fingertips. Only one more to try, the one beside his brother, *his* compartment. He prayed he would not be forced to break into those that were sealed.

He propelled himself forward with his elbows, the stone walls closing around him.

Emma's voice echoed behind him. "You will find it this time."

He forced his eyes to examine the black void.

At first there was nothing; then a mere pinprick of light so small, he thought his eyes played tricks on him. When he blinked, the light was still there.

"Emma, I have found it." He pulled out his dagger and poked at the crack of light. It suddenly grew larger, about the size of a ha'penny.

Emma's voice sounded closer, as if she stood next to him. "I can see it!"

As he hoped, the mortar was crumbling. He scraped and chopped at it, pushing against the stone, which was about a foot square. When he felt it loosen, he crawled out of the space and went back in, feetfirst. He kicked at the stone until it fell away. Light streamed in, along with the fresh-scented air of a spring morning.

"We can do it, Emma."

He climbed out again, and she stood in the glow of sunlight. He enveloped her in a joyous embrace.

When he went back in to hack at another stone, she called after him, "I'll fetch your greatcoat."

The mortar on the adjacent stone above the other one gave away equally as well, and Spence kicked it out making a bigger hole. "Two more and we are free."

He turned around to hack at the other two stones. These were more stubborn. He chipped away at the mortar until his arm ached with the effort. When he finally felt he'd weakened the stones, he kicked at them with strength that increased with the promise of escape. The two stones fell away.

"Now, Emma." He climbed back into the mausoleum and helped her into the compartment. She scrambled toward the light and he stuffed his greatcoat out behind her. A moment later he, too, was outside, gulping in the fresh air.

Emma raised her arms and face to the sun. The sky was dotted with clouds, but blue. The grass and trees were bright green. He caught Emma and together they twirled around, laughing.

He picked his greatcoat off the ground, taking the pistol from its pocket, wrapped the coat around her. "I am taking you back to Kellworth. I'll deal with Reuben later." He tucked the pistol in the waist of his trousers.

She looked as if she were about to protest, but she said, "Very well."

They crossed the cemetery and hurried out the gate to the path Reuben had taken Spence down the night before. The path led around to the front of the church, passed the vicarage, then to the road, to the place where they could cross the fields, muddy as they were, the quickest way to Kellworth. To home.

As they started down the road in front of the church, Spence heard a sound behind him. He whirled around, his hand closing on the barrel of the pistol. He had not reloaded it.

"Spence!" called Reuben from the doorway of the church. Spence pushed Emma behind him.

"Do not think you can escape me a second time." Reuben lifted a pistol from behind his back as he advanced on them.

Spence pulled out his own pistol and aimed it at his cousin. "I did not know vicars wore firearms, Reuben."

"'God helps those who help themselves.'" Reuben smiled, looking every bit as beatific as he did in the pulpit.

"No!" cried Emma.

"Stay behind me!" Spence demanded.

The two men were about ten paces apart, aiming at each other, much as Spence and Esmund had done in the duel. This time more than honor was at stake. His body was the only barrier to stop the ball from hitting Emma; yet, if Spence were hit, she would be Reuben's next victim. Spence faced his cousin knowing what was at stake—Emma's life. Their happiness together.

He also knew he had no shot to take.

"Stay well behind me," he repeated to Emma.

Spence watched Reuben's face and saw his moment of decision. Reuben's pistol shot cracked loudly in the tranquil morning. Spence saw the fire from the barrel and braced for the feel of the ball penetrating his flesh. Instead, he heard the ball whiz past his ear. The cloud of smoke obscured him momentarily, and before Reuben could realize what had happened, Spence charged him, knocking him to the ground. Man-to-man Reuben did not stand much of a chance against his stronger cousin, but he fought viciously.

As Spence was holding him down, Reuben's arms flailed and his hand closed on the dagger and pulled it from its sheath. Spence jumped to his feet, moving out of range. Reuben came at him, slicing the air with the sharp blade.

Emma cried, "I will get help!"

"Run, Emma!" Spence commanded.

She started for the house, several yards away.

Reuben continued to advance, but Spence moved back, watching. Reuben lunged at him again, but this time Spence caught his wrist, knocking the dagger from his hand.

Both men dived for it. Spence's hand closed on it first, but still Reuben grabbed for it. Spence snatched it away, but the blade sliced into Reuben's palm.

Reuben broke away. Holding his bloody hand before his eyes, he wailed, "You cut me!"

Emma stopped and started back toward Spence, but he gestured for her not to come too close.

"Are you hurt?" she asked Spence.

"No." The shot had missed him. This time there had been no sharp pain, no falling backward, no last regrets.

Reuben fell to his knees, holding his fisted hand against his stomach and rocking back and forth.

Spence dropped down to his side. "Let me see the wound."

Reuben jerked away, refusing to let Spence pry his hand open. Blood squeezed through his fingers and stained his coat. "It hurts."

The sound of horses' hooves made Spence look up. Four riders approached. He recognized two of them as Blake and Wolfe. As they came closer, he saw Tolley was with them and—astonishingly—his uncle.

"We heard a shot. What is it? What has happened?" Uncle Keenan fired questions even before the men dismounted.

Tolley held the horses.

"He's cut," Spence told him.

"Cut?" His uncle hurried over, crouching next to Reuben. "Is it very bad?"

"It is mortal!" wailed Reuben, still clutching his hand.

"It is not mortal," Spence said. "But he will not let me see it."

Keenan, his face awash in concern, reached for his son's hand. Reuben reluctantly allowed him to examine it.

"He tried to kill me." Reuben whimpered.

Emma fought her way to Keenan's side. "It is lies, Mr. Keenan. It was Reuben who tried to kill us. He locked us in—"

"I know," Keenan said sadly, pulling out his handkerchief and wrapping it around his son's hand. "The question is, what to do with him?"

"What to do with me!" Reuben wailed. "Father," he pleaded. "Do not believe them. They killed my groom and are trying to blame it on me."

"Now see here—" started Wolfe.

"Enough!" shouted Keenan, glaring at his son. "Your deeds have caught up with you."

"Let's take him into the house and tend to him. We can discuss the matter there," Spence said.

Keenan and Blakewell helped Reuben to his feet, each taking one of his arms, Reuben was forced to walk between them to the vicarage. Spence glanced over to Tolley. "Good work, Tolley. Can you stay here and see to the horses?"

"Yes, my lord," Tolley replied.

Spence wrapped his arm around Emma and followed the others to the house.

Keenan demanded water and clean bandages from the alarmed housekeeper. They took Reuben into his drawing room. His father sat Reuben in a chair and unwrapped the handkerchief. There was a deep gash in Reuben's palm, but the bleeding had already slowed. Reuben no longer pretended to whimper.

When the housekeeper came with the water and bandages, Wolfe took them and closed the door on her.

Keenan gently cleansed his son's wound and rebandaged it.

He glanced to Spence. "Tell me what happened."

As briefly as possible, Spence related the events of the previous night, their entrapment, the dead groom, their escape, Reuben's wounding.

Keenan frowned. "What will you do now?"

"What will he do?" broke in Wolfe. "Send for the justice, I daresay. The man ought to hang!"

"Wolfe," cautioned Blakewell, shaking his head. "It is for Spence to decide."

Spence stared at his cousin for a long moment. He squatted down so he could look Reuben directly in the eye. "Give me one reason why you should not hang."

Reuben's eyes filled with hatred.

Spence's uncle answered the question. "He is my son. Your cousin." The older man looked pale.

Reuben laughed. "Oh, now you show concern for me, Father. When I was a boy, it was always Stephen this, or Stephen that. 'He is the earl.' That is all I ever heard from you."

Keenan's face contorted in pain.

Spence glared at Reuben. "Did you kill Stephen, too?"

Reuben gave a sardonic grin. "No. *You* performed that deed. I will admit that was when I first got the idea I could be earl. Thank you, Cousin."

His uncle looked toward Spence. "Australia, perhaps? The West Indies?"

Reuben wailed. "I will not go to those god-awful places!"

Spence rose. "How can we, Uncle? He has killed more than once. He tried to kill Emma. I see no other choice but to send for the squire and to see him prosecuted."

"Prosecuted?" Reuben cried. "Like a common criminal? A man of the cloth?"

Spence looked over at Emma.

She stared back at him, the enormity of what they were discussing written all over her face.

Spence shook his head. "We must send for Squire Benson. A trial must decide his fate."

Reuben leapt to his feet, and before anyone could stop him, ran to the door, pulling it open. Spence chased him up the stairs to his room, but Reuben had been too quick.

He reached his bedchamber, slamming the door and turning the key in its lock.

"Reuben!" Spence shouted.

The others reached the hallway.

Spence stepped back to kick at the door, and just as his boot shattered the wood frame, the loud report of a pistol sounded in the air.

Emma screamed, "Spence!" Blake held her back.

This pistol ball had not been meant for Spence. As he entered the room, his cousin lay sprawled on the bed, dead from a shot to the head.

Hours later Emma sat on her bed in her bedchamber at Kellworth, bathed, freshly dressed, and fed. The room was comfortably unaltered, making it seem as if she had never left Kellworth, had never gone to London, had never been trapped in a living tomb.

A wave of nausea hit her, and she curled up on her bed.

Spence, his uncle, his friends, and Justice of the Peace Squire Benson had been below stairs for ages discussing some way to minimize the scandal. Was there any palatable story to explain the death of the parish vicar?

She must have dozed, because she woke to the sound of mewing. Tom and Puss climbed the bedcovers to reach her, purring and rubbing against her.

"My little darlings," she murmured, sitting up again. "I have missed you."

The door connecting her room with Spence's opened. Spence walked in. "The little rascals are still with us, I see."

He sat upon her bed and picked up little Tom, ruffling its fur until Tom squirmed and Spence released him.

Emma gazed upon her husband's handsome face. Her body ached with the nearness of him and with how close she had come to losing him.

"Is everything settled?" she asked.

He nodded. "Reuben killed his groom and then himself when his deed was discovered. It is close enough to the truth and not nearly so scandalous as the whole story." Tom pounced, back for more roughhousing. "It satisfies my uncle."

"I felt sorry for him." Emma had never expected to feel any such emotion toward Mr. Keenan, but his pain at his son's deeds was palpable, and the man had been so visibly grieved.

"I do as well." He lounged on the bed, resting on his elbow. "How do you fare, Emma?"

Her breath caught with the force of his gaze. "A little unwell, but I suppose that is because of all that has happened."

Concern showed in his eyes. "Unwell?" He felt her forehead.

She took his hand in hers. "Not feverish. A little nauseous. The feeling comes and goes. It has ever since the curricle accident."

His eyebrows rose and he placed his hand on her belly. "Could there be a baby?"

She started to shake her head, but stopped. "I don't know."

"When was your last . . . your last . . ."

"My courses?" She felt herself blush talking about it. "I thought it came the day you left for London, but it was very little bleeding, nearly gone the next day."

He rubbed his hand across her belly and winked. "If I were a wagering man, I'd wager you are carrying a boy."

She covered his hand with both of hers. In spite of everything, a deep fear returned. "If there is a baby inside me, our bargain is complete." She twisted around to search his face. "You would be free to leave."

He placed his fingers gently on her cheeks. "I propose a new marriage bargain."

She was afraid to breathe. "What?"

He kissed her lips, a long, soft kiss that made her feel like butter melting near a fire.

He moved his lips away enough to murmur, "Till death do us part."

About the Author

When Diane Perkins was a little girl, she thought everyone had stories filling their heads. It never occurred to her to write down her stories, even though she loved reading, especially reading Historical Romance. Instead, she spent a career as a county mental-health therapist helping other people craft real happy endings. It took a lull in Diane's busy life for her to finally put fingers to the keyboard and bring her stories to life. Once started, she never looked back, even going on to win the Romance Writers of America's prestigious Golden Heart Award, the Royal Ascot, and other romance writing prizes. She now writes Regency Historical Romance full-time. Happily married and the mother of a grown daughter and son, she and her husband live in Northern Virginia with three very ordinary house cats. Diane would love to hear from you. Contact her through her Web site at www.dianeperkins.us.

THE EDITOR'S DIARY

Dear Reader,

Ever think fate is getting a little chuckle at your expense? Whether it's husband hunting on a deadline or a second chance at your first marriage, pick up our two Warner Forever titles this October and join in the fun.

Romantic Times BOOKclub raves **Wendy Markham's** last book is "touching and humorous" and "will keep you glued to the page." Well, cancel your plans—you won't be able to tear yourself away from her latest, **BRIDE NEEDS GROOM!** Dominick Chickalini rejoices in his bachelorhood. In fact, he's on his way to Las Vegas for a decadent weekend of drinking, flirting, gambling, and ignoring the fact that everyone in his life is married. But as he boards the plane, he notices the most beautiful woman he's ever seen is sitting right next to him... and she's wearing a wedding dress. Mia Calogera has to get married. Her wealthy grandfather has threatened to cut her off financially if she isn't married by his 85th birthday and it's just about time for him to blow out a few candles. As much as she hates to admit it, she just can't go back to the hand-to-mouth lifestyle she led before. Her plan: to marry a man she met over the Internet. But will this gorgeous bachelor throw a wrench into her otherwise fool-proof plan?

Emma Chambers from **Diane Perkins's THE MARRIAGE BARGAIN** knows a little something about fool-proof plans failing too. When Spence Keenan married her, he rescued her from a distasteful union to a lecherous old codger. But he was far from her white knight. He disappeared off to war without a backward glance and has ignored Emma's pleas since. Now he's returned to her, delirious with fever and in desperate need of her care. As Spence slowly regains his health, he can't help but be grateful to this beautiful woman who has kept his estate running. But what begins as gratitude soon becomes much more . . . until mysterious "accidents" threaten both Emma and Spence's lives. Can Spence convince Emma of his love? Or will his past behavior threaten their current happiness? *Booklist* called Diane Perkins's previous book "emotionally intense and richly romantic...simply superb" and this one is even better! So run out and grab a copy today.

To find out more about Warner Forever, these titles, and the authors, visit us at www.warnerforever.com.

With warmest wishes,

Karen Kosztolnyik

Karen Kosztolnyik, Senior Editor

P.S. Destiny takes a hand and love follows in these two irresistible novels: Amanda Scott delivers the sensual tale of a man whose family secret threatens his life and the life of the beautiful, intriguing woman who must become his wife in PRINCE OF DANGER; and Candy Halliday tells the hilarious and sexy story of a woman whose perfectly planned life is turned upside down by a patrol cop in MR. DESTINY.

Want to know more about romances at Warner Books and Warner Forever? Get the scoop online!

WARNER'S ROMANCE HOMEPAGE

Visit us at www.warnerforever.com for all the latest news, reviews, and chapter excerpts!

NEW AND UPCOMING TITLES

Each month we feature our new titles and reader favorites.

CONTESTS AND GIVEAWAYS

We give away galleys, autographed copies, and all kinds of fun stuff.

AUTHOR INFO

You'll find bios, articles, and links to personal Web sites for all your favorite authors—and so much more!

THE BUZZ

Sign up for our monthly romance newsletter, and be the first to read all about it!

If you or someone you know
wants to improve their reading skills,
call the Literacy Help Line.

WORDS ARE YOUR WHEELS
1-800-929-4458